Gift child

Giftchild

JANCI PATTERSON

GARDEN
NINJ
BOOKS

GIFTCHILD

Edited by Kristina Kugler
Cover Design by Melody Fender

Cover photograph from istockphoto.com/Photolyric
Back cover footprint image by Melody Fender
Author photo by Michelle D. Argyle

Published by Garden Ninja Books

JanciPatterson.com

First Edition: December 2014

0 9 8 7 6 5 4 3 2 1

For my mother,

Who always believed I could do this

Even when I didn't.

Chapter One
Week One

When Mom texted me to tell me that my baby sister was about to be born, I nearly dropped my camera out of a tree. I gripped it in one hand, using the other hand to let go of the branch I was braced on and reach for my phone. My foot was wedged against the trunk and a lower branch, which wobbled, showering raindrops onto my friend Rodney below.

"Careful," he said. "Don't get your lens wet."

I twisted my wrist around so the lens hood faced down. Trying to dry the lens in this tree would be like toweling off while still standing in a shower. Climbing the tree had been a bad idea in the first place, since it had only barely stopped raining, leaving the branches slippery and wet. Sap streaked down the sleeve of my windbreaker. Water seeped through my jeans and sweatshirt, and even through my tennis shoes. If I was at this much longer, I was going to have wet socks as well.

Rodney had asked me three times if I was sure my shot was worth it. It had better be, or I was going to hear about it for days.

Rodney stood below me, looking up through the branches. "Penny," he said. "Are you *texting* up there?"

"No," I said. "Just checking. It's from my mom." *Lily's in labor*, the message said. *I'm packing for the hospital now.*

"Right," Rodney said. "I think tree climbing is a non-texting activity. Like driving. Or making out."

He was never going to let that go, even though it had been nearly six months. "You know, that time was also my mother. She's important, too."

"Tell me about it," Rodney said. "Mood killer."

I narrowed my eyes at him, but he grinned up at me.

I turned my attention back to my phone, partly because Mom really was important, and partly because Rodney told me not to.

Mom was packing? She'd only spent the last two weeks arranging and rearranging her hospital bag, like *she* was the one who might go into labor at any moment. She'd had a plan—mapped it all out, like an emergency evacuation. Lily would text Mom to let her know that she was at the hospital. If it happened during the day, Mom and Dad would both meet there, then Mom would stay with Lily through her labor, just like Lily asked her to. Dad would be on call to get Mom and Lily anything they needed. My older sister Athena would stay at her dorm and generally pretend that nothing was happening. And I would stay at home, *without* Rodney. Mom had reiterated that last point about six times, even though I told her she didn't need to. It wasn't like I'd be asking Rodney to spend the night.

But, like all of Mom's plans to have a baby, this one seemed to have already gotten derailed. It didn't really matter—Mom was just worried about all the things she couldn't plan for, so she over-accounted for all the things that she could. She didn't know how long Lily's labor would be, and she wanted to be at the hospital as much as possible. And Lily wanted her there, unlike the other birth moms, who we'd barely known. Mom took it as an omen that this was the time that was going to work out. Her plan was a shield against the loss of this baby—the tragedy that always seemed to befall our family.

I just hoped that her failure to follow the plan now wasn't a bad omen for the rest of the birth, and the signing of papers after.

Rodney squinted up through the branches at me. "Are you

seriously still messing with your phone?"

I shoved it back in my pocket, jarring a branch with my elbow so drops rained down into Rodney's eyes. I smothered a smile. "I'm putting it away," I said. "Hang on." I obviously needed to get home soon to help Mom, but after making Rodney boost me up the tree, I couldn't climb down until I had my shot, mock-worthy or not.

I lifted my camera, steadying my arm on the branch in front of me. The raindrops glistened on the pine needles, sparkling like bunches of bells strung on a green wreath. I wanted to get one particular bunch of needles in focus, against the backdrop of other branches behind. But one misshapen bunch poked up right in my way. I stretched my fingers out to pull it off the branch, but I couldn't quite reach.

"I agreed to help you up there," Rodney said, "but I'm not going to catch you when you dive back down."

"Fine," I said. "You're the one who's going to have to explain to the coroner why your best friend belly flopped onto the ground."

"I'll tell him I've never met you," he said. "I just stopped to talk the lunatic out of the tree."

"Shut up," I said. "You love me too much to let me die."

Rodney was quiet for a moment, then he waded through the grass to the base of the tree. "Fine," he said. "I'm coming up."

I smiled, but as Rodney hauled himself up by his arms, feet scraping against the bark, the branches rattled, bringing fat drops down on me. "Hey!" I said. "Careful! You'll spoil my shot."

Rodney's body pressed against me from behind, his arms taut against the branches. "Nah," he said in my ear. "I'm just rearranging it a little."

A shiver ran down my arms that had nothing to do with the cold. I held still. At least shivers were invisible. I didn't like letting him in on the effect he could have on me. He'd never let me live it down.

9

With Rodney holding on to my shoulders, I snatched the wayward branch, peeling it back until it hung from the tree by a thread. I stretched out my camera, snapping photos of the sparkly needle bunch. Fresh drops strained at the bottom needles, catching glimmers of the other needles around them just before they fell. I snapped shots three, four, five at a time, until I had enough that one or two of them had to be perfectly in focus.

I twisted around, holding onto Rodney's arm to stay balanced in the tree. Rodney's grip on the branches tightened. "Hey," he said. "You're not bringing me down with you."

I inclined the camera screen so he could see. "Well?" I asked. "Worth it?"

He squinted at my picture. "Worth it," he said.

I poked him in the chest. "Are you only saying that to get us out of the tree?"

He released a branch with one hand, which showered more drops down onto us. Rodney's hair stuck to his forehead, but instead of wiping it away, he wrapped his arm around my shoulders protectively. "Maybe," he said. "I'll tell you once we're down."

I poked him harder, and he grinned. More drops rained down on us, and one of them hit me smack on the eye. My eyes squeezed shut. Rodney laughed, but he steadied me as I reached up to wipe them off.

When I opened them again, Rodney's face was inches away. I could feel his warm breath on my cheek, and I wondered for a moment if he was going to kiss me. When was the last time Rodney and I made out? A month ago, almost. We weren't officially together, so it wasn't like we did that all the time. A soaked, spiny, sap-covered tree wasn't exactly the most romantic of locations, but Rodney had kissed me in stranger spots. And I had to admit that I wanted him to, more than I probably should have. More than I had in a while, now that I thought about it.

What had I been so distracted about?

Mom.

10

Who was at home, freaking out, right at this minute.

Rodney's face inched closer, and his eyes dipped to my lips.

"I'd really better get home," I said. Then I grinned. "Rain check?"

Rodney groaned. "If I didn't have to be the one to talk to the coroner, I would seriously shove you out of this tree."

"Come on," I said. "It was punny. Admit it."

He jabbed me in the ribs, and I had to cling to his arm to keep from falling. Rodney took advantage of my grip to swing me closer to the ground, and I hung on until my feet were close enough to the ground to jump down. When he hit the ground beside me, he turned, arms out. "All right," he said. "Face the consequences for your punning."

I wanted to believe he wouldn't tickle me to the ground on a cold, wet day, but I wasn't about to call his bluff. I turned and ran toward his car, both of us racing through the park. Our shoes pounded through a puddle, kicking water up all around us, so we both had to hide our cameras under our shirts to keep them dry. When I arrived at his car, my sides ached. Rodney slammed into the car next to me, and I turned to him.

"Lily's in labor," I said.

His smile faded. "Oh," he said. "*Oh*. Then you really do need to get home." He held open the car door for me and I climbed in, dripping sneakers and all.

I made Rodney come into the house with me, even though he offered to leave. I probably should have let him, but to be honest, I didn't want to face my mother's mental state on my own. When I opened the front door, I found her running frantically around the house, scooping things up at random and dumping them into her bag. From the way it bulged, I gathered she'd been doing this for a while.

"Mom?" I asked. "Did you hear anything else from Lily?"

Mom charged down the stairs, waving her checkbook, and put her other hand to her forehead. "Didn't I text you?" she asked.

"Yes," I said. "That's how I knew you heard anything at all."

Mom let out a breath of relief. "Oh. Right. I must have remembered that earlier."

Rodney hovered in the doorway, as if he wasn't sure he should be here. I motioned him into the living room. From the look of things, Mom would be gone in a minute anyway.

I motioned to Mom's checkbook. "What are you doing with that?"

Mom tossed it into her bag. "I just thought I might need it," she said. "You never know."

"Mom," I said. "You're not buying the baby. And I think the hospital gift shop would take a card."

But Mom was already in the kitchen, rifling through a drawer. "I think I forgot to pack a pen."

I leaned against the door frame in the kitchen. My clothes were still damp, and my shoes were sinking wet footprints into the carpet, but Mom was too insane to notice. "I'm pretty sure they'll have pens at the hospital. Or in the gift shop. Or Dad could bring you one if you really need one."

But Mom resurfaced with two pens, each with a mismatched cap. "Found one!" she said.

I sighed, peering into Mom's bag. She obviously wasn't thinking clearly, so I tried to remember all the things she couldn't. The things she should *actually* be doing, instead of scrambling around for pens. "Where's Dad?" I asked. "Have you called him?"

Mom nodded. "I'll meet him at the hospital."

I looked at her trembling hands. When Mom made that plan before, it had sounded fine. But in this state, she might cruise through a stoplight and die. "Um . . ." I said. "Maybe he should pick you up?"

Mom looked at me blankly. "Why?"

Because, Mom. You're not fit to drive. "Because then you'll only have one car there," I said.

Mom's eyebrows met. "Do you need one? I could leave you my car. But we can't put the car seat in Dad's truck. It's already installed in mine—"

"Okay," I said. "So have Dad come here and drive you in your car."

Mom squinted at the air in front of her, like she was trying to solve an impossible puzzle. "You can't drive your dad's work truck."

"I know," I said.

She dashed upstairs again, this time returning with an extra pair of socks. She'd already packed four. "So we'll take two cars. Stick to the plan. It'll be fine." She unzipped and rezipped the pocket on her purse without putting anything into it.

Wrong answer, Mom.

I searched for a reason for Dad to come here, instead of meeting her at the hospital. An answer that would not involve telling my mother that she was clearly losing her mind. I didn't want to say that to her now; however crazy she might be for the next few days, it was nothing compared to the depression she'd sink into if this adoption fell through like the others.

Finally, lightning struck. I put a hand on Mom's arm. "If you both go in your car, you'll be able to both drive home with the baby, you know? You'll want to be together for that." Dad was technically my step-dad, or he had been before he adopted Athena and me. He'd never had an infant before, and I knew he didn't want to miss a single moment. And Mom didn't want to miss a single moment of it with *him*.

Mom nodded. "You're right. Of course you're right. Thank you for thinking of that." She pulled out her phone to text Dad.

That's what I'm here for, I thought. Then I dug my phone out of my pocket. "I'll do it. You finish packing."

Mom ran up the stairs again to grab who-knows-what while I sent a message to Dad. *Mom's nervous. Shouldn't drive. Come pick her up?*

I got a message back a second later. *On my way.*

I nodded. That was just what I wanted to hear.

Rodney leaned into the living room doorway. "Should I leave?"

"No," I said. "Mom will be gone in a few minutes, and then it will be quiet." Too quiet. I didn't want to be left alone in the quiet.

I was hoping that with Rodney out of sight in the living room and Mom halfway out of her mind, she'd forget that Rodney and I weren't allowed to be in the house alone. But she reappeared at the top of the stairs right then, a blank baby book in her hand. As if this child was going to begin to have milestones that she had to write down before they even got home from the hospital.

"Mom," I said. "I think you can leave that here."

She balanced the book on the corner of the banister at the top of the stairs, and put her hands on her hips. Rodney had disappeared back into the living room again, and Mom lowered her voice, even though I was sure he could still hear.

"What are you two going to do?" she asked. "Your father will be here any minute."

"We'll go grab food somewhere," I told her.

She raised her eyebrows. "What if it rains again?"

I sighed. "It was raining when we left school. Rodney can drive just fine in the rain."

She nodded. "And what will you do after that?"

I leaned against the wall. Mom could be really paranoid about leaving me alone with Rodney. I'd told her a million times that we weren't really together—high school relationships didn't last, and I didn't want to waste what Rodney and I had on some fleeting fling. I'd explained that to Mom, but she still worried. And I got that. She'd married and divorced her high school sweetheart—my birth father—before she was even twenty. Everything went better at home if I just didn't do anything with Rodney to make her worry. Which is why she didn't need to know about how often we made out, just-friends or not. I could

14

tell her we'd go to Rodney's house, where we would be equally alone, but that sure wasn't what she wanted to hear.

"After that he can drop me off at Athena's," I said. "And she can bring me to the hospital after the baby is born, so I can take pictures for you, okay? Like you planned?"

Mom nodded. "Okay," she said. She picked the baby book up again, brought it downstairs, and shoved it absentmindedly into her purse.

I hoped she remembered that arrangement and didn't call me in five minutes worried about where I was. A few minutes later my dad swept in the door, hefted Mom's bags and her worries, and directed her into her car.

I waved goodbye to them on the porch. When I went back into the house, I sank onto the couch beside Rodney and let my breath slide out of me. I loved my mother, but I couldn't help but feel a little bit glad that she'd gone, and taken her hurricane of stress and worry with her. A tiny pocket of it remained, though, swirling in my stomach. This time was going to be different. This one was going to last.

It had to.

Rodney rubbed my shoulder. "You'll be fine," he said. "Are you ready to go get something to eat?"

I shook my head. "I just told her that so she wouldn't worry. I don't think I could eat anything." To tell the truth, I was only slightly less nervous than she was. "Do you want to go home?" I asked. "My head is noisy today. I'll probably be crappy company."

Rodney rested an arm around my shoulders. "My house is too quiet," he said. "I like the noise."

I smiled and leaned into his shoulder, and, ironically, we were *both* quiet. I got what he was saying, though; there was a difference between the quiet of an empty house—Rodney's parents both worked crazy hours—and the quiet of sitting in comfortable silence with someone who wanted you around. This was the good kind of quiet—the kind Rodney and I made

15

together. That kind always made me feel better, no matter what.

And since adoption day was coming, that might be the only kind of quiet I could find for a while.

Mom didn't call that night, though Dad did send me a steady stream of update texts. Through the night and the next day at school, I checked my phone obsessively. Lily was at a three, a five, a seven. They were giving her an epidural. She was pushing. The baby was born. Mom got to hold her. Mom was already calling her Anna—the name she and my dad had picked.

As the updates came, I tried to breathe through the anxiety. Nothing was final until the paperwork was signed.

Then Anna would really be ours.

It took until the next evening before Mom called to tell me they were ready for me to come meet my baby sister. I would have been happy to wait until Anna officially came home, but Mom wanted nice, professional-looking pictures of Anna and Lily at the hospital, and I wasn't going to tell her no.

"Can Rodney bring you?" Mom asked.

I rolled my eyes. She'd already forgotten where I was supposed to be, and who I was supposed to be with.

Oh well. At least if Mom had forgotten the plan, I wouldn't get in trouble for not following it exactly. "Athena will drive me," I said. "I already asked her."

"Right," Mom said. "Thank you. I knew I could count on you."

Athena did drop me off, but she parked at the curb with the engine running.

"Are you sure you won't come with me?" I asked her.

Athena's hands hung limp on the wheel. "I will if you need me to."

It was Mom who might need her, not me. I hadn't seen her since she left the house, but I couldn't imagine she was any less of a mess. "Don't you want to meet our new sister?"

Athena shrugged. "I'll wait until the paperwork is done."

I fiddled with my lens cap, twisting it round and round. That's what Mom should have done, too. But she always charged in, wanting to be there for every possible minute, in case this was the child that would, at last, be hers. "This time will be different," I said. "Lily's almost part of the family."

"I know," Athena said. "That's what I'm worried about."

We'd only known Lily for two months, since she chose Mom and Dad to be the adoptive parents of her unborn baby. In the four weeks since Athena moved into the dorms, Lily had hung around our house more than Athena. She and Mom had negotiated an open adoption with visitation and everything, so after she signed the papers, she'd always be part of our lives.

Athena wouldn't say so, but I was pretty sure she'd stayed away partly *because* of Lily. Lily might be more likely to go through with the adoption because she got to be more involved than the other girls had, but she also had more power to hurt Mom. If Lily backed out, Mom would have two holes in her life to fill, instead of just one.

When I opened the car door, Athena gave me a worried look. "Are you sure you want to do this?" she asked.

"Yeah, of course," I said. "Mom asked me to."

Athena sighed. "I just don't think it's fair of her to do this to you."

I squeezed my camera. "I'm fine," I said. "If you need to worry about someone, worry about Mom."

"Okay," Athena said. But she didn't look convinced.

I took the elevator up to the maternity ward and gave them my name and pass phrase through the courtesy phone. The door buzzed, and I pushed it open.

Dad sat in the front waiting room. He stood and came over to me, giving me a hug. "Is Mom doing okay?" I asked.

Dad made a wobbling motion with his hand, which was pretty much a non-answer. "She and Lily are in with the baby."

"Anna," I said.

Dad nodded. "When the paperwork's final." He cringed. "But don't tell your mother I said that."

He knew I wouldn't. "Are they signing tonight?"

"That's the plan."

I sighed. I wished he'd talk about it with more confidence, if only for Mom's sake. She needed us all to be supportive, to be sure.

Otherwise, the stress was going to kill her.

I couldn't blame Dad, though. We were all tired. This was the last leg of a long race. We had so little left to go, but I still wasn't sure if we could make it.

Dad walked me down the hall to Lily's hospital room. Lily sat cross-legged on her bed, with the quilt Mom had made for her wrapped over her knees. She wore a hospital gown, but she'd already put on eyeliner, though not as thick as she usually wore it. I guessed Mom had told her I was coming to take pictures, and she didn't want to go without it.

Lily waved at me as I walked in the door. "Penny!" she said. "Come hold the baby!"

Mom had the baby in her arms, but she beamed up at me as I walked toward her. The infant was wrapped up in a tight little bundle, with only her head showing. She had about an inch of dark black hair already, though Lily's was blond.

"Anna," I said.

Lily wrinkled her nose. "Maybe. We were talking about Tina, too."

I frowned, and looked at Mom. She had been calling this baby Anna for the last month. I'd never heard anyone talk about Tina.

Mom didn't argue, but she didn't agree, either. She just ran a finger through the downy hair of the baby—my little sister.

Lily was only six months older than I was. To tell the truth, it was easier to think of *her* as my sister, since she was right between me and Athena.

"Do you want to hold her?" Mom asked.

"Pictures first," I said. I walked to the door, making sure that every light in the room was on. I knelt on the floor in front of Mom, snapping some shots of her looking down at the baby.

"Can I have her?" Lily asked. "Would you take some with me?"

I lowered my camera. I'd only just begun taking pictures of Mom. I opened my mouth to tell Lily to give us a minute, but Mom was already taking the baby over and placing her in Lily's arms.

Lily leaned down over the baby and smiled. I dragged my camera over and snapped a few photos from the end of the bed, and then moved closer, kneeling on the floor to get some of Lily looking down at the baby.

"That's enough," Mom said to me. "Don't overwhelm her." But when Lily looked down at the baby, she didn't look overwhelmed. She looked happy.

"It's okay," she said. "You can take a few more."

Please, I thought at her. *Don't do this to my mother.*

I stood above her, snapping away.

I'd give her all the pictures she wanted. Hundreds. Thousands. I'd give her pictures of her daughter from now until Anna graduated from college, if only Lily wouldn't break my mother's heart.

Rodney picked me up outside the hospital half an hour later. I wanted to stay until the papers were signed, but I could tell I was jittering, watching Lily hold the baby in her hospital bed like *she* was the mother. Once Anna came home, we could start feeling our way into a new normal, with our two new family members.

"How'd it go?" he asked as I climbed into his car.

"Good, I think," I said. "Let's go to my house. I can show you the pictures before we study for physiology."

"The first part sounds great," Rodney said. "Sure your parents won't freak out?"

I shook my head. "They're too worried to notice. Plus, studying. They can't argue with that, right?"

Rodney did not look pleased.

"It's a necessary evil," I said. "The test is tomorrow." I flipped through the photos on my camera's screen. It was sometimes hard to tell if I got anything good when the pictures were so small. I hoped the well-composed ones were in focus.

"You should have taken these," I said. "You're better than me. Plus she's a baby. They don't really move around much."

He smiled. "Moving, I can handle. But people want baby pictures to look cute. I don't do cute."

I rolled my eyes. He needed to get over that. We'd been talking about running a photography business together, and the easiest jobs to get were in family portraits. "Once Anna's home, you can take some edgy black-and-whites, okay? Maybe Mom will let you pose her with a tomato. You can pretend it's a still-life."

"Yes," he said. "I'm sure edgy is exactly what your mom will be looking for."

I shrugged. "I bet there will be a lot of poop. Remember that guy who took stills of his own feces? It'll totally be museum worthy."

Rodney laughed. "Dadaist baby photos. Could be a niche market."

"See," I said. "I knew I could get you to agree."

But he shook his head, like he hadn't. If Anna came home, I'd have to let her win him over herself.

When Anna came home. *When*. Not if.

The house was dark when we arrived. I unlocked the door and turned on all the lights as we walked upstairs.

Across the hall from my room, I could see through the door to Anna's new room, with her name spread across the wall in polka-dotted letters. There had been two names on the wall before hers. Mom had the rest of the alphabet stashed in the downstairs closet.

I'd told Rodney I'd show him the pictures, but instead I left my camera on my dresser. There would be plenty of time to fall in love with the pictures tomorrow, once Anna was really ours.

I sat cross-legged on my bed, opening my physiology book. Rodney sat on my chair, leaning back so his legs stretched halfway across my floor. I held the chart up for him to see. "Which one is the inferior nasal concha?"

"Come on," Rodney said. "Aren't you too distracted for this?"

I shook my head. "This *is* the distraction."

"I can think of a better one. I'll buy you dinner. We could order pizza."

I hadn't eaten, but I still wasn't hungry. I turned the chart so I could see. "It's this one," I said, putting my finger on the chart. When I checked the book, I had to slide my finger over half an inch to find the right spot for the label. "Whatever. I know it's in the nose. Isn't that enough?"

"Do me a favor," Rodney said. "Don't become a doctor."

"Come on," I said. "Save me from the madness of waiting for my parents to come home."

Rodney eyed Anna's room across the hall. "All right," he said, twirling his finger in the air. "Pin the anatomy on the chart. The ethmoid sinus is . . . here."

I checked the key in the book. He'd pointed right at it. "Never mind," I said. "Now I'm just depressed. I didn't even have to tell you what it was called."

"Meh," Rodney said. "I got lucky."

Lucky, my ass. We both knew it didn't matter how many hours I studied or how many he didn't. He would score half a grade higher than me on the test, like he always did.

My cell phone rang, and I pulled it out of my pocket. It was Dad. My heart thudded. I'd just seen them at the hospital. Why would he be calling me now?

Rodney snapped open his handheld game system, no doubt glad for the distraction from the studying. It also let him avoid staring at me while I was on the phone.

I took a deep breath. It didn't mean anything. Maybe they

were calling to tell me that they were coming home.

Maybe.

"Hey," I said into the phone.

"Penny?" Dad said. His voice sounded strained.

It took me a second to answer. "Yeah?"

"We're on our way," he said. "But we're not bringing the baby with us."

No, I thought. *No, no.*

And then he said it. The last words anyone in my family wanted to hear: "I'm sorry," he said. "But Lily has decided not to go through with the adoption."

I closed my eyes.

We'd been through this before, but instead of getting easier, each time got worse. Mom couldn't go through this again. *I* couldn't go through this again.

And yet, here we were.

Chapter Two
Week One

S he can't do that." I said. Lily had eaten dinner with us more often than not this last month. She'd gone out with us on my birthday. I'd helped her with her algebra.

"She can," Dad said. "We haven't signed anything. She still has rights."

Rodney shifted in his chair, but I didn't look up. He could probably tell what was happening just from the look on my face. I kept the phone pressed to my ear and bit a nail. "So she can just use us and then . . ."

Dad's voice got sharp, though I could tell he was trying not to let it be. "She's not using us," he said. "She's still the baby's mother."

"Anna," I said.

"Tina," he said. "She's naming her Tina."

Tina. Where had that come from? "I can't believe this."

"I know," Dad said. "We made a mistake, getting so close to her. I'm sorry."

Getting close wasn't exactly the problem. "What is she going to do? She doesn't have anybody but us."

Dad spoke slowly. This was the same voice he used to talk Mom down, when something like this went wrong. "I don't know, honey. That's not really any of our business."

I chewed on my lip. None of our business? We were supposed to be like family now. And Lily was just going to walk away from that?

Of course she was. She'd do it for her baby. Mom cried for weeks after the last one, but she said she understood. You didn't walk away from someone who had that tight a hold on you. You didn't just leave them with a stranger. She said placing a baby for adoption was the hardest thing in the world to do, because all your instincts said to take care of that baby, whatever the cost.

But if Lily couldn't let go, knowing Mom, knowing how good a parent she was, practically being parented by Mom herself, who would?

I sighed. "Is Mom okay?" Stupid question. "Don't answer that."

Dad sounded tired. "We'll be home soon, okay?"

"Okay," I said. Even though it wasn't.

Dad hung up the phone; I glared at the ceiling.

When I looked down, I found Rodney fiddling with his game system. "Things went bad?"

"Yeah," I said. "Again." I stood up and walked into Anna's room—the nursery, as we would resume calling it—and pulled all the letters down off the wall. I stashed them in the top drawer of the dresser, on top of the perfectly folded rows of onesies. Then I turned off the light, and shut the door.

I pulled mine closed as well, leaving only the necessary crack. Once Mom and Dad came home, we were allowed to be in my room as long as the door was open a little. I'd never say this to them, but the rule didn't matter. We could close doors at Rodney's house all we wanted.

But today, Mom and Dad weren't going to be thinking about rules. They'd only be thinking about what they'd lost.

Then I reached for my camera and started deleting the photos of Anna. Mom could never see these.

I never wanted to see them again.

Then I picked up my phone to call Athena. "Did you hear?"

I asked when she answered.

"Yeah. Dad texted me. Do you think I need to come over?"

"Probably not," I said. "I'm hiding in my room with Rodney. You don't really want to be here, do you?"

"I don't," Athena said. "But I don't want to abandon you there, either. You want to come have a sleepover? I'll let you take the bed."

"I'll be okay," I said. "I'll just make Rodney stay for a while."

He nodded at me. Of course he'd stay. That wasn't even a question.

"I wish Mom hadn't done this to you," Athena said. "It's not fair."

I groaned. "She's not doing it to me," I said. "Lily is doing this to her."

"I guess," Athena said. "But it was Mom's idea to let her into your lives."

I closed my eyes. Athena always said that Mom was looking for another daughter because we weren't enough. I knew it stung that Mom practically replaced Athena just as she was leaving the house, what with Lily being around all the time. But I didn't care if we were enough for Mom or not.

I just wanted the crying to stop.

"You should call Mom tomorrow," I said. "Lily will change her mind."

"Don't count on it," Athena said. "And don't say that to Mom."

"I won't," I said. It was probably wrong to get her hopes up. Though at this point, if she didn't have hope, what did she have?

Nothing but pain, that's what.

"Call me if you want to get out. Day or night."

"Done."

Then I turned off the phone. "I'll be right back," I told Rodney. Then I moved through the house, turning off the ringer on all the phones. The last thing Mom needed was every friend and family member calling to congratulate her on the new baby. If

Dad was smart, he'd sent out a mass text about it, so everyone would know. But then they'd all call to console her, which wasn't what she needed, either.

When I returned to Rodney, he'd collected the anatomy chart and book from my bed. "Sit," he said. "I'll quiz you."

I heard Mom and Dad come home ten minutes later. Rodney and I stayed in my room, and Dad didn't swing the door open like he usually did when we were up here alone.

"I can go anytime," Rodney said. "But I'll stay as long as you want."

"Thanks," I said. "You can go back to your video game, if you want."

But he didn't.

An hour later, when I walked Rodney out to his car, we found Mom sitting alone on the porch swing. She wore sweats, and had her hair pulled up in a ponytail. I could see the remnants of her makeup pooled at the corners of her eyes, and smeared across the outline of her jaw, but she wasn't crying now.

"Night, Rodney," she said.

He waved at her. "Goodnight."

That was one thing I loved about Rodney. He was never awkward with anyone. "I'll see you in the morning," I said to him.

Rodney nodded. "I'll pick you up." Then he walked to his car, and was gone.

I stood in the doorway, not sure if I should disappear upstairs, or stay. "Do you want company?"

"Sure," Mom said.

I sat down cross-legged beside Mom. The swing creaked as we swayed back and forth.

"I'm really sorry," I said.

"Me, too," Mom said. "You'd think I would have learned by now not to let someone into our lives like that."

Letting Lily in wasn't the problem. She wouldn't have regretted that if she had a baby in her arms right now. "She seemed like she liked us."

"She did," Mom said. "She liked us, but she loved her baby more. Someday, when you hold your own child, you'll understand."

I didn't know if I would do either. Athena told me she was never having kids, not after what we'd been through with Mom. What if she had one, or two, and then wanted more and couldn't have them? What if it consumed her, like it did Mom? But me, I just tried not to think about it.

"What will you do now?" I asked.

"I don't know," Mom said. "Try again, I guess."

I dug my nails into my palms. The thought of letting some other girl into our house, letting her sit at our dinner table and tell us that Mom could have her child, made me want to punch Lily right in the nose. I didn't see how Mom could trust another birth mother again.

I knew *I* couldn't.

"Let's talk about something else," Mom said. "How's school?"

Mom always got *really* interested in my life right after she lost a child, like she needed to remember that she was actually a mother, even if she wanted more kids than just the two of us. It bugged Athena when Mom did that; Athena just wanted Mom to butt out. But I didn't mind.

I leaned back, trying to think of a good story to tell her. "We have a physiology test tomorrow," I said. "Facial respiratory anatomy." That wasn't a brilliant tale, but it was on my mind.

Mom nodded, slowly. "Are you ready?"

"I'm nervous about it."

"Did you study?"

"Yeah. But it all blurs together after a while."

"I'm sure you'll do fine. You always do."

"I'll pass," I said. "But Rodney will do better."

"You'll beat him one of these days."

"Not likely."

"It'll happen. But there's got to be something more interesting going on in your life than that."

"Well, my mother lost a baby," I said.

Mom gave the swing a hard shove with her feet. "Something that doesn't involve your mother, maybe?"

"Okay," I said. "Here's some real drama. My friend Kara's boyfriend just dumped her over a text message."

"Ugh," Mom said, making a pained face. "Dating used to be hard enough. I'm so glad I married your father before the invention of the text."

I remembered when Mom dated Dad—I was six, and Athena was eight. Mom liked him because he was a gentleman. He called ahead for dates, and even paid for her babysitter, so she could go out without having it add to her single-mom financial stress. That had been the biggest four years in my family's life—year one: dating, year two: marriage, year three: adoption of Athena and me. And then year four, the year I turned ten. The first pregnancy.

Things hadn't changed much since then.

"Dad wouldn't have dumped anyone over a text message," I said. "Then or now."

"Not as an adult. Maybe in high school. Boys that young just aren't capable of commitment."

Mom would know. My biological father split when I was just a baby. "Yeah," I said. "Kara's a mess."

"How long had she been dating this guy?"

"A year."

Mom groaned again.

"Yeah. She sobbed for three days, and then she saw him making out with some freshman in the quad."

Mom turned to me. "And that made her cry less?"

"It made her angry, which is an improvement over weepy."

Mom gave a sharp nod. "That's what I need," Mom said. "Someone to be angry at."

"Lily," I said. The name was out of my mouth before I realized it was an inappropriate thing to say.

"No," Mom said. "I can't be mad at her for loving her baby."

28

Mom would have let her love Anna. That's what the open adoption was for. "Well, I think she's crazy for not wanting you to be Anna's mom."

"You have to say that," Mom said. "You're my daughter."

I stabbed a finger in the air. "Not true. Most people at school hate their mothers."

"Ah, right," Mom said. "Maybe you should try that. Tell me you hate me. Be a normal teenager for once."

"Nah," I said. "I'll save that for a text message."

For a moment, I thought Mom might smile. The corners of her mouth twitched upward, but then they wilted down again. "We should both go to bed," she said. "I'm exhausted, and you have that test tomorrow."

"Okay," I said. We kept swinging for a moment longer. I tried to think of the perfect thing to say—something that would really make her feel better. There were no perfect words. I already knew that. We'd been through this before.

"You are the best mom ever," I said.

I sounded like a greeting card, but Mom didn't care. She wrapped an arm around me and pulled me into her shoulder. "Love you," she said.

And I knew that didn't make everything better, but it certainly didn't make it worse.

We climbed the stairs together, and when Mom opened the door to her bedroom, I could see that Dad still had the light on. Mom closed the door behind her and their voices talked in quiet murmurs; I couldn't hear what they were saying.

I went into the bathroom, and closed the door behind me, leaning against it in the dark. The latch rattled against the door frame.

My family couldn't do this anymore. We'd all had enough of believing that this next time would be the right one, that Mom would finally get to have more kids. She'd had Athena when she was my age, married her high school boyfriend, and then had me two years later. They'd lived in his parents' basement

29

until he'd left her, and then she'd spent five years as a single parent, doing daycare to pay the bills. Mom thought when she married Dad that she'd finally get to have the big family she always wanted, but that didn't work out, not through fertility treatments or adoption.

We couldn't let another birth mom into our home. I couldn't pretend that one more girl my age was supposed to be like a sister to me. I couldn't watch Mom try to open her heart to another one, like she was her daughter.

I was *already* her daughter. And if I were pregnant right now, I'd choose Mom and Dad to parent that baby in a second.

I flipped on the light and looked at myself in the mirror. Lily was only six months older than me, so she'd been younger than me when she got pregnant. If she'd given Mom the baby, she could have done anything she wanted after.

Mom needed a pregnant girl who didn't want to keep her baby. She needed someone who loved her enough to make her a mother again, since she and Dad couldn't. And if love for a baby was that strong—if someone who liked us as much as Lily did couldn't make the sacrifice—then Mom needed someone who loved her so much that she could.

Someone just like me.

My fingers trembled. I couldn't do that, could I?

But in my mind, I heard the things I learned in sex-ed. You can get pregnant, even the first time.

The more I thought about it, the more it made sense. There was no one in the world better to be the daughter Mom needed than me.

The daughter she already had.

Chapter Three
Week One

I didn't remember falling asleep that night, but I did remember waking up knowing that I was losing my mind. I'd fallen asleep with my knees curled up under me, still thinking about the possibility of getting pregnant for Mom. As if that were a thing I could even think about doing. That was crazy, right? It had to be.

I stretched my arms above my head and tried to forget about it, like any sane person would.

Then I heard Mom's voice in the hall.

"I don't see why we can't try again," she said.

Dad's voice was weary. "It's just so much money."

I hugged my knees. My door was still closed, and my alarm clock wasn't due to go off for another half an hour. It was never a good sign for them to get started this early in the morning, and it was an even worse sign for them to be arguing so soon after a loss.

"I could get a job," Mom said.

I didn't have to see Dad to know the look on his face, lips pursed, like he was trying to hold in the things he really wanted to say. They'd gone into debt to afford the first set of fertilized eggs, and the medical treatment that went with implanting them. But now they'd lost all of those babies, and even if the doctor would do it, they couldn't afford to try again.

They couldn't afford adoption, either. But Mom kept pushing. Mom didn't give up. "We could borrow against the house. We have the equity."

I couldn't hear Dad's sigh, but I knew it was there. I tried to bury my head in my pillow, but my stomach twisted. There was no way I was going back to sleep. Instead, I rolled out of bed, opened a dresser drawer, and slammed it closed again. Sometimes, if they knew I could hear them, they'd cool down before things really got going.

Footsteps moved past my door and downstairs. I hadn't ended the argument, just relocated it.

That should have made me feel better, but it didn't. If I couldn't hear them, who knew how upset they might be getting? I wavered. If I followed them downstairs, they might stop. Or one of them might turn on me, and then I'd be in the middle of it. I didn't want Dad to storm off to work—that would just stress Mom out more.

I moved across the hall to the bathroom and climbed into the shower, trying to get rid of the queasy sensation, but the longer they were out of earshot, the more my stomach tightened. Who knew what they might be saying to each other when I couldn't hear?

I turned up the heat of the water until it nearly scorched my skin, and let it slowly drain lukewarm as the hot water ran out.

Breathe, I told myself. *Breathe.*

The answer to all of this couldn't be for me to get pregnant. But.

But.

The possibilities swirled in my mind. If I were pregnant, Mom and Dad wouldn't have to pay nearly as much as they did for adoption, or infertility treatments. There would be doctor's bills, sure, but they paid Lily's, and she wasn't even covered by our insurance.

I stood with my face under the water, holding my breath.

I couldn't really do that. Of course I couldn't. If I wanted to get pregnant I needed to have sex, and Rodney and I didn't do that. Sure, we'd made out more than a few times, but we both thought it was stupid to be in a committed relationship that would inevitably lead to a breakup. I couldn't stand the idea of losing Rodney. If we weren't officially together, our relationship could ebb and flow naturally, instead of needing labels that might inspire us to split over text message. I'd always figured I'd date Rodney eventually, like when we were both in college and old enough to make serious decisions about our lives.

Like having a baby.

I turned off the water and stood in the steamy tub, dripping. I squeezed my eyes closed, trying to wring out the thoughts, to let them run down the drain with the water.

My heart beat faster. I climbed out of the shower and ran my fingers across the mirror, revealing my striped reflection. The thoughts were still there, spinning at the back of my mind.

And the worst part was, they made a crazy kind of sense.

When I turned off the bathroom fan, I could hear Mom and Dad's voices downstairs. I got dressed as quickly as I could, and then stood on the stairs, gripping the banister.

"What is one more payment?" Mom asked. "When compared with a child?"

My hair dripped onto my shirt, soaking my shoulders. If it took them this long to arrive there, they must be arguing in circles.

"Nothing," Dad said. "But it never happens. We spend the money, and something goes wrong."

I gripped my hair, wringing water onto the carpet. Dad was right, but he still shouldn't say that. Not when this new loss was so fresh.

Mom's voice shook, like she was hanging on to hope by a thread, and Dad was threatening to cut it. "Don't be a pessimist."

Dad's voice softened. "I'm talking about *reality*."

Mom's edged toward hysterical. "You're talking about *money*."

"I'm really not," Dad said.

I sucked in my breath. The argument paused for a heartbeat. *Don't*, I thought.

"What, then?" Mom asked.

"I can't watch you go through this again," Dad said. "I can't. And Penny can't, either. I swear she's going to move into that dorm with Athena."

I bit down on my lip. It wasn't fair for Dad to use me as an excuse.

But he also wasn't wrong. I'd had that thought, too. Repeatedly.

Jeez. What kind of a daughter was I? Did I really want what was best for Mom, or not?

I heard Mom sniffle. "I'm sorry," Dad said.

Mom didn't respond. Dad wouldn't push her any further; he'd only said what he did because Mom dragged it out of him. I wished he'd held back even then, though. Mom might stew on it for days before she asked me if that was true, and then I'd have to tell her that it wasn't. Of course we'd stand by her again. Of course. That's what families did.

But a voice nagged at the back of my mind: *families help each other. Aren't you willing to do everything you can?*

I heard one of my parents sink onto a couch. "I'm sorry," Dad said again. "I didn't mean . . ."

I took a deep breath. At least the fight was over, for now. I crept downstairs and into Dad's office as quietly as I could, and sat down at his computer.

I still had ten minutes before I was even supposed to be awake, and unless I wanted to run into Mom while she was crying, I needed to lie low. I pulled up a photo I was editing—a picture I'd taken while lying down in the roots of a redwood with the top of my head against the trunk. I'd focused on a felty strip of bark halfway up the tree, with the branches and the rest of the trunk in fuzzy focus on either side.

A minute later, I heard the front door close. I figured Dad had gone to work, but then the office door opened behind me, and Dad stood in the doorway. He hadn't even gotten dressed yet. "I'm sorry you had to hear that," he said. "Are you okay?"

I guess I didn't sneak downstairs as quietly as I'd thought. "I'm fine," I said. "What about Mom?"

"Not okay," Dad said. He hesitated. "That's my fault. I shouldn't have said those things."

I understood. Sometimes it was hard not to. "Where did she go?"

He waved a hand toward the front door. "I think she just needs some space."

Space was good when she came back better, but sometimes she came back worse. "I could talk to her if you want."

Dad shook his head. "Let's both let it go, unless she brings it up again, okay?"

I squirmed. "You're still going to have to decide what to do though, aren't you? About the future?"

Dad leaned against the door frame, like the weight was too heavy to carry. "We will," he said.

We both looked down at the floor. There were no easy answers, I guessed. Dad would never suggest that I should have a baby for Mom. He'd never even *think* it.

And if I told him about it, he'd tell me that I shouldn't be thinking it, either.

"What are you working on?" Dad asked.

I leaned back so Dad could see the photo.

"Is it finished?"

"Not started, actually," I said. "I'm about to correct the colors." Since the tree provided too much shade, I needed to adjust the white balance and the exposure, to bring out the green in the needles and the burgundy brown in the trunk.

"You're still thinking of studying this in college?"

I shrugged. Stressing about money always got him asking about my educational plans. Neither he nor Mom had college degrees, and he always blamed that whenever they couldn't afford things, as if people with college degrees never had money problems. "Probably," I said.

"Doesn't pay well, does it?"

"I think it depends on what you do with it."

Dad gave me a sharp nod. "You better find out before you start."

"I will," I said. "Don't worry."

"I'll worry all I want," he said. But he was already walking up the stairs to get ready for work.

Athena was majoring in English teaching, which meant that even with a college degree, she'd never make more than Dad did. Dad kept hoping she'd change her mind, but Athena wasn't the mind-changing type.

I saw his point, though. If photography and editing wouldn't make money, I'd find something else to major in. Then Dad could quit stressing about it.

I was upstairs drying my hair when Dad knocked on the bathroom door. I turned off the blow-dryer.

"I'm leaving," he said. "Your mom isn't back yet. Do you need a ride to school?"

"Rodney's picking me up," I called.

"Great. Have a good day."

As his footsteps plunked down the stairs, I heard him mutter, "Someone should."

I turned the blow-dryer back on, to muffle anything else he might have said.

If ever there was a morning I wanted to rush off to school, this was it, but I finished getting ready with time to spare. I went back down to his computer, where I'd left my photo. I selected the tree bark and toyed with the colors, pushing them from yellow to blue and then back again. My fingers trembled, and I had to use the keyboard to move the slider, to be sure I found a happy equilibrium.

By the time Rodney arrived, I'd been pacing back and forth in the living room for twenty minutes. In our four-year friendship, I'd never been nervous around Rodney. This was ridiculous.

There was nothing to be nervous about anyway. He'd never agree to have a baby with me, would he? I mean, given his opinion of taking pictures of kids, I knew he wasn't interested in being a father.

But that was kind of the point, wasn't it? He *wouldn't* be the baby's father. That was the point of adoption: he wouldn't have any responsibility to the baby.

I paced faster.

When I heard his car door slam, I walked into the kitchen and grabbed a glass of orange juice, trying not to look like I'd been waiting. Rodney knocked on the door and then just opened it. He walked right through the living room to find me in the kitchen.

"Hey," he said. "Can I have some of that?"

I nudged the carton of orange juice his way, and he opened the cabinet and pulled down his own glass. I tried to relax. Any guy who knew where to find the glasses in my kitchen was not a guy to be nervous around.

"How's your mom?" he asked.

"I don't know," I said. "She left the house this morning before I got up."

"That's good, right?"

The first time Mom lost a baby, she stayed in bed for four days. "It's better. But she left because she and Dad had a fight."

"Ugh. Not good. Sorry." Rodney guzzled his orange juice down in a series of gulps. I stood against the counter, trying to decide what to do with my hands.

The last time Rodney and I made out was a month ago, on the last weekend of summer break. We'd driven over the hill to the Santa Cruz boardwalk and wandered around. After three spins through the bumper cars, we walked down to the water and Rodney scooped me off my feet and dunked me into the waves. My breath flew right out of me when the icy water hit my skin, and when I caught it again, I screamed. Rodney stood above me, waves washing up to his thighs, laughing and laughing.

When the seventh wave came, I rolled right into him and knocked him onto his butt. His arms circled over his head like a drowning man trying to do a butterfly stroke, and then the wave bowled me right over him, tangling us together, and that's when he kissed me.

We didn't drag ourselves out of the waves until a kid on a boogie board nearly ran us over, and then Rodney pulled me to my feet and held my hand up the beach and all the way back to the car. We drove to the point above Seabright beach and made out in the front seat as the sun went down over the ocean. Even in my memory it felt more frantic and silly than romantic. Kissing Rodney was always like that.

But now we weren't doing anything silly, or frantic. We were just standing in my kitchen like we did on all the mornings that Rodney drove me to school.

Rodney raised his eyebrows at me as he finished his orange juice. "What?" he asked.

"Just admiring your juice-chugging skills," I said.

He grinned. "I am the champion."

My return smile twitched, but Rodney didn't seem to notice.

Argh. I wasn't ready to bring sex up with Rodney when I'd just begun to think about it myself. What would we talk about on a normal day?

Physiology, and *not* the sexual kind. Until that moment, I'd forgotten about the exam. We both had that class before lunch, so there wasn't much time left to study. Rodney had the test first period, and I had it third. At this moment, I couldn't remember half the terms that would be on it. Maybe if we'd been labeling reproductive anatomy, I'd have had better luck.

"Are you ready for the test?" I asked.

"I think I might need a donut to get my brain running. You mind stopping by the grocery store?"

I looked at the clock. We had time, if we hurried. "Sure," I said. "As long as it's your treat."

"A whole donut," Rodney said. "I don't know that my wallet

will ever recover."

I stiffened. The donuts were always his suggestion, so him paying for me didn't make it a sign of our relationship status or anything. Yesterday I wouldn't have worried about it. But today that month since we'd last made out seemed like a long time. He didn't kiss me in the tree. But he'd wanted to, hadn't he?

Was I crazy thinking he'd even *want* to have sex with me?

On the way to his car, Rodney glanced at me sideways. "You're quiet today," he said. "Are you that worried about the test?"

"Maybe," I said.

"You always do fine," Rodney said. "Even after you worry."

Today I *wished* that was the biggest thing on my mind.

Chapter Four
Week One

After school, Rodney had a chess match. On chess club days, I sometimes waited around for him and sometimes I caught a ride with Kara. I could always text my mom for a ride, but today, I didn't want to. That was selfish, and I knew it. If she was lying at home in a pool of darkness, I should call to drag her out.

But instead, I called Athena. She answered on the fourth ring. "Hey," I said. "Are you busy?"

"I should be," Athena said. "I'm supposed to be writing a paper, but my eyes were crossing."

"Can I come over?" I asked.

"Sure. Can you catch the bus?"

"No problem." That was the benefit of having Athena on the college campus; the bus went straight there. I texted Mom to tell her where I was going, got off the bus at the student center, and hiked up the stairs to the dorms. When I arrived at the foot of her high rise, I texted Athena so she could come downstairs and let me into the building. She opened the door in her pajama bottoms and a t-shirt, her long brown hair pulled back.

"Didn't you have class today?" I asked.

She shrugged. "Yeah. I changed when I got back."

We ran up the stairs to her room, Athena's ponytail swinging to the waistband of her PJs. "How's Mom?" she asked. "I'm guessing it's bad, right?"

I groaned. "She and Dad had a fight about whether they're going to try again."

Athena looked at me over her shoulder. "So that's why you're here."

I rolled my eyes. "I also like you a little."

Athena waved a hand dismissively. "I'm avoiding my paper; you're avoiding home. I'm not going to judge you."

We reached the top of the stairs. Athena unlocked her door and flopped onto her bed. I sat next to her with my legs crossed under me. "Thanks for letting me come over," I said.

"Stay as long as you want," Athena said. "Though you can't avoid Mom entirely unless you move in."

She was right. The last adoption, Mom didn't fall apart completely until the week after she lost the baby, when she had to face her next period. Some girls tracked their own periods on a calendar, but I tracked Mom's. If I wasn't careful during those days, I might be the one who made her cry.

Mom was only thirty-four. We still had a lot of years of periods ahead of us.

Athena kicked her feet up, resting her heels on the wall. "So did you hear if they decided anything?"

I played with the edge of her blanket. "No. Mom wants to do in vitro again. Or international adoption."

Athena rolled her eyes. "If they'd done that the last time, they might have a baby by now."

"Maybe," I said. "But don't say that to Mom."

Athena shook her head. "She won't listen, anyway."

I picked up a piece of lint and rolled it between my fingers. "Then Dad told her that he didn't want to watch her go through it again."

Athena's eyes widened. "Really? I didn't think Dad had it in him."

I sighed. "Yeah. And then Mom left the house."

Athena looked up at the ceiling. "Even odds say by tonight they'll both be pretending he never said that."

That would be better, wouldn't it? Except then we'd be going through this again in a few months, back in this same place like we were riding a horrible merry-go-round none of us knew how to get off.

Athena ticked us off on her hands, "You avoid Mom. I avoid homework. Mom avoids the truth—"

"Please," I said. "You avoid Mom, too. Don't even."

"Fine," Athena said. "But now that I don't live there, I can pretend that I don't."

"And the truth!" I said. "That's three for you, and one for each of us. You lose."

"Or I win," Athena said. "Ding ding ding! The most out-of-the-house award goes to—"

I kicked my legs out from under me and flopped down next to her. "You know, if I wanted to talk about this stuff, I would have gone home."

"No," Athena said. "When you want to avoid things, you talk to Mom and Dad. You come to me when you want to discuss."

I sat up and looked at my bare arm where a watch might have been, if I wore one. "Gee, look at the time. Guess I should get—"

Athena smacked me in the arm. "Shut up. You just got here. If you want to talk about something else, tell me about Rodney. Is he calling himself your boyfriend yet?"

I lay back down, taking up half of Athena's pillow. "No," I said. "And he won't be anytime soon."

"Please. I dated Taren all through high school, and our relationship looked exactly like yours."

I couldn't decide if I hated or loved the way Athena had to announce everything that she thought. Mom hated it—they fought all the time when Athena lived at home.

For me, I think it was half and half.

"And you broke up as soon as you graduated," I said, "which

proves my point."

"Touché," Athena said. Though that wouldn't stop her from bothering me about it next week. She was a little stuck on labels, but Rodney and I were better than that. We didn't need the label to know that we cared about each other.

I closed my eyes. Though, having a label would have made it more clear whether I could, say, have sex with him without screwing everything up. "Why didn't you sleep with Taren?" I asked. I knew she hadn't, because two weeks after graduation, he dumped her for a girl who would.

Athena's eyebrows disappeared under her bangs. "Where did that question come from?"

I waved a hand in the air, trying to play it off. "I was just wondering. You think you're the only one who gets to pry?"

She laughed. "I was scared of getting pregnant. You'd think I wouldn't have been, 'cause of Mom."

I froze. "Because you would have given the baby to her?"

Athena's mouth dropped open. "No, psycho. You think I want to be one of her pet birth moms?"

"Ouch." That was harsh, even for Athena. I didn't want to be Mom's *pet*.

I probably shouldn't have taken it as such a slap to the face. Athena tried to fly under Mom's radar as much as possible. She wouldn't be able to handle Mom paying that much attention to her. But Mom and I got along fine. Plus, it would only be for nine months.

Athena rolled her eyes. "I meant because she's proof getting pregnant isn't always that easy."

My stomach dropped. Way to be obvious, Penny. "Oh. Right."

Athena didn't even notice. "I think dealing with her just made me hyper-aware of the possibility." She gave me a suspicious look. "But seriously, why do you ask?"

I held up both palms in surrender. "I was just wondering, that's all. I swear." I sounded guilty, though. After that comment about Mom, would Athena put two and two together?

She squinted at me. "You and Rodney aren't having sex, then?"

Oh. *That's* what she thought I sounded guilty about. "No," I said. "Not yet."

She grabbed the sleeve of my t-shirt and dug her fingers in. "Not *yet*? Didn't you just finish telling me about how you're not even together?"

"Um," I said. She had a point. If we did have sex, what would that make me? Not a slut, exactly. Easy? Not if it took four years of friendship, right?

"But really," Athena said, "why would you want to sleep with the guy if you're not committed?"

My face flushed. Why indeed.

Her eyebrows waggled dramatically. "Unless you *are* to-gether. . ." Her mouth dropped open, waiting for me to fall into her trap.

Not a chance. "It was a hypothetical! I'm not planning anything."

Athena snorted. "You guys must be doing *something*, if you're thinking about it."

"We've made out a few times." Or forty or fifty, over the years.

Athena rolled over on her side so she could look me in the eye. "Just be careful. Even Mom got pregnant quick, when she was our age."

Literally our ages, now that I thought about it. With Athena when she was my age, and with me when she was Athena's. "I know," I said.

And I did know. That's what I would be banking on—that I could get pregnant quick, when Mom couldn't, anymore.

Jeez. What was I thinking?

Athena was right. I *was* a psycho.

Athena played with the end of her hair. "And it's not just that. Having sex without commitment complicates everything, because it means different things to girls than it does to guys.

My roommate comes home after spending the night at a guy's place, and she thinks they're really together, you know? But to the guy, nothing's changed. Spending the night didn't make them any closer than they were before, and it certainly didn't mean a commitment."

Ouch. "Sucks for Wendy," I said.

"Yeah," Athena said. "But especially with Rodney not even being your boyfriend . . ."

Please. Even the label of husband hadn't been enough to keep our birth dad around. Kara thought being Ryan's girlfriend meant they'd last, but they obviously didn't. I sighed. "But if sex isn't a big deal to him, then it wouldn't mess up our friendship any, right?"

Athena's eyes went wide. "That's not what I meant for you to get out of that story."

I sat up. "It's okay," I said. "I get it. Don't worry."

But Athena was still studying me. I climbed off the bed.

"Really," I said. "Thanks for letting me talk about this stuff."

Athena lowered her feet over the edge of the bed and crossed her arms over her chest. "You haven't really said much. I've just been lecturing you, which I know isn't helpful. I'm sorry, okay?"

"I'm fine," I said. "Really."

"And you don't have anything else you want to tell me?"

I shook my head slowly.

But once again, Athena didn't look convinced.

When I got home that night, Dad's truck wasn't in the driveway. At this point he might just be working late, but another twenty minutes would push it over into clear avoidance territory.

So that made all of us.

I walked through the door to find a stack of brown paper bags lining the floor of the living room. In the bags were stacks of onesies, diapers, even the mobile that had been hanging above the baby's bed. I could hear noise coming from upstairs, and

I went up to find Mom lying on her back on the floor of the nursery, ratchet in hand, disassembling the crib.

"Mom," I said. "What are you doing?"

"What does it look like I'm doing?" she asked. I'd expected anger in her voice, even tears, but she sounded calm.

I steadied one side of the crib for her. "This isn't what Dad meant for you to do."

She sighed. "So you heard."

"Yeah," I said. "Let's put this back together before he gets home, okay?"

"I already talked to your father," she said, pulling the side off the crib. "He's fine with it."

I slowly lowered my side of the crib, so the pieces rested on the floor on either side of Mom. "Okay," I said. "We can put everything in the closet, and you can put it back up when you're ready."

Mom shook her head decisively. "No. Your dad's right. I have to deal with reality. I have two daughters, and that's enough." Her jaw set, like she was determined to believe that, even though she didn't. And with good reason. If Mom could really just give up on a child so easily, she would have done it years ago.

"Reality can change," I said.

Mom gave me a hard look, like she didn't believe that, and didn't think that I could, either. And I felt a sudden stabbing of guilt that I hadn't thought about getting pregnant earlier. If I had, could I have saved us from these last few years of pain? Would Mom already have a baby in the nursery? Would she have been spared waiting so long that she felt the need to take apart the crib?

Even in the bright light of the nursery, long shadows stretched across her face. If she gave up now, I'd be looking at them for the rest of our lives. If I had children someday, I'd know she wished it was her.

And *I'd* know that it could have been her, if I'd just tried harder to help her. I sank against the doorway, and that's when

46

I knew.

I had the power to change my mother's life. It would be selfish of me *not* to do it. "Please, Mom," I said. "Let's store it in the garage. For now."

Mom hesitated, and a flicker of hope crossed her face—not for long, but long enough for me to know that this is what she wanted. She didn't want to give up hope. She just didn't want to live with the pain anymore.

I could fix that. I could make it better. And if the last years were any indicator, I was the only one in the world who would.

"Please?" I said again.

Mom looked around at the remnants of the crib, and nodded. "At least then it will be out of the way."

"Exactly," I said. Mom's dreams, tucked quietly out of sight— far enough away that the reminder wouldn't sting, but not so far as to be out of reach.

Chapter Five
Week Two

The next morning I caught Dad in the hall, looking at the empty nursery. When he heard me behind him, he shut the door and turned toward me, rubbing his forehead.

I stood in my doorway and leaned against the frame. "I convinced her to leave everything in the garage."

Dad's eyes looked tired, and it was only seven AM. "That's probably for the best." His eyes caught on one of the baby pictures hanging in the hall—a portrait of Athena holding me, when she was three and I was barely one year old. Dad looked away quickly and faked a smile at me, but as he did, the same long shadows I'd seen on Mom's face stretched across his.

I collapsed against the door frame. Dad wasn't that old, either—only thirty-two to Mom's thirty-four. Plenty of people had their first child at that age. Dad had raised Athena and me as his kids, but he'd never had a baby. He hadn't even met me until I was six. I'd seen him look at our baby pictures that way before—like he wished he could have been there. I wished that, too. He should have been my father from the very beginning.

But he wasn't. And Mom wasn't the only one who wanted a baby in her arms.

"Love you, Dad," I said.

He put a hand on my shoulder. "Love you, too. Check on your mom before you head to school, okay?"

I nodded. "Okay."

And then Dad walked down the stairs and headed out the door to work.

I walked down the hall to Mom and Dad's room.

Through the gap between Mom's door and the door frame, I could see the lump of her lying in the middle of her bed, covers wrapped around her like a cocoon.

My stomach knotted. She rarely overslept, except on the bad days. If I was already pregnant, then she wouldn't be in this state now. I turned her door handle and pulled the door the rest of the way shut, letting go slowly to avoid even the slightest click.

It was time to put my plan into action. I opened the hall closet to find her ovulation predictors. If I was going to get pregnant, I needed more information about what my body was doing. It had been a week or two since my period, but I wasn't sure exactly how long. But I'd been living with Mom long enough to know how to track my fertility: she'd used ovulation predictors for years.

But as I reached for her stack of rectangular boxes, the ones she kept wedged between the extra tubes of toothpaste and tablecloths for special occasions, I found the space empty. Our red-and-green Christmas napkins slid out of the center of the tablecloth pile, the whole stack slouching into the new space.

I sighed. The nursery wasn't the only thing Mom had been cleaning.

In the garage, I found the place where Mom and I had stacked the crib, against the wall below the weed-whacker. I poked through the tops of the bags of onesies and burp cloths and thin, flannel blankets, but found nothing.

I stepped back, thinking I'd try the kitchen trash, when something crunched under my foot.

I stepped aside and looked. Where my foot had been, I found a shard of tan plastic, smaller than a dime. Amid the layers of dust and leaves and last summer's grass clippings, I found more of them—tiny, brittle chunks of plastic in irregular shapes, like someone dropped a pair of glasses, but broke only the frames.

I saw the hammer sitting on top of Dad's toolbox, and felt like I'd been socked in the gut. I hurried out the side door to our garbage cans, already knowing what I was going to find.

The morning air was thick with mist, but I could see the few feet to the garbage cans just fine. I lifted the lid on the one for trash. On top of one of the bags of garbage were the shattered remains of several ovulation predictors and pregnancy tests. They lay spread over the top of a white liner from the kitchen garbage, and smelled of rotten orange rind. Stuffed in the side of the recycling can were the cardboard boxes, torn open on one end like they'd been ripped in a hurry.

My stomach twisted tighter, and I closed the lid again. When had Mom done this? Last night? Yesterday? Before or after she dismantled the nursery?

What must she have been thinking?

I grabbed the edge of the garbage can, afraid I was going to be sick in it, but I breathed in the wet air, and my body relaxed.

I was going to fix this.

I walked quietly back up the stairs and waited outside Mom's door again. I could let Rodney drive me to school, but I pictured myself walking Rodney to the women's hygiene aisle. *So*, I'd say casually. *I was thinking I'd get pregnant.*

A headache began to form at the base of my neck. No. I'd have to introduce the idea to him somehow, but not like *that*.

I knocked quietly on her door.

"Hmm?" Mom called. "Yes?"

I nudged the door open. "Can you drive me to school?"

Mom sat straight up in bed, the covers unwinding from around her shoulders.

"Not now," I said. "In half an hour. I need you to drop me off at the Walgreens to get some snacks for a class party."

Mom blinked at me, and then leaned over, pulling aside the bottom of her curtains. Fog wafted across the lawn. "I can wait for you in the parking lot," she said. "Then you won't have to walk in this weather."

If there was one thing you didn't announce to your mother, it was that you were about to try to have sex. Mom would talk me out of it. She'd *have* to. So it'd be better if I didn't tell her until after. "It's fine," I said. "I'll take my camera. I like to walk in the fog."

Mom squinted out the window, and I could see her measuring the risk in her mind. Was it dangerous for me to walk? Would some car fail to see me?

"Okay," she said.

"Thanks," I said, and I pulled her door closed again. I only hoped she didn't decide to take the hammer to the crib while I was at school. After she'd lost her first adoption, I'd faked being sick to stay home with her, but Dad told me I couldn't babysit her all the time.

He was right, but that didn't stop me from wanting to.

I texted Rodney: *I need to run to the drugstore before school. Mom's taking me. See you at lunch.*

I braced for what I knew was coming. My phone beeped.

I could take you.

The phone felt slick in my palms. *It's girl stuff,* I texted back. All Rodney said in response was *K.*

I dressed quickly, wondering what he thought that meant. He'd been with me when I bought tampons before; it embarrassed me way more than it did him. Other guys might have cracked jokes, but not Rodney. He'd just stepped away from the register so I could buy my tampons in peace.

I packed up my camera in my backpack, and Mom drove me to Walgreens at about five miles an hour.

"What are you getting for class?" she asked.

"Chips, I think," I said. "I have a note somewhere."

Mom nodded.

My headache began to pulse. I could tell her. I *should* tell her. But I knew what she'd say—what she'd *have* to say. No, Penny. Don't do that. Don't even think about it.

And who could blame her? No one wants their teenage daughter to be pregnant. She was going to flip when she found out what I'd done. But there'd be no undoing it. And would my pregnancy really hurt her more than the years of longing, and the pain of giving up hope?

I looked at the circles beneath Mom's eyes as she squinted into the fog before turning into the parking lot of the Walgreens. There was no way anything I did could make her situation worse.

I opened my door before Mom had the car parked. "Thanks!" I said. "See you after school!"

I sounded far too chipper, so I closed the door before Mom could respond, and ran into the store without looking back.

There were a couple girls from school on the cosmetics aisle, smearing the sample lipsticks onto their hands. I didn't know any of them by name, and they probably didn't even recognize me.

I hoped.

I found the pregnancy tests near the tampons and the tubes of Monostat cream. As I reached for them, my stomach turned. Pregnant meant fat, it meant nausea, it meant labor.

I swallowed, and pulled a two pack of tests off the rack. Labor meant pain. Lots of pain. Supposedly more pain than I'd felt in my life.

The edges of my vision turned white. I leaned over, putting my hands on my knees, and gazed down the row of ovulation predictors.

Mom had been through pregnancy and labor twice. She survived, and more than that, she wanted to do it again. She wept for years that she couldn't. Nine months was just a school year. The same length as sixth grade, when I grew breasts before every other girl in school and Cassandra Templeton hung an endless stream of lacy, worn, second-hand bras on my locker. I lived through *that*.

Four predictors came off the rack. I held the boxes in both

hands. A baby would mean an end to the crying.

I could do this.

I went through the line cashiered by the middle-aged woman, instead of the one with the twenty-something guy. If the cashier did happen to make a comment, it would be less embarrassing this way.

I stood behind a woman with a toddler and a stack of ads, holding the boxes down at my side and waiting for the cashier to price-match every item in her basket.

The male cashier waved at me as his line cleared. "I can help you," he said.

I shook my head. "I'm good."

His confused look was interrupted by the lipstick girls bearing cans of soda.

I should have told Rodney. He'd have breezed over and handed this guy the boxes without a second thought.

When the lady with the ads left, I stepped up close to the register and set my purchases down at the end of the conveyor belt. The cashier picked one up and looked at it. "Are these the ones that are a dollar off?"

I blinked at her. "I don't know."

She picked up the phone next to her register. "Let me have someone check."

I spoke too quickly. "I don't care."

Now she looked at one of the predictors. She looked at me. *Crap.* I hadn't meant to draw attention.

"It's for my mom," I said.

The cashier squinted at my pile of products. "She might care."

I squirmed. "She'll care more if I'm late to class."

As they passed by, cracking open their sodas, both girls looked at the predictor in the cashier's hand. *Just ring it up*, I thought. *Just put it in a bag.* When she finally did, I realized the bag was translucent.

Outside the store, I wrapped the bag around and around the boxes and then shoved them in the top of my backpack. I couldn't take them home where my mother might find them, and I couldn't put them in my locker where Rodney kept his book for trig. Maybe after I talked to him about it, but certainly not before.

My gym locker would work. As I walked to school, the fog was lifting, only shading the passing cars as if through a veil. But instead of feeling relieved, I just felt exposed. Even if no one knew what I was doing today, I still didn't want to be seen.

In the locker room, I stashed the predictors and the pregnancy tests underneath my long gym pants. It was still too warm to be wearing those anyway. Unless they did some spontaneous locker search, no one would find the tests there.

I unwrapped one of the predictors, pulled out the stick and the instructions, and carried them up my sleeve into the bathroom. I passed a couple girls coming in to change for first period gym, but if they noticed anything, they didn't speak.

I unwrapped the predictor with shaking hands, peed on the stick, and stayed in the stall, checking the time on my cell phone and waiting the two minutes for the results.

Only one line appeared. I wasn't ovulating yet.

Relief rushed through me, followed by a wave of guilt. I *wanted* to be ovulating, didn't I? The longer I had to wait, the longer Mom had to suffer.

But I'd also have longer to talk to Rodney about it—longer to figure out exactly the right thing to say.

I held the stick with two fingers. I couldn't flush it—it was too long, and probably wouldn't even go down. Instead, I wrapped it in the instructions and stuck it in the little metal box inside the stall where you're supposed to put used pads. A janitor probably wouldn't look too hard at the contents of that. Plus, if they did find the stick, there wouldn't be any way to tie it back to me.

It's not like anyone was going to run a DNA test on the locker room trash.

Rodney had chess club again at lunch, so I spent the day thinking about what I was going to say to him. I drummed my fingernails on the classroom desks, rehearsing. *You know my mom has been trying to get pregnant forever. You know how hard that's been on my family. Well, I was thinking . . .*

In history class, I took furious notes. By the end of the period, I'd written down about every word of the lecture, but I didn't remember a bit of it. Instead, these words kept running through my mind: *Hey, we're friends, right? So let's have sex and give my mother a baby.*

Shoot me now. Rodney was a sensible guy. There had to be a way to explain this that didn't sound like he needed to check me into a psyche ward.

I was no better off at the end of the day, when I found him waiting at my locker.

"Hey," I said.

"Hey," he said back. He didn't even look up—just finished shoving his books into the locker and then held it open for me.

It's just a normal day, I thought. A normal day on which we might kiss or we might not. A day like any other in the history of our friendship.

I wiped my palms on my jeans. What if he was. . .*over* me? Could you get over someone you'd never actually crushed on? Was that a thing?

As we headed out to the parking lot, Rodney gave me a sideways glance. "So, are we not talking about it, then?" he asked.

My heart picked up pace. "About what?"

Rodney raised his eyebrows at me. "The test?"

My eyes went wide. How could he know? The girls from the store? Had someone seen me in the locker room? Did half the school know already?

Rodney looked confused. "Didn't you get yours back?"

My face flushed. Physiology. Duh. The test Rodney was supposed to know about.

Way to act like a spaz, Penny.

I let my hair fall into my face, trying to cover my blush. "Yeah," I said. "I got it."

Rodney waited for a long moment. "And?"

I sighed. "C plus."

Rodney winced. "Ouch," he said. "No wonder you didn't bring it up."

Yeah. It totally wasn't because I was distracted by other things. "What about you? B?"

"A minus."

Ugh. His usual half a grade was funny. A full letter and a half was just sad. "Like, ninety percent, squeaking by?"

"Ninety-four percent."

"That's not even a minus."

"Depends on the scale." Rodney bumped me with his shoulder, like he was waiting for me to laugh, but I didn't. Even on a regular day, it wasn't that funny.

We reached Rodney's car, which he'd parked at the back of the parking lot. His mom had given him her old station wagon, which still had a bumper sticker announcing that his kid was on the honor roll. Rodney tried to compensate by hanging a stuffed Moogle from his rear view mirror, but it didn't work. The upside of the car was that we could have fit just about everyone we knew into it, even though it was usually just him and me.

Rodney unlocked the door for me, and I climbed into the passenger seat and leaned back, putting my feet on the dash and taking deep breaths. This was my opportunity to talk to him, and I knew it. But my heartbeat kept thudding in my throat, and I didn't get the words out. I just kept thinking them over in my head: *I was wondering . . . I was thinking . . .*

It wasn't until we'd driven a couple of blocks that Rodney broke the silence.

"Seriously, what's up?" he asked.

I dug my nails into the armrest. "What do you mean?"

"You're all quiet again. That's the second time this week."

"Sorry," I said. "I'm just . . . steaming about the test."

Rodney waved an arm at me, and for a second, I thought he was going to touch me, but he didn't. "What do you need physiology for anyway? You're not going into medicine."

I crossed my arms. "I need it to get into college." Oh, jeez. College. My grades. What if I was really sick in the mornings and missed school? Junior year was supposed to be the year colleges cared about most.

Rodney shrugged. "What's the worst that can happen? Say you fail physiology, and that messes up your applications. Then you have to go to a community school for a year or two first. Would that be the end of the world?"

I took a deep breath. Rodney always knew how to put things into perspective. "You're right. Thanks."

Rodney smiled. "That's what I'm here for."

I squirmed in my seat. I had to talk to him about what was really bothering me, but I would die if I asked him to sleep with me, and he turned me down.

What we needed was to do something normal. Then I'd be able to work up some nerve.

"Do you have your camera today?" I asked.

Rodney nodded. "It's in the trunk."

"The leaves are turning at the park," I said. "Maybe we could stop on the way."

"Done," Rodney said, and he took the next right, driving the few blocks to the park near the city center.

The leaves weren't just turning. They were also falling. We walked beneath the towering trees on a carpet of red and yellow and orange, each with our cameras in our hands. I aimed my lens at the treetops, taking pictures of the branches backlit against the sky. I focused on my camera, avoiding eye contact with Rodney. I kept glancing at him and then glancing away, but he just fiddled with his own settings, like he didn't notice.

I couldn't believe so many leaves had dropped when the trees looked as full as ever. Still, leaves rained down around us. One caught in my hair, and Rodney turned his lens on me.

I lowered my camera. "What do you want me to do?" I asked.

Rodney smiled. "Just hold still."

I turned so the sun would fully light my profile, to give him more to work with.

"Check it out," Rodney said, inclining his screen toward me so I could see the shot. "Once we color correct that, it's going to be awesome."

Rodney had tilted the lens, so I looked off balance. The line from my forehead to my nose pointed to the vibrant red leaf.

"We'll have to brighten the leaf," I said. "Make it look larger than life."

Rodney grinned. "Exactly."

I turned my camera back to the sky, and then thought again and flopped down in the leaves.

"Are you getting anything from down there?" Rodney asked.

My heart thudded. "Come down here and see."

Leaves crunched as he lay down beside me and leaned into my shoulder so he could see my screen. I squinted at my camera, letting the exposure alternate bright and dark, depending on whether I focused on the branches or the sky.

"Switch it to manual," Rodney said.

I fiddled with the settings, finally bringing out the crisp, dark branches against the bright sky. I punched the shutter, taking bunches of shots at a time. My skin prickled, like every hair was aware of how near he was.

"Nice," Rodney said. He turned his camera along the ground away from me, focusing on a leaf four feet away. I propped my head on his shoulder so I could see, and he snapped a picture. The foreground and background blurred, but the leaf looked crisp, on the small screen at least.

Rodney turned back toward me, his face only a few inches from mine. I held my breath to keep from hyperventilating.

"That's a keeper," he said, still looking at the camera screen.

The corners of his mouth turned up in a smile, and a tendril of hair fell into his eyes. This was my moment. My heart beat faster. What was wrong with me? Was I laying a trap for him? Sneaking up to surprise him?

No. I was just trying to relax. Then we'd talk. I held my breath, and leaned in until my nose brushed his.

Rodney's face faded to serious, and he lowered the camera. His eyes wavered on my lips. A breeze picked up, scattering a bucketful of paper-thin leaves over the top of us. One caught behind Rodney's ear, and as he reached up to grab it, I kissed him. Leaves crunched under my hair as he leaned into me, rolling over me on the grass. More leaves tumbled over us, and our hips pressed together. Rodney's arm wrapped around my shoulders, pulling me closer. For a moment we moved in tandem—my mouth against his, his knees wrapped around mine. The world blurred like an out-of-focus picture as we disappeared beneath the shifting pile of leaves.

Then my stomach started to tingle, like a wriggling worm.

I giggled. Our mouths broke apart.

"What?" he asked. "Is my breath bad?"

I laughed harder. Rodney rolled over and watched me struggle to catch my breath. "No," I said finally. "It's nothing."

Rodney turned back to his camera. "Sure," he said. "I totally believe you."

But he didn't push. Rodney never pushed.

I brushed the leaves from my shirt, and they skittered away, becoming part of the traveling detritus.

Rodney held his screen up, pretending to look at it, but I caught him eying me.

"What?" I asked.

He smiled and shook his head. "You still have leaves in your hair."

I shook my head, trying to free them. "Help."

Instead, he held up his camera, snapping a picture of me.

I threw a fistful of leaves at him. "Sure," I said. "Take my picture when I look ridiculous."

Rodney bit his lip.

"What?" I asked.

"You look gorgeous," he said, looking down at his screen. "You always look gorgeous."

I collapsed in the leaves, the wind knocked out of me.

Kissing, check. Attraction, check.

Sex couldn't be that big of a jump from here, could it?

Now I just needed to find the right words.

Three days later I was lying on Rodney's bed with his laptop open in front of me, watching his pictures upload while Rodney played a game on his handheld, oblivious to my repeated glances in his direction. That morning, just after gym class, two lines had appeared on my ovulation predictor. According to the instructions, this meant I had about a three-day window to get pregnant, and I still hadn't talked to Rodney about it.

Rodney eyed my hands, where I'd been unconsciously balling his comforter in my fists. "How's your mom?" he asked.

Mom had driven me to school that morning, her eyes puffy and red, like she'd fallen asleep crying. "Meh," I said. "The usual."

My heart lodged in my throat. This was my cue. I had to tell him. But my voice froze. I couldn't speak. Rodney's photos finished uploading, and I opened one, stalling. "You were right about this one of me with the leaves," I said. "It's striking."

Rodney fiddled with his game. "Don't fish. I already told you you're gorgeous."

I squinted at the screen. "I'm not fishing. It's obviously your camera skills at work here, not *me*."

"Ugh," Rodney said. "Now you're really fishing."

I threw a pillow at him. "I am *not*." Even though I totally was.

I pulled that picture into an editing program. Rodney flopped down on the bed next to me, watching me work. He was so close, I could feel his body heat through my jeans.

"Seriously," I said, tilting the screen toward him. "Look at that. Someday you're going to be famous."

"Please," Rodney said. "It's not that good a picture."

"*I* like it."

"You have questionable taste."

"I must," I said. "I like *you*."

Now he whacked me with the pillow. I took it from him and shoved it under the laptop.

"Besides," I said, "I'll be your business partner, and I'm *clearly* a genius."

"And we'll do what? The money's all in portraits. I don't want to be taking pictures of people's kids for the rest of my life."

I turned back to the photo. "Some people make a living taking pictures of objects."

Rodney looked skeptical. "Sure. Product photography. I could make ads forever. That's *lots* better."

I looked at Rodney's walls, which were hung with his art and mine, but no one else's. "People buy art."

"But they only buy Ansel Adams."

I rolled my eyes. "Fine," I said. "Abandon me. I'll start up our photography business on my own."

Rodney looked at me out of the corner of his eye. "You start a business, and you can hire me. *If* you can afford me."

I laughed. "You can't ask much, if you refuse to do portraits."

Rodney leaned toward me so his shoulder was against mine, looking at the picture he'd taken of me. My whole body tingled in response. I held perfectly still.

"I'll do portraits," he said, "if they can all have leaves in their hair."

His eyes ran over the image of me, and he smiled.

My pulse picked up. Okay, I thought. Tell him. I tilted my head so our faces were only an inch apart.

But I waited a moment too long. Rodney's chin tilted toward mine, and then he kissed me. My body melted into his, every muscle responding to him. His body swallowed me, his intensity leaving no room for argument.

61

I snapped the laptop shut and set it beside me on the bed. Rodney rolled over me, putting a hand on each side of my shoulders.

I struggled to breathe. This didn't feel anything like the silly kissing at the park. Maybe it was me; maybe it was him. But serious energy crackled between us, and I couldn't break away.

I want to get pregnant, I thought. *Tell him.* But when I finally surfaced for air, I couldn't get the words out.

"You ever wonder what it's like?" I asked finally.

Rodney brushed my hair behind my ears, his lips brushing mine as he spoke. "What?"

"You know." I moved my hips against his, pressing our bodies together, kissing him harder.

When we pulled apart, his voice caught in his throat. "Oh," he said. "That."

"Well? Do you?" And I knew that was a stupid question to be asking a sixteen-year-old virgin, so I kissed him again, so he didn't have to answer if he didn't want to.

And he didn't—not with words.

But he moved the laptop to the nightstand. I wrapped my wrist around his neck as he pressed his whole body against mine and kissed me, his hands inching up my waist. Blood rushed in my ears and my body curled into him reflexively. I pushed aside the thought that if we couldn't say the word "sex" to each other, we couldn't possibly be ready to share it.

Rodney's lips paused against my earlobe. "Wait. Is *this* what you were giggling about the other day?"

I laughed. "No," I said. "Maybe."

His fingers brushed my hips, edging up under the hem of my shirt. "Wouldn't we . . . need something?"

Protection. *Tell him*, I thought. *Tell him.*

"It's okay," I said.

He rested his forehead against mine. His lips broke out in a smile. "No way. You planned this?"

My lips trembled, and instead of answering, I kissed him

again, and I felt his whole body relax as he leaned into me. He thought I was on the pill or something. He thought this was about me and him.

I *had* to tell him.

His hands slid up to my bra hooks, and my head fuzzed. Rodney took his shirt by the hem and pulled it off over his head in one fluid motion. His bare skin was smooth against me, and as his mouth moved down my neck and over my collar bone, my body arched against him. The time for talking was over.

As I squeezed my eyes closed, one thought cut through: that took a lot less convincing than I'd thought it would.

Chapter Six
Week Two

Afterward, I lay curled under Rodney's covers, my heart pounding in my ears. Rodney's forehead rested against the nape of my neck, his breath heavy against my shoulder. *It's not a big deal*, I told myself.

But my heart didn't slow. My body ached to turn into Rodney, to burrow into him and lose myself. His hand rested at my bare hip, a gentle reminder that we were both, incomprehensibly, naked.

But it's not a big deal. It's just sex. Guys don't care about sex.

Rodney's nose grazed my shoulder, and I had to fight to keep my body from arching into him. Ugh. Maybe Athena was right. Maybe girls weren't capable of detachment.

That wasn't the only thing that hadn't gone as expected. I'd read the books; I'd sat through the lectures. I knew sex wasn't supposed to be good for girls in the beginning. I was supposed to be in pain; I was supposed to fake it.

But for a little while, my body had taken over, responding to Rodney like a part of me had always been waiting to be close to him, clothes and reservations stripped away.

My cheeks burned. I hadn't had to fake anything.

Rodney's teeth tugged gently at my earlobe. His voice was low in my ear. "I'm trying to think of something eloquent to say. At the risk of sounding like a Neanderthal, I think I'm going to go with *whoa*."

I squeezed my eyes shut. Only Rodney could start with "eloquent" and end with "whoa." I should follow his tone. I should keep this light.

His arms squeezed around me. My back pressed against his chest, and I fought to breathe. I should be clear that I didn't mean to start anything serious.

Too late.

I smiled and turned to face him. I waited to respond until I was sure I had control of my voice. "Was that a complaint?"

"No," Rodney said. "Never." He bit his lip, looking into my eyes.

My heart hammered harder. *No big deal*, I thought. *No big deal. No big deal.*

Rodney nuzzled his nose against mine.

And that's when the front door opened downstairs.

Rodney leapt off the bed and pulled on his boxers. I turned away from the flash of naked Rodney flesh and curled up tighter, torn between the need to dress and the desire to stay covered.

Rodney saved me by tossing my clothes at me one piece at a time. Bra. Underwear. Shirt. Jeans. All landed one by one atop the comforter, and as Rodney jumped into his own pants and shirt, I scrambled under the blanket, wiggling into my clothes like a sixth-grader dressing out for gym class.

Keys hit a table downstairs. Rodney finished dressing and smiled sheepishly at me. His hair stuck up funny in the back. Minutes ago, my fingers had been knotting it.

"Brush your hair," I said. I crawled out of the bed and started to smooth the covers, but stopped with them halfway on. Rodney never made the bed. *That* would be suspicious.

I dashed to the bathroom across the hall before anyone could come up the stairs. I looked at myself in the mirror. My hair looked normal enough, but I felt disheveled. My body felt sticky, but a shower would have to wait.

I flushed the empty toilet and ran the sink. As I was reaching

65

for the door to leave, the stairs creaked outside. "Rodney?" his mom called.

"Hey, Mom," Rodney called back. To his credit, he sounded totally normal. *I* was the spaz who couldn't deal.

But I also couldn't avoid her forever, so I opened the door.

Rodney's mom smiled at me as I stepped out of the bathroom. I tried to smile back, even though I was pretty sure I had *sex* written across my forehead in permanent marker. "Are you staying for dinner?" she asked.

I couldn't maintain normal for that long. And I really needed a shower. "Not tonight," I told her. "I need to get home."

"I'll drive you," Rodney said.

"Come right back," his mom said. "I've already ordered a pizza." Then she walked past me to her bedroom, like nothing was out of the ordinary.

I guess to her, nothing was.

Rodney grinned at me and tossed me my backpack. "Come on," he said. "Let's go."

In the car on the way to my house, Rodney sighed. "You're being quiet again."

My chest felt like I was wearing one of those lead vests for x-rays. It weighed so heavily on me I could barely breathe. I wasn't stupid; I knew having sex once didn't automatically mean I was pregnant. But if I was, then I'd just tricked him into it, and if I wasn't, then we'd need to do this again. How would I explain to him that I hadn't been on birth control the first time? If I told him the whole truth now, he'd think I only wanted him for his sperm—that it didn't mean anything to me.

My chest tightened. It wasn't *supposed* to mean anything to me. Was it?

Rodney gave me an alarmed look; I still hadn't answered him.

"Maybe I'm becoming a quiet person," I said.

He laughed. "Right. That'll happen."

"You never know."

He looked at me out of the corner of his eye. "Seriously,

though, are we okay?"

"Yeah, of course," I said. But from the way he chewed on his lip, I wasn't totally sure he believed me.

For the rest of the ride we were both quiet people, Rodney smiling to himself, and me sinking lower and lower in my seat. Something about the way that he smiled made me uneasy. Did sex mean something to *him*? Did he think we were together now? I wanted to ask, but I waited, thinking any minute now *he* would bring it up.

But we reached my house in silence, because apparently we could have sex, but we still couldn't talk about it. And in addition to sticky, I now felt sick to my stomach.

I walked into my house with even steps, trying to look normal. I'd been hoping to sneak upstairs to the shower, but Mom stood in the living room, two inch fabric squares scattered all over the furniture. Mom had tacked a blanket-sized piece of felt above the front windows and was studiously pinning the tiny fabric squares into place, starting with a burst of oranges and reds in the center.

Thankfully, her eyes were clear of puffiness—she'd taken refuge in distraction. On a normal day, I would have been relieved. Sometimes it took her weeks to find the desire to *do* anything.

Today, though, relief wasn't in my vocabulary. I stayed in the corner of the living room, as far from her as possible. I could smell Rodney's skin on mine, and I didn't want her to catch a whiff. I pretended to look over her quilt. "Sunset?" I asked.

Mom stood back and squinted. "It's supposed to be."

Her reference photo peeked out from beneath a pile of blue squares. It was a photo I took last year in the redwoods, the sun reflecting over the ocean and casting a glow through the clouds above.

"That's a hard one," I said.

"I know," Mom said. "But if I get it right, it's going to be beautiful."

67

I nodded. She'd picked it as a challenge, then—a powerful distraction. That might buy me some time, but for what? To find out I'd tricked my best friend into getting me pregnant? To have the awkward conversation with him about how I wanted to be?

My stomach turned. "I'm going to take a shower," I said. "Have you had dinner?"

Mom looked at the clock, and then shook her head as if to clear it. "Dinner. Right."

"Is there anything in the freezer?"

"Pot pie," Mom said. "Would you throw it in the oven?"

"Sure," I said. "That'll give me time to shower before dinner."

Mom was already shuffling the red and orange squares around, unpinning and repinning. If I did have *sex* written across my forehead, she hadn't looked at me to notice.

I pulled the pie out of the freezer and shoved it in the oven, then shut myself in the bathroom. I balled up my clothes and wrenched on the water, jumping in the shower and letting the water pour over me.

It's not a big deal, I told myself. Surely Rodney didn't think it was, either. I was just imagining things. I was such a cliché, a stupid girl assigning meaning where there was none.

Hot water saturated my hair. I stood still, hiding my face beneath the stream, letting the afternoon wash off of me. And I couldn't help but wonder if Rodney was doing the same.

At midnight, my phone beeped. I climbed out of bed to grab it and found a text from Rodney: *you okay?*

I wanted to crawl under my pillow. Rodney was more than amazing. It was bad enough that I'd misled a guy into thinking I was on birth control when I wasn't. Did I have to do that to Rodney?

Sure, I replied. *You?*

Miss you.

I shoved the phone under my blankets and buried my face in

my hands, but my phone chirped again. I had to look.

Come out on your roof?

The room seemed to tilt off-kilter. *It's only Rodney*, I told myself. But that didn't stop my skin from tingling.

I opened my window and popped out the screen. As I climbed across the garage roof, Rodney's head appeared at the other end. He climbed from our garbage can onto the roof of Dad's shed, and then onto the shingles with me. I sat at the edge of the eaves with my feet dangling in front of the garage door.

"Hey," I said.

He settled down next to me, close enough that our knees touched. "Hey," he said. "Are we okay?"

My stomach dropped. *Keep it light.* I whacked him in the shoulder with the back of my hand. "You already asked me that. Twice. Did you come all the way over here just to ask me again?"

Rodney rubbed his hands together. "I don't know. I just wanted to make sure you weren't . . . regretting anything."

He couldn't use the S word, either.

The cold night air made my skin break out in goose bumps. "Of course not," I said. Another lie, though only a partial one. It wasn't the sex I regretted, exactly. It was more that I should have been honest with him, first.

But now, the last thing I wanted was for things to be awkward. I put my hand on his knee. He relaxed and wrapped his arm around my shoulders.

His body felt warm against mine, drawing me nearer. I scooted over until we were right next to each other. Rodney bent down and kissed me on the temple. I leaned into his sweatshirt, breathing him in, and my body melted into him reflexively.

Had he always smelled so good?

Rodney sounded relieved. "So we're okay?"

"Yeah," I said. "Unless your mom wised up."

Rodney laughed. "Ha. Thankfully, no. I think we made some kind of a record getting dressed that fast."

Rodney pressed his face against my cheek, nibbling on my

ear. His breath grew deeper, faster, and my body responded in kind, drawn to him as if by a magnet.

I resisted, pulling away.

Rodney's gaze flicked from one of my eyes to the other, as if searching for something. "Talk to me?" he asked.

"Okay," I said. "Okay." But if I told him the whole truth, he might be the one pulling away from *me*. For a horrible moment, I thought about going to a clinic, and asking for Plan B.

No. I'd be evicting possible fetuses from my womb even while Mom pined after a child. I wouldn't do that. I couldn't.

"I'm scared," I said. "I don't want things to change."

Rodney looked up at the few stars you could see over the city lights—no constellations, just isolated dots on the dark sky. "Not all change is bad."

I couldn't breathe. "I like things the way they are. Don't you?"

Rodney's face turned serious. "I guess that depends on what things you mean."

My stomach sunk. "Us," I said. "I didn't mean to mess anything up."

Rodney must have seen my panic. He leaned back, forcing a smile. "Hey," Rodney said. "I'm fine with us if you are."

But he wouldn't be if I told him why I'd come on to him like that. "Fine with us as what?" I asked. Saying the words "just friends" to him right now might spark exactly the kind of change I was trying to avoid.

Rodney sighed. "Look, Penny. I can't read your mind. So tell me what you want, and it's yours, okay?"

Hadn't I already said that I wanted things to stay the same? "Since when am I the only one who gets to decide?"

He squeezed my shoulder. "Since you're the one freaking out about it."

Oh, right. Here I was, spazzing out again. So much for keeping it light.

I made myself smile. "I'm not the one climbing onto your roof, needing answers in the middle of the night."

He held up a hand, leaving the other arm around me. "Who said I need answers?"

But he did, and I could tell from his sheepish smile he knew it. Rodney pushed my hair back over my ear, and kissed my forehead. "Look, I'm not complaining. This is good. Better than good. Nothing has to change."

Rodney was quiet then, but he didn't pull away. He stayed there, with his breath in my ear and his arm around my waist, just looking out at the streetlights and the suburban haze that blocked most of the stars. I nuzzled into his neck and breathed him in. His collar smelled like the leaves in the park, and I wanted to freeze that moment and live in it, just the way it was, forever.

But Rodney pulled me closer, his fingertips running down my back and resting on my hips. My body ached, and my mouth moved reflexively against his throat. He moaned softly, and I could feel the vibrations of his voice against my lips.

For a moment, all I wanted was to invite him in. We could slip through the window and curl up in my bed, and no one would know about it but us. I wanted it in a way that had nothing to do with getting pregnant. But if going to bed together was a thing that Rodney and I were going to do on a regular basis, then we were either in a serious relationship, or seriously screwed up.

I leaned back on my hands. Gravel from the shingles dug into my palms, and I concentrated on the sting.

Things clearly *had* changed. What if there was no going back? Did that mean that I was destined to lose him? Was I repeating my mom's history, even as I tried to avoid it?

Ugh. I rubbed my forehead. When had my life become such a drama?

I looked up at Rodney, and found him watching me. "I better go," he said.

He looked worried again. And all I wanted was to pull him inside and prove to him that everything was okay between us.

But if sex was a part of the problem, it couldn't also be the solution.

"Okay," I said. And Rodney scooted off the roof and onto the shed.

I wrapped my arms around myself, trying to stay warm. When we'd made out last summer, it was hard and fast and fun. We'd laughed and teased each other, and started whenever we wanted and stopped when one of us got laughing too hard. Which, now that I thought about it, was always, always me.

But now things felt serious. Heavy. Was it just the sex that changed things? Or was it something more?

Rodney stood on the roof of Dad's shed. He put one hand down, ready to hop off, but seemed to think better of it and stood back up, looking at me. "Penny," he said.

My skin tingled, as if it knew what was coming even before I did. "Yeah?"

Rodney looked at me and the light from the street lamps lit up his face. "You're the best."

The whole roof seemed to tilt. I hugged my knees to my chest, trying to maintain my balance. And that's when I knew for sure, the thing I'd been trying not to know.

Rodney was in love with me.

And for the first time in our friendship, I was completely unworthy of it.

Chapter Seven
Week Two

I woke up to my alarm and slammed down my snooze button. My head ached, and I was sure it wasn't just from lack of sleep. My fingers inched across my stomach.

One time. We'd had sex one time. So I probably wasn't pregnant. Lots of women had sex while they were ovulating and didn't get pregnant. Right? Because having a baby with a boy who was in love with me would be a whole different game than the one I thought I was playing.

Mom banged on my door a few minutes later. She shouted through the door, "Is Rodney driving you today?"

"No," I yelled back. "He has a chess game."

"Hurry. I'm headed out."

As I dressed, I brought myself to my senses. Rodney was in love with me. But he wasn't acting differently than he always had. So either this was an age-old development, or he was handling it with class.

And if he could do that, so could I. I didn't have to cling to him, to miss him every second, to pull him into my bed and absorb all his warmth like a leech.

I could be cool. That's all I needed to be.

Downstairs, out the door, into the car, all the way to school, I wore a smile like an ID badge. Hello, My Name Is *Cool*.

I had this.

Mom dropped me off fifteen minutes early, and I strode into the building, throwing the double doors open before me and stalking right down the middle of the hall.

Act like it's fine, and it will be.

It had to be.

I got to my locker, and spun in the combination, my confident smile still pasted to my face.

And that's when I found the single red rose lying on top of my math book, petals fanned out over the cover.

The ground sunk out from under me. I put a hand on the locker above mine to keep from being swallowed by the floor. Only one other person had my locker combination, and only one person had cause to give me a rose on a random Friday.

I picked up the flower by the stem, which Rodney had bent some to fit into the locker. A single, red, thornless, long stem rose, that Rodney had bought early in the morning, before his chess game with Parker, on a night when he'd been out late.

Last year, I'd gone with Rodney to buy flowers for his mom for Mother's Day. "Buy the yellow ones," I'd told him. "Red roses are for romantic love."

Be cool, I thought.

Who was I kidding?

I shut the locker and leaned against it. The first bell grew closer, and the press of students around me thickened. I couldn't stand for fear of falling.

"Hey, Penny," a voice said. I looked up to see Kara waving at me. "Are you okay?"

"I'm not feeling well, actually," I said.

"Who's the flower from? Secret admirer?"

The room swirled. "No," I said. "I have to ask you a stupid question."

"Shoot."

"How long has Rodney been in love with me?"

Kara's shriek fell somewhere between mocking and glee.

"Shut up!" I said. "Just answer me."

74

"Since like seventh grade," Kara said. "Remember how he used to wait for you outside the locker room after gym?"

I remembered him leaning against the wall, pretending to play with his phone, but really obviously waiting for me. That was *four* years ago. "No way," I said. "He liked Sarah Kim in seventh grade."

Kara shook her head. "Maybe. But he liked you more."

The floor seemed to move out from under me. "How could you not tell me this?"

"I think I did," Kara said. "Besides, everybody knows."

I flopped my hands against the locker. "Seriously?"

Kara grinned. "What's the matter with that?"

I narrowed my eyes at her. "Aren't you supposed to be against romance?" I asked. "After the text message?"

"Please," Kara said. "That was last week. This week I want to live vicariously."

I sunk the rest of the way to the floor. "How was I this clueless?"

Kara extended her hands to me, pulling me to my feet. "Honey, get a grip. You love him. He loves you. This is not an issue. Now come on. We've got to get to class."

When I didn't follow, Kara left me standing there, rose hanging in my hand.

I was sure if I thought about it long enough, I would think of an aspect of my friendship with Rodney that didn't look like a serious, committed relationship. Any minute now, it was going to come to me.

I went through the next few classes with the rose stem-down in my backpack, bloom peeking out the top of the zipper. I didn't want Rodney to see that I'd left it behind, or crushed it entirely by shoving the blossom under the zipper, but I also didn't want to carry it around in my hand for everyone to ask about. Instead, the flower watched me as I sat in class, reminding me that things had, in fact, changed. I glanced down at it

75

every few minutes, but it was always there, watching me with its velvety, soft petals.

So much for cool.

Rodney caught me in the hall at lunch. "Hey," he said. He put out a hand and rested it on my arm, which was something he might have done any day, but today I stepped reflexively into him, standing only inches away, and his hand ran up my arm and around my shoulders.

My spine tingled. "Hey," I said back. "Thanks for the flower."

He reached for my backpack and ran his thumb around the bottom of a petal. "I woke up feeling like a jerk," he said, his voice low so only I could hear. "I didn't want you to think I was using you, you know?"

My head pounded. *No, Rodney. I was using you.*

"I've got another game today," he said. "But Xander told me about this abandoned warehouse by the golf course—he said the roof is falling in. Could be good for pictures. Want to check it out after school?"

That sounded like a normal thing, and I could sure use a dose of normal. "Sure."

"Great. I'll see you then." Rodney bent down and kissed me on the cheek. Then he reached down to take my hand, right there in the hall, in front of everyone.

My face flushed. *Oh, no,* I thought. *If it looks like a couple, and it walks like a couple . . .*

I was the biggest idiot who ever lived.

After school, I jittered my way to my locker to meet Rodney. He smiled at me, and brushed my arm casually with his fingertips, but when I didn't respond to it he didn't take my hand.

He didn't push. Of course he didn't. How long had he been following my lead, beat by beat, moment by moment? How could I not have noticed before?

We walked out to his car, and Rodney opened the car door

for me. He'd always done that, because he was the one with the keys. But as he walked around the car to climb in, I obsessed over it. Did he do that for other people, or just me? By the time he started the car, I already had the radio all the way up.

The golf course was on the outskirts of the city, next to the freeway interchange. It had been built over the top of an old landfill, which backed up to a lumberyard and a recycling center. Behind the rows and rows of wooden planks, past the factory that reeked of tangy aluminum and dried soda, beyond a barbed wire fence to keep people out of the recycling piles, stood the building industry forgot. It probably had been a warehouse, like Xander said, but half of the roof had tumbled inside and lay warped and sunken in the afternoon sun.

I dug my camera out of my backpack while Rodney grabbed his from the trunk. I held it up, took a test shot of the building, and adjusted the settings. The shape of the structure was too square to look interesting backlit by the sun.

"The light's pretty bad here," I said. "Let's walk around the other side."

Rodney followed me, kicking a soda can across the empty lot as we went.

"Why do people let this happen?" I asked, surveying the sunken roof.

"Cheaper to let it rot than to tear it down, I guess." Rodney sunk to his knees in front of the building. I crouched behind him to see his screen. He angled the shot so the camera was closer to the foundation than the roof, making the building loom menacingly.

"Nice," I said.

Rodney stood and beckoned me toward the building. "Come on."

The door had fallen half off its hinges, so it jutted out from the building at an awkward angle. In the window next to it hung a tattered sign announcing the building's condemnation by the county inspector.

Go figure.

Rodney walked up to the door and peered inside.

"You aren't going in there," I said.

He lifted a foot over the hanging door and stepped through the gap. "Why not?"

I grabbed him by the arm. "Because the roof is caving in?"

Rodney craned his neck to look farther inside. "Not over here."

I stood on my tiptoes to look past him. From here, I could clearly see the splintered mass of metal and wood that used to be the ceiling. "Please," I said. "Breathe wrong and you'll get squashed by a falling beam."

Rodney grinned back at me over his shoulder. "What's the matter? Can't live without me?"

I tightened my grip on his arm. "I'm more worried about myself," I said. "Your car is a stick shift. I can't drive home if you die."

Rodney pointed his camera up at the ceiling, taking a picture of the falling detritus against the sky. "Come in with me, then," he said. "You wouldn't want me to die alone."

I walked up to the building and peered through one of the empty window frames. The ceiling above the door did seem to be intact. "Fine," I said. "But only because I can't let you get all the good shots."

Rodney stepped his other foot in, and reached back to help me over the fallen debris. I moved in behind him, choosing my steps carefully to avoid broken glass.

The place had been emptied. All that was left were three wooden crates, the sides facing the fallen roof rotting away from exposure.

I knelt down, catching the corner of one of the boxes with a sparkling maze of glass shards spreading in front of it.

I held my screen up for Rodney to see. "I win," I said.

He inclined his screen toward me, revealing a high-contrast shot of the sunken roof against the windows beyond, the curving line of the collapsed beams standing in sharp relief to the square angles of the window frames. It was better than mine by a mile.

"Fine," I said.

Rodney wrapped an arm around my shoulders and took my camera away, looking through my last few photos. "Better luck next time," he said.

"Whatever," I said. I held his camera out at arm's length and turned the lens on us. "This is the winner. Smile."

Our foreheads knocked together as we both faced the camera. I clicked the shutter, and then turned the camera around to see.

Rodney was making a fish face.

I put a hand on my hip. "You ruined my masterpiece."

"Retake," he said, holding my camera out just as I had his. But instead of turning toward it, he ducked down and kissed me just as I heard the click.

When the kiss ended, Rodney still held me close. I could feel his breath on my cheek, and my heart pounded. "Now there's evidence," I said.

"Of what?" Rodney asked. And he pulled back grinning, like he was daring me to say it. Of our relationship. Of how we were so totally not even pretending to only be friends.

I hesitated; he waited. Then the wind scattered leaves across the floor, and the ceiling above us groaned.

I grabbed Rodney by the hand. "We are leaving," I said. "Now."

Rodney laughed, but he followed.

Safely outside again, we completed our lap around the building, stopping next to some concrete slabs that might have been parking barriers once upon a time.

I knelt next to one of them, taking a picture of the corner of the broken roof against the clouds. I could feel Rodney behind me, looking at my screen, breathing on my ear. My heart hammered harder, and I dug my teeth into my lip, willing it to slow down.

We couldn't go on like this. I had to talk to him. Now. I

wheeled around. "What are we doing?" I asked.

Rodney was staring up at the building again. "Trespassing for the sake of art."

I punched his arm. "You know what I mean. We're supposed to be friends, but—"

When Rodney turned back to me, he was no longer smiling. "Penny," he said, "It's okay. We don't have to have this conversation."

I was finally trying to be open with him, and *he* didn't want to talk about it? I threw up my hands in surrender. "So roses are okay, but not discussions?"

He rubbed my shoulder. "I'm just saying, if *you* don't want to talk about it, don't push it. I'm fine with everything. Really."

I crossed my arms. That was Rodney's specialty—being fine with everything. But would he be, if he knew? "Forget about me for a minute. What do *you* want?"

Rodney sat down on a slab of concrete, leaving me space beside him. I sat next to him, and he put a hand on my arm. "All that stuff about breaking up being inevitable, that was your idea. I just went along with it because it was what you needed."

Was that true? Why didn't he *say* something? "You agreed to just be friends, though. Even if it was my idea."

Rodney wavered. "Maybe I did," Rodney said. "But now I think we were idiots."

I'd proved that pretty well on my side. "So are we together, then?"

Rodney looked like a man treading carefully over slippery rocks. "We can be," Rodney said. "If that's okay with you." He looked at me, waiting.

It wasn't about what I wanted. It was about what I'd done. A slow burn crept over my face. "First I have to ask you another question."

A trace of worry passed over his face, but he gave me one solid nod. "Go."

I scratched at the edge of the concrete slab with one fingernail, loosening some pebbles. "I've been thinking a lot about what I can do for my mom."

Rodney rested his elbows on his knees, adjusting to the change of subject. "Did you come up with anything?"

"Yes," I said. "I kind of want to get pregnant."

Rodney whistled. He leaned back slightly, as if absorbing the blow.

"I was just thinking about it . . . since you and me . . . you know . . ."

He hesitated. "Are you asking me to father a child for your mother?"

It was all I could do not to cover my face with my hands. *Own up to it*, I told myself. "You don't have to."

Rodney squinted at the sky. "Obviously."

Burn. "I'm just saying—"

Rodney looked at me, like he couldn't believe what he was hearing. "You're serious?"

It would be so much easier to play this off as a joke, but I couldn't. Rodney would know the difference. "I am."

The rays of the setting sun shot through what was left of the dirty windows, illuminating the inches between us.

I watched Rodney carefully, but he sat calmly, watching the building, giving nothing away. "Say something," I said.

He shifted uncomfortably. "That's a sweet thing to want to do for your mother," he said. "It comes from a place of love. I get that."

"But?" I said.

His voice was strained. "But we can't do that. I mean, not that I mind the process . . ."

I smacked him on the arm and he put a hand on my knee. The line of the light passed across his sleeve.

"I'm sorry," he said. "You get why, right? I mean, it's one thing for your mother to adopt a stranger's baby, but for the baby to be ours . . . that's weird."

My cheeks burned even brighter. I'd been a total idiot not to talk to him about this beforehand. "I get it," I said. "It's okay." I felt like the concrete slab was slowly sinking. What if I was pregnant already?

It was once. Just once. Women who were trying to get pregnant sometimes had to try for months. You couldn't even get an appointment with an infertility specialist unless you'd been trying for a year.

"So," Rodney said slowly. "Was that an ultimatum?"

"What?"

He gave me a sideways look. "Are you going to find someone else to . . ."

"No," I said. "Don't be stupid. There's no one but you."

He elbowed me. "I suppose there're always sperm donors."

I smacked him on the arm again. "Be serious."

"Hey," he said, waving a hand at me. "You're the one who wants to get pregnant. If you want to talk crazy, we can talk crazy."

"No," I said. "You're right. It's a bad idea."

"Terrible," Rodney said. "Sweet, but terrible."

"So we're still together," I said. "Even though I'm crazy?"

Now he leaned over, bumping me with his shoulder. "What's this still? I thought you said we weren't together." I opened my mouth to answer, but Rodney rolled his eyes. "It's fine," he said. "I'm used to the crazy."

He took my hand and led me toward the car. "Not that I'm complaining," he said, "but how long had you been planning . . . you know."

Heavens. He still couldn't say the word.

I spoke too quickly. "Not that long," I said. Crap. Birth control took a while to work, didn't it? "I mean, a while, but not, you know?"

He looked at me sideways. Of course he didn't know. That made no freaking sense.

"Um," he said.

I had to put an end to this, before he started thinking about the exact moment that things changed. The day after Lily decided to keep the baby. "I guess I'd been thinking about it for a while."

Rodney looked surprised. "You could have fooled me," he said. "I thought you didn't think about me like that."

My chest throbbed. I'd backed myself into a corner. If I told him the truth—that I'd tricked him, that I'd as good as lied—I'd lose him. "I came to my senses, I guess."

Rodney opened the car door for me, but now his face had turned serious. He had to have noticed that I'd dodged his question. I could almost see the wheels turning in his mind. He was going to put it together.

When he sat down in the driver's seat, I rubbed the back of his arm. "Are you sure you're okay?" I asked.

Rodney's jaw set. "I'm fine," he said.

But his formerly easy grip on the steering wheel tightened to a grasp. As we drove, he was the one who was quiet. And I tried to silence the voice that said he was putting together the pieces of my lies in his head. They made a warped puzzle, and I wasn't sure how to diffuse his doubts without assembling the whole ugly picture for him to see.

Chapter Eight
Week Two

When we pulled up to my house, Rodney left the engine running. "Don't you want to come in?" I asked.

Rodney shook his head, avoiding my eyes. "I should get home."

My hand shook on the door handle. "Maybe we could do something tomorrow?"

Rodney adjusted his sun visor. "I've got family stuff."

I hesitated. Rodney never had family stuff. His dad was a big time realtor and his mom ran an insurance agency—they were always working weekends, and when they weren't, they were too tired to actually do anything. "Are you sure?"

Rodney sighed. "I'll call if I have time, okay?"

"Okay," I said. I leaned over and kissed him on the cheek. I expected him to pull away, but instead he leaned in, catching me by the shoulder and kissing me on the mouth.

I lingered, drawing the kiss out as long as I could. I'd never meant to hurt him. Maybe he'd get that message, even though I didn't know how to say it out loud without making it worse.

A minute later I saw the blinds rustle in our front room window. I pulled away. "Later," I said.

He nodded, still refusing to look at me, and put the car into reverse. I shut the door and waved to him from the driveway. *Wave back*, I thought. *Please wave back.* And he did, but he still wasn't smiling.

But when I walked into the living room, Mom was.

I closed the door carefully behind me. "Watching us?" I asked.

Mom looked embarrassed. "Not intentionally. I heard the car and wanted to see if it was you or your father. I didn't expect there to be anything else to see."

I shifted from one foot to the other. "Yeah," I said. "Um, Rodney and I are kind of together now." Still. Hopefully.

Mom nodded like she was expecting that, which, since she'd watched us make out through the window, she probably was. "So is this new? Or were you afraid to tell me?"

I sure hadn't been meaning to break the news today. "No, it's new. Today, actually."

Mom looked surprised. "He could have stayed for dinner."

Right. Because *that* wouldn't have been awkward. Even so, I wished he'd stayed, if only so I'd know how badly I'd messed things up. "I asked him in, but he needed to get home."

Mom nodded slowly, watching me. That's when I realized I'd been backing up toward the door, literally into the corner. She had to have noticed that I didn't seem happy. "You really don't mind about this? I mean, you always said getting serious in high school was a mistake."

Mom opened her mouth and closed it again, like she wasn't sure how to answer. It was then that I realized Mom might not have known it was serious. I hadn't even considered that it might not be. This was Rodney. Any commitment put our whole friendship on the line.

That was why I'd avoided it for so long.

"I like Rodney," Mom said finally.

My stomach squeezed. "Yeah," I said. "Me, too."

Mom gave me a funny look. "I would hope so."

Oh. Right. I tried to think of something natural to say, but just ended up flailing my arms a little.

Mom stood up, heading for the kitchen. "I suppose it'll be fine," Mom said. "Athena dated Taren all through high school, and she survived."

Survived? Sure she did. But they broke up.

My cheeks went red. At least Rodney wouldn't be dumping me for refusing to sleep with him.

I spent Saturday morning holed up in Dad's office, working on photos. Rodney might have been busy with family stuff, but he wasn't too busy to dump his pictures of the abandoned building into our shared folder so I could see them. I added mine, then combed through them, pulling my favorites into my editing software.

Among my shots, I found the one Rodney had taken of the two of us kissing. From a photography standpoint, it was painfully bad. My head was closer to the camera than Rodney's, casting a shadow over part of his face. But I pulled the photo into the software anyway, and applied some filters to give it a stylized grain. I blurred the edges, so only our faces remained crisp. We looked dramatic like that, like the world spun around us, with only the two of us standing still.

We looked like we were in love.

I saved the edited photo to the folder, and added a note next to it. *What do you think?*

By Saturday night, Rodney had responded. *Don't fish. (You're gorgeous.)*

I bounced up and down in my chair. I was just being paranoid. He was just tired, or legitimately busy. If he was really putting things together, he wouldn't still be calling me gorgeous.

I spun around once in my chair, and almost whacked my knee against Dad's filing cabinet.

"You're happy," Dad said.

I turned around to find him standing in the hall.

"Yeah," I said. "A little."

Dad looked over my shoulder at the picture of Rodney and me on the computer screen.

"Nice work," he said.

My face flushed, and I closed the window. "Thanks."

Dad scuffed his toe on the carpet. "Your mom told me you two are dating."

Yes! Still! I smiled at Dad, and toned the answer down for him. "I guess so."

He gave me a questioning look. "How exactly is that different from what you've been doing?"

I squirmed, eying the screen where the photo had been. "Kissing."

He folded his arms. "Right."

My blush deepened. Dad didn't know we'd been doing that before, did he? It wasn't like we'd been big on the PDA, but we hadn't exactly been hiding, either.

Dad got this concerned look on his face. "I can't help but worry about you," he said.

Now my cheeks burned. "Dad," I said. "It's fine."

But Dad wasn't giving it up. "I just want you to be careful. You guys have been friends for years. When you already know the person you're dating, things can move fast."

His warning hit me like a punch to the gut. *No kidding, Dad. Thanks for the heads up.* "I'll watch it," I said.

Dad put a hand on the back of my chair. "I was a sixteen-year-old boy once, too, and you know what your mom's experience was like."

I did. And I knew Dad was just trying to protect me, but the idea that Rodney was someone I might need protecting *from* made me even more nervous about the leap we'd taken. He'd never hurt me intentionally. But people in relationships hurt each other unintentionally all the time, didn't they?

Like *I'd* done to *him.* I sank back into my chair. "I get it."

Dad nodded. "You're a good kid. I know you'll be smart."

As he headed back toward the kitchen, I rested my forehead on the desk. Dad trusted me. Rodney had, too.

I was totally going to hell.

I spent Sunday with my phone ringer turned all the way up, trying not to check it obsessively. I should have gone to Athena's, because homework and photo editing were not enough to distract me from staring at it, willing it to ring. But Rodney didn't text, and he didn't call.

I made it to the afternoon before I broke down and texted him.

Busy?

He responded immediately. *Ish. What's up?*

I was thinking about dragging my boyfriend to a movie. Could I call him that? I deleted and retyped the word "boyfriend" twice before hitting send.

When the phone vibrated, I squinted at it through one eye.

Hope you two have fun.

I couldn't help but smile. I set my phone down and counted as the seconds ticked by. Slowly.

A minute passed. Two. Three.

My knee bounced up and down. Was he really going to blow me off like that? I picked my phone back up, and began to type my comeback when he finally texted again.

Pick you up at six?

I breathed a sigh of relief and answered: *You'll make my boyfriend jealous.*

I'll try.

My pulse picked up, and I flopped back onto my bed. It's okay, I told myself. The awkwardness was probably all in my head.

Be cool.

I spent the hour before Rodney showed up flattening my hair, so it hung long and sleek down my back. I put on makeup I didn't usually wear—mascara and eyeliner and lip liner, too. I wore a pair of skinny jeans with no-nonsense boots and a loose, flowing shirt with chiffon sleeves floating down to my wrists.

When I came down the stairs to wait for Rodney, Mom and Dad were both sitting at the kitchen table, bills and budget sheets spread out before them.

"Careful," I said. "Don't overdo the fun."

Dad looked up at me over his reading glasses. "Going out?"

"Yeah," I said. "Rodney's picking me up. And we're going to a movie. In a public place, see?"

Both Mom and Dad smiled, and I tried to return it. I was a good daughter. I *was*.

When I caught sight of myself in the entryway mirror, I wondered if they'd both been laughing at me. I'd overdone it, big time. I'd never dressed up to see Rodney before. But some things should be different now, shouldn't they? Why couldn't this be one of them?

I jumped when Rodney knocked on the door. He opened it right away, like he always did when he was expected. He stepped inside wearing a plain white t-shirt and jeans. The only thing different about him was the way he looked at me, staggering slightly as he took in my face, then letting his eyes travel the length of my body.

I'd been checked out before, of course, and it usually made me want to hug my chest and hide. But today my pulse quickened, my body soaking up heat, not from embarrassment, but from the sheer thrill of being *wanted*.

"Hey," he said.

"Hey," I said back. And we both shifted, like we'd suddenly forgotten what to do with our hands.

I turned to the coat closet to get my jacket—mostly for something to hold—and I caught Dad leaning around the corner and watching us. "Goodbye," I shouted.

"Have fun!" Dad yelled back.

"And be safe!" Mom called.

But I couldn't help but think that if Rodney and I got in a car wreck, I wouldn't have to explain any of this to them. Ever.

We walked to the car, and Rodney unlocked my door and held it open. And then he stood there long enough for me to climb all the way in, so he could close it for me as well. I settled into my seat, like I had a hundred times in Rodney's car. But this time felt surreal. This was really happening. Rodney and I were really together. And, just like I'd always thought it would, that fact gave me so much more to lose.

Rodney climbed into the car beside me and started the engine. And in addition to not knowing how to dress, I also didn't know what to say. "What movie do you want to see?" I asked.

Rodney shrugged and looked over his shoulder, backing the car out of the driveway. "I thought you were the one with the plan."

I hadn't even checked the showings. "Sorry. I hope I didn't interrupt anything important."

"Eh," he said. "Nothing big."

Nothing big? He couldn't see me at all this weekend for *nothing big*? "You didn't have plans with your family?"

He shrugged again. "My dad's showing a big old house in San Jose. He let me go with him yesterday to take pictures."

"Really?" Rodney's dad never did that—he thought photography was a waste of time. It was no secret that he didn't think Rodney was ambitious enough.

"Yeah," Rodney said. "I think his normal photographer was out of town, and he needed some shots in a hurry."

That was the irony with his dad; he'd employ photographers, but still thought going into photography would make Rodney unemployable. The part that really ticked me off was that Rodney believed him. "That's great," I said. I stared at the dash, trying not to add the obvious: *You didn't invite me?* Finally, I settled for, "Get anything good?"

Rodney wobbled a hand. "I'll upload them. You can tell me."

An uneasy silence settled between us, and for once, Rodney didn't call me on it. I was grateful I'd suggested a movie and not dinner. The less talking required, the better.

When we got to the theater, though, Rodney grabbed my hand, and we walked up to the box office with our forearms touching from elbow to wrist. My skin hummed against his,

90

but it wasn't enough. As we looked up at the marquee, I stepped in front of Rodney and pulled his arms around me, so he held me from behind. I could feel his heart beating against my back, pounding out a steady rhythm, and I wished I could align my nerves to that beat.

We found a six-thirty showing of a disaster movie. The theater was all but empty, and I pulled Rodney up the stairs to the very back row. At that moment, I didn't care about the movie, only about the heat of Rodney's arm against mine.

When we reached our seats, Rodney pulled up the armrest so I could squeeze up against him, but even the thin layers of his shirt and mine felt like too much between us. So I shifted up into his lap with my feet resting on my own seat, took his face in my hands, and kissed him.

He kissed me back fiercely, like he hadn't seen me in months. By the time the previews started, Rodney already had his mouth on my neck, and the last thing in the world I wanted to do was pull away.

We barely watched the movie. We flipped up the armrests and lay down across the empty row, hands up under each other's shirts, heat burning so intensely I was honestly surprised when the seats didn't go up in flames around us.

After the movie, Rodney parked in my driveway and kissed me long and deep, like he didn't want to let go any more than I did. In all the times we'd made out before, I'd never been so aware of him, of the slight dampness behind his ears, of the subtle way his back arched when I kissed his neck.

My parents could have been watching us from the window. The living room was dark, so there was no way for me to know. I put my hand on the car door handle, but the idea of retreating alone into my dark room was unbearable. I ran my fingertips over Rodney's forearm, raising goose bumps. "Come in," I said. "Go park the car around the corner, and meet me at my window."

Rodney bit his lip, meeting my eyes. His body swayed toward me even as his fingers tightened on the gear shift. "Are you sure?" he asked.

I didn't want to think twice. I slipped my nails under the collar of his shirt, and Rodney groaned.

There was no way I was letting him go. "See you inside," I said. And I climbed out of the car and shut the door.

I stood on the doorstep while Rodney drove away, and then ducked inside. Mom and Dad had already gone up to their room; they had the door open and the TV on. I breathed slow and steady for a while, to make sure I could be calm before I passed by.

"Goodnight," I called.

"How was the movie?" Mom asked.

"Lame," I said. "I'm exhausted, so I'm going to bed."

"Night," Dad called. And they both turned back to the television.

I was glad for it, because the noise would cover the sound of me locking my door and opening the window. I stood in my room with the pane pushed aside, breath steaming into the night air, waiting in the dark.

Rodney appeared on the roof a few minutes later, and eased himself over the windowsill. He had his hands on me before he was even all the way in the room. When his feet hit the floor, he whispered in my ear: "Are you sure I should be here?"

I slid my tongue up the outside of his ear. "Yes," I said.

He pulled off his jacket, and we sank onto my bed. Rodney barely took his mouth off mine, except to pull both our shirts off over our heads. The rushing of my ears drowned out the sound of my parents' TV down the hall.

The weight of him on top of me sent shivers over my body. As I ran my fingers around the waistband of his jeans, reaching for his zipper, Rodney fished something out of his pocket—a square, shiny wrapper.

The room spun. I'd lied to him about the birth control.

And he *knew*.

I floated, suspended in time. But instead of confronting me,

Rodney drew close. His teeth grazed my shoulder. I breathed him in and let the tide roll me under until we landed, beached and breathless, on the shore.

When Rodney left, he looked like I felt, shadows pooling in the hollows of his eyes. The cold air that swept in after him chilled my sheets, and I curled up on my pillow, clinging to the last traces of warmth where he had been. I knotted my fingers up in my pillow until they cramped, squeezed my eyes shut, and begged for sleep.

But the empty darkness rang in my ears well into the night.

I woke up in the morning to a text message—Rodney had a chess game. Could I get a ride from my mom?

I dropped the phone over the side of the bed and crunched down under my covers. What was wrong with me? Rodney often played chess in the mornings. It wasn't like it meant anything.

But when I got to school that morning, there was no rose in my locker.

Chapter Nine
Weeks Three through Five

Rodney's chess games went on, mornings, lunches, afternoons. The district chess tournament was three weeks away. Usually Rodney didn't even mention it until the week before, but this year he couldn't get enough practice. Rodney buried himself in his game, and I buried myself in our photos, and I wondered if either of us would see the light of day again.

When we ran into each other at my locker, or in the halls, Rodney would take my hand, brush my hair behind my ears, and kiss me on the cheek. It was sweet in an aching kind of way, but he didn't make any effort to get me alone, or to go further. And I didn't push him either. Since our night together, a hollow pit gaped in my chest, and whenever Rodney touched me, it seemed to bore deeper.

It was my fault, of course, not only for lying, but for the hanging uncertainty. I could be pregnant, even now, and every cramp, every twinge, every uneasiness in my stomach made me hold my breath. The day before my period I could take the test. And once I knew I wasn't pregnant, Rodney and I could figure out our relationship with no doubts hanging between us.

My mother still wouldn't have a baby, of course. But Rodney was my boyfriend now, and he'd already said no. I hadn't waited this long to be with him just to screw that up.

Days passed. Rodney texted me in the morning about his

chess opponents, and in the evening about the editing work I'd done. But when we were together, I'd catch him looking at me out of the corner of his eyes, like he, too, was holding his breath.

A week later, Mom came into Dad's office while I was sitting at his desk, working on one of the pictures Rodney had taken of the house his dad was showing. It was an old Victorian, and Rodney had dumped the whole set of shots into our folder, including the boring, full-room shots he'd taken for his dad's work. Rodney must have carted a step ladder from room to room, because the angles in the photos made the house look roomy—something Victorians rarely were.

The second half of the photo set told a different story. The series of art photos showed doorways cut in half, banisters with grooves worn in the paint, the dirty corner of a window with a single, star-shaped chip in the glass. Rodney had taken shots from the bottom of the stairs, focused on the worn dips in the wood where feet had bent them down from decade upon decade of trodding.

I had one of the stairway photos pulled into my editor, and played with the levels, trying to keep the photo bright without the light from the top of the stairs pulling the center of interest off balance.

"Where is that?" Mom asked.

"It's a house Rodney's dad is showing," I said. "He went without me."

Mom looked pensive. "I haven't seen Rodney around the last few days."

I waved a hand dismissively. "He's got a chess tournament coming up."

"So it's not because of what your dad said?"

I looked over at Mom. She hadn't been there when Dad talked to me, so they'd obviously had a conversation about it when I wasn't around. Perhaps several. "No," I said. "It's got nothing to do with that."

"Good," Mom said. "Your dad was worried."

Worried. But not enough to talk to me.

Mom tapped her nails on the desk, like she was trying to work her way up to something.

"What's wrong?" I asked.

"Nothing," Mom said. "Nothing's wrong. I just wanted to talk to you."

I swallowed. "Did the agency contact you about another birth mom?"

"No," Mom said. "I asked the agency to take me off the list. That's what I wanted to talk to you about, actually. I know you wanted me to keep the baby things in the garage, but I'm thinking of donating them. They aren't doing any good sitting there, and your dad needs the space."

Dad's tools overflowed into all the empty spaces in the garage, but if she wanted to free up space for him, she could have gotten rid of the boxes of old toys or school papers. She didn't have to get rid of the crib.

Mom stood to leave. My heart beat in my throat. If I was pregnant, what then? We'd need those things—the crib, the clothes, the car seat.

It had only been one time. I still felt normal. I couldn't tell Mom I might be pregnant until I knew for sure.

But I couldn't let her get rid of the things, either.

"Wait," I said.

Mom turned around in the doorway.

"Where are you going to donate them?" I asked.

Mom shrugged. "I was thinking of asking at the hospital where Lily delivered. They probably see a lot of young moms pass through who could use the help."

"Let me call," I said.

Mom shook her head. "You don't have to."

"I want to," I said. "You don't really want to know who you're giving the stuff to anyway, do you? You don't want to picture who might be using it, if it isn't you."

Mom closed her eyes, and I cringed. I'd gone too far.

But then she nodded. "Okay," she said. "You can do it."

I let out a long breath as Mom left down the hall, hopefully not to cry in her room. I hadn't meant to hurt her. I just needed her to hold on a tiny bit longer.

And once the test came up negative, we could all let go.

On the Monday before I expected my period, I skipped breakfast, not only from nervousness, but because the idea of putting food in my mouth was utterly repulsive. A tightness bore down on my sternum, right above the xiphoid I'd labeled on that week's physiology homework.

It's nerves, I told myself. Morning sickness would make me nauseous. But the power of those nerves kept me far away from the kitchen.

I left a note for Mom saying I had a study session, and then took an early bus to school.

By seven, I walked onto campus. The place was deserted—the only cars in sight were in the staff parking lot. The side door to the locker room was locked, so I walked around to the main gym doors. For a moment I was afraid they would be locked, too, but they swung open, and I moved through the gym and into the locker room without running into anyone.

After opening my locker, I wrapped one of the tests in my gym shirt and carried it into the bathroom. As I went, I tried to come up with excuses for why I was there so early, but I couldn't think of anything. My mind buzzed blankly. I couldn't think about anything but the test.

Pregnancy tests were designed to torment jittery women. I peed on the strip and then sat it on top of the sanitary napkin box, timing it with my cell phone. Ten seconds past. Fifteen. Twenty. It was probably bad luck to stare, but I couldn't help it. All the time I kept telling myself it was going to be negative. It had to be negative. Mom was moving on; Rodney was against it. After this, we could all go on with our lives. No one would ever have to know what an idiot I'd been. No one but me and this little white stick.

After a minute and thirty seconds, two pink lines appeared. I double checked the instructions twice. I checked the time again. I picked up the test and held it upside down. I waited all the way to two minutes, just to be sure. The result didn't change. White spots filled my vision, and I leaned against the wall.

I was pregnant.

All the blood seemed to drain from my body. I wasn't sure how long I stood there, holding the test. After waiting too long, the instructions said the test result could falsely change. But it didn't. Those two lines just kept staring at me.

As I held it, I actually thought about going to a clinic to get rid of the problem. I could just pretend that everything was fine. No one would have to know—not my mom, not Rodney.

I could tell Athena. She'd make the phone calls for me. She'd drive.

But already I could feel myself folding in on those thoughts; I could not become that statistic. I'd heard Mom quote it with tears in her eyes: one million girls a year terminated their pregnancies instead of letting Mom adopt their babies. The way she said it, she probably believed she could have adopted them all.

And here I was, thinking of a child as a *problem*. What was wrong with me? I'd chosen this. I'd *planned* this.

Now I had to own it, whatever the consequences might be. And in the end, whatever happened to me, at least Mom would have her baby.

If I couldn't do anything else right, at least I could give her that.

While walking to first period I realized I should have waited to take the test until after school. Whatever agony it would have been to wait that long, waiting to tell Rodney was going to be much, much worse. I couldn't tell him in the middle of the school day. He needed time to react—to yell or to hate me or to break up with me.

Oh, please, I thought. Please, please. Don't let Rodney break up with me. That would be the end of everything—our four year friendship, every possibility for the future. How could I have messed with that, after waiting for it so long?

Rodney had a chess game at lunch, so I hid in the locker room and took the second pregnancy test. The two lines appeared again. I shook the test. I squinted at it. But the two lines just stared back at me, unmoving.

This wasn't a false positive.

I knew I should eat, but I couldn't. The thought of putting food in my mouth made my throat close up, and as I walked to Rodney's last period class, I felt so nauseous I was glad that my stomach was empty. And after seeing the tests, I could no longer pretend that it was nerves. Curse whoever called this morning sickness. It was almost three in the afternoon. If my body kept up this way, I wouldn't need to tell Rodney anything. I'd starve to death before I started to show.

No doubt the mortician would find the fetus in the autopsy.

I waited for Rodney outside his last-period trig class, tying the ends of my backpack straps into knots. I promised myself I would say something as soon as he came out. I owed him that.

When Rodney saw me, one corner of his mouth quirked up. "Hey," he said.

"Hey," I said. "Do you have a minute?"

"I have a game with Ryan."

"You always have a game," I said. "Cancel it."

Rodney looked at me. That was the first time I'd ever asked him to skip a game for me, so he must have known I was serious. "What did you have in mind?" he asked.

For once I fulfilled my promise. "We need to talk."

Those had to be the worst four words in the English language, especially when they came from someone you'd been sleeping with. Rodney gave me an uneasy smile. "Okay," he said. "Shoot." People pushed by us in the halls. No one seemed to be paying attention, but I still couldn't tell him here.

"Let's walk," I said.

We walked around the baseball diamond at the back of the school to the bleachers. I was being too quiet, again, and from the uneasy silence, I could tell that Rodney noticed. He walked up the bleachers to the very top and sat down, leaving room for me on the aisle.

"You didn't text Ryan," I said.

"Ryan will survive," he said. "Look, I know I owe you an apology. I've been so busy. But the tournament is this weekend, and after that—"

"It's not about that," I said.

He was quiet for a second. "You're right. I should have talked to you before. I'm sorry."

"No, really," I said. I reached for his hand, trying to connect with him. He took it, but kept talking.

"You just freaked me out with that stuff about your mom, you know? But I should have been honest with you about it. There's no excuse—"

"*Rodney*," I said. "I'm pregnant."

Rodney's grip tightened on mine. He swayed backward, and I was afraid he was going to fall off the bench, but he steadied himself.

"I'm sorry," I said. "I didn't mean to just blurt it out like that."

"You're pregnant," he said. "Right now."

"Yeah," I said. "I just found out today."

He rubbed his temples with his free hand. "You said it was okay. I thought that meant you were on the pill or something."

"I know," I said.

"But you weren't."

"No," I said. "I'm so sorry."

Rodney pulled his hand away and pressed both his palms to his forehead. His voice sounded far away. "I knew it," he said.

Everything I hadn't eaten in two days threatened to rise into my mouth. Of course he knew. This was what we hadn't been talking about for days. It was so thick in the air we'd both choked on it.

He went on. "You planned this. For your mother. That's what this was about all along."

I could see our short relationship unwinding before his eyes. I hadn't wanted him, only a baby. "It wasn't *all* about that," I said.

He looked at me, waiting for me to elaborate.

"You're," I said. "I mean . . . I wanted to *be* with you—"

Rodney rolled his eyes clear up under his eyelids. "Yes," he said. "I'm clearly irresistible."

I couldn't breathe. I wanted him to know what I'd felt, but everything I could say sounded like an excuse. "I'm sorry," I said. "It was a terrible idea, like you said."

He turned to me, staring me down. "*Yeah*, it was. How could you do this to me?"

My hands and feet went cold. Yes, Penny. How could you? "I didn't think it through."

"Obviously," he said.

I looked up at the sky. I'd given him the worst answer of all, when it came from someone you loved: I did this life-altering thing, and I didn't even think about how it would affect him.

"I was an idiot for not realizing this would hurt you," I said. "But we always said that we weren't serious. We always said we weren't really together. Maybe it was my idea, but you went along with it so I thought that—"

"Of course I went along with it," Rodney said. "What else was I supposed to do? You're saying to me, gee, Rodney, you're so important to me that I don't ever want to lose you, so we can't be together now." He threw his arms open. "Tell me what I was supposed to say to that."

I'd never thought of it that way. "I guess . . . I guess that is what I was saying."

"I know, right? I didn't want to be the guy who wants something so badly now that he throws away what he wants later."

I buried my face in my hands. What he meant was, he didn't

want to be like me.

"But this," Rodney said, gesturing toward me. "This has nothing to do with me." Rodney folded inward, knees together, arms resting on his legs. A cold breeze blew between us.

I hugged my arms around myself and scooted closer to him on the bench. I couldn't let him leave here thinking he meant nothing to me. I had to say something, anything, to get him to stay with me.

"I love you," I said.

Rodney's hands fell to the bench, his knuckles striking the metal with a clunk. "How can you say that to me now?"

I wanted to insist that I meant it, but the words wouldn't come. I wanted to mean it. The crushing weight bearing down on me had to mean something, didn't it? "I just want you to know . . . that I didn't mean any of it to hurt you. Being with you meant something to me. I just didn't know how much until after."

Rodney looked up at the sky as a cloud passed over the sun. "It meant something," he said. "But not enough to tell me the truth until after you knew that you had to."

The knife struck so far into my gut that it stuck out the other side. I fought the urge to get on my knees and literally grovel. "I'm so sorry," I said. "Tell me what I can do to make it better."

Rodney examined his fingernails for a long moment. My heart sank. There was nothing I could do, and to illustrate the point, he was going to ignore me.

But instead, Rodney cleared his throat. "You could marry me," he said.

I about fell off the bench. "I could *what?*"

He flicked some dirt from under his thumbnail. "You could marry me." Then he looked up, his eyes boring into mine. Begging me. Daring me.

The whole world stood still. "You cannot be serious."

But Rodney didn't even blink. "I am if you are."

My lungs constricted, and for a terrifying moment, I couldn't draw breath. I looked at him wide-eyed, but he stared back with that calm steadiness that I so loved about him.

And I knew.

He still loved me. My stupidity hadn't erased four years of history. He was giving me the chance to take it back. We could go on pretending that I got pregnant by mistake. I could marry him, to prove to him that I loved him. To prove to him that I knew I'd screwed up. I wouldn't have to lose him. We could still be together.

Pregnant at sixteen, not for my mom, but for real.

Blood rushed in my ears. "We're too young," I said.

Rodney rolled his eyes again. "That's what you keep saying. And look where it's gotten us."

How could he do that? How could he stare me down, like what he was saying wasn't completely, utterly crazy? "We're talking about a baby, here. You don't even *like* kids."

Rodney shook his head. "I don't like to babysit other people's kids. That doesn't mean I don't ever want to have them."

That was news to me, but also beside the point. "Okay," I said. "But you don't want to have them *now*."

"I don't get a choice in that, do I?"

I cringed.

"Jeez," Rodney said. He reached across the bench and took my hand again, his fingers loose in mine. "I'm sorry."

"No, I deserved that."

"Maybe," Rodney said. "But it was still a dick thing to say."

I squeezed his hand. "Where would we live?" I asked. "What would we do?"

The breeze ruffled Rodney's hair. "We could live with your parents, or mine. Finish school. Start that business you keep talking about."

Raise a child. Me, in my mother's house. With a baby I'd intended for her.

My skin prickled. Married even younger than her. A doomed high school marriage.

Rodney moved closer to me, so our arms touched. His skin was cool from the wind. "I didn't mean to say you're the only one involved, here. I did this, too. I'll take responsibility, if you'll let me."

My heart pounded. This was what I wanted, wasn't it? For Rodney to forgive me, to keep him forever. It's what I'd always wanted. It was more than I deserved.

But bile still rose in my throat. Not like this. This would just be another way to cover up for the things I'd done. A commitment to a lifetime of ignoring my lies. Our relationship, warped as it was, wouldn't survive it.

"No," I said. "I can't marry you."

From the look Rodney gave me, I could tell he knew I meant it. I could also tell I would have hurt him less by slapping him in the face.

"Say something," I said. "Is this the end? I don't want it to be. I'll do anything."

Anything except be honest with him. Anything except think about his feelings first. Anything except marry him.

Even I couldn't believe me.

Rodney closed his eyes, like he was trying to hear something very, very faint. I held my breath, afraid the slightest movement would tip us off balance, and we'd fall.

I put a hand on his arm, and he stared down at it, like he didn't know what it was. I held my breath, waiting for him to pull away. Waiting for him to tell me it was all over.

"Do you remember our first kiss?" he asked.

I blinked at him. Of course I remembered, though it had been years, and we'd never talked about it. No one forgets their first kiss, and our first was also *the* first, for both of us. We were still in middle school. Rodney had just gotten his first SLR for his birthday—a camera way nicer than the point-and-shoots we'd been using to take pictures after school. We'd walked to the gas station and bought fudgesicles from the freezer section, and then went to the park. I'd told him to get out his camera to take pictures of some kids feeding the ducks.

"You wouldn't touch your camera until our popsicles were gone," I said. "You didn't want to get chocolate on it."

Rodney nodded. He focused on something far away in the outfield, or maybe something invisible, far back in his memory. No doubt he remembered every detail of that day at the park, as I did. We'd finished our popsicles, and thrown away the sticks, but still he wouldn't get his camera out.

"You have chocolate on your face," he'd said. Then he'd stepped close to me, and wiped my lower lip with his thumb. He had the slightest smudge of chocolate at the corner of his mouth. I don't know if it was the sugar buzz or the soft brush of his thumb to my lip, but in a rush of electric bravery I leaned in, brushing it with my lower lip. He turned into the kiss at the last moment, and our mouths collided. We stood there in the park, in full view of the pond and the ducks and the bread-wielding children, kissing each other with limp lips, making it crystal clear that neither of us knew what the hell we were doing.

Rodney shook his head slowly, like the memory offended him. "I should have told you then how I felt."

Then? I blinked away dizziness. *That's* how long this had been for him? How could I not have realized?

I stuttered. "Why—why *didn't* you tell me?"

Rodney gave me a regretful look. "I didn't want to scare you off."

I hadn't thought it possible to regret the past more than I had already. "You were right," I said. "I would have been scared."

"I should have said it anyway."

I gripped his hand. "You're saying it now."

Rodney's eyes turned hard. "Too late."

My chest burned. I wanted to go back and be that girl again, kissing her best friend and giggling over it. I wished I knew the right thing to say now, the magic words that would transform us back into who we used to be, to give us a do-over.

"Don't get the wrong idea," he said. "I wasn't in love with you then. Just hopeful."

My mouth went dry. I didn't miss the implication, the admission that he was, in fact, in love with me now. It didn't make it better that he wasn't back then. The hope of a thirteen-year-old boy felt like a delicate thing. And what had I done? I'd squashed it.

I spoke quietly, hoping to push him toward happier memories—the ones that would convince him our relationship was worth salvaging. "When, then?" I asked.

He sighed. "You called me in the middle of the night," he said. "After your mother had her last miscarriage. Your parents had a big fight—"

"I remember." The fight had been about in vitro. Mom wanted to try again; Dad wanted to stop. "You stayed on the phone with me for hours. Even after I had nothing left to say." We'd both fallen asleep on the phone; I wasn't sure who had disconnected first. That had been two years ago, in the fall of our freshman year.

"I wished I could drive," Rodney said. "So I could come over to be with you. You sounded so sad, and all I wanted to do was make it better."

"You did make it better," I said.

"And the next day I got sent to the office for sleeping through class."

I scrunched my eyebrows. "I don't remember that."

Rodney breathed out a long, slow sigh. "That's because I didn't tell you. I didn't want it to stop you from calling me again, if you needed to. Because I cared more about what you needed than I did about me."

No. No, no, *no*. I saw this knife coming. I could have dodged. But instead I sat there. Waiting.

"That's how I know you don't love me," he said.

I hugged my waist. I deserved that. If it hadn't been true, it wouldn't have cut. But it wasn't as if he'd given me the chance to be there for him like that. He didn't call me in the night crying.

Rodney didn't cry; he didn't fall apart. He just strode through life with a steady balance.

Rodney shuffled his feet on the metal bench. That sounded a lot like the end of the conversation, but I couldn't let it be.

"I want to," I said. "Does that count for anything?"

He looked at me, considering. I held my breath. I didn't deserve another chance, but I wanted one.

"I don't know," he said. "I need time to think."

I squeezed my eyes shut. The last thing I wanted was to be away from him. But time was a chance. Time was not the end.

Not yet.

He put me first. If that's what love looked like to him, that's what I needed to give him.

"What do *you* want?" I asked. "And don't say it's to get married and have a kid, because I know you."

Rodney was quiet for a long moment. "Honest truth?" he asked.

"Yes," I said.

He turned and looked me right in the eye. I'd never seen him so intent, so focused. My heart pounded, and my head spun, and I wished I could melt into him and hold on tight.

"I want to be with my best friend forever," he said, "and take millions of pictures and be stupidly happy. She's the most beautiful thing in my life. Everyone in the world would wish they were us."

That picture slammed into me like a speeding truck. And for a moment, I could see it—the life he described. But it felt like a dream, or a wish. Something far, far away that I once knew, but then forgot.

I leaned closer to him. "We could get through this," I said. "And still have that. Couldn't we?"

Rodney shook his head slowly, the way I imagined a doctor might when asked to give a diagnosis for a dying family member. "That's not us," he said. "Maybe it could have been, but it's not."

If I hadn't been sitting, my knees might have buckled. This was the status of our relationship: dead on arrival. I should have known that. I'd killed it myself.

I shivered. Like a relative in denial, I couldn't accept the prognosis. I reached out for his arm. "Don't you want *anything* I can give you now?"

Rodney's hand slid slowly out from under mine. "If I think of something," he said, "I'll let you know."

I bent over my knees. I really was going to retch. *Be cool*, I thought. *Be cool, be cool. Do* not *let him see you hurl.*

Rodney stood, his boots echoing on the bleachers. "You need a ride home?"

"No," I croaked. Breathe in, breathe out. My head started to clear.

"Penny?" he asked. "Are you okay?"

I looked up at him, at his brow etched with genuine concern. Only Rodney would offer to help me after a blow like that. I wanted to hang on to every minute I had left with him. But he wanted time to think, and the sooner I gave that to him, the faster he'd be able to figure things out.

"I'll be fine," I said. "Are you going to call me?"

He looked past me. "I don't know," he said. "I don't know anything."

And then he turned and walked away. The aluminum bench rattled under him with each step. The sides of my eyes tingled like I was going to cry, but instead they just burned.

Rodney never looked back.

Chapter Ten
Week Five

I sat on the bleachers for what felt like hours, my arms wrapped around myself. What I'd done was awful. But the worst part was, I'd done it to Rodney, who was willing to stand by me even now, if I was just willing to do the same for him.

I could text him right now. He might let me change my mind and marry him.

I closed my eyes. We had almost two years of high school left. Neither of us had a job. Getting married had to be the worst possible plan. But an ache throbbed in my chest. If I didn't, would he ever forgive me?

The wind blew stronger as the sun dipped lower in the sky. Finally, I stood up. I couldn't sit here forever.

Next I had to face my mother.

Mom was going to yell, of course. She was going to be upset. How could she not be, when her teenage daughter was pregnant? But she'd have to see reason. I had something she needed, and after what I'd done to Rodney to get it, she had to see how important it was to me that she have the child.

But I couldn't tell her about that, could I? If she knew I'd done this on purpose, she might feel bad, like she pressured me into it. And she didn't—this was my choice. Better to let her think it was an accident. Things like this happened all the time. Why shouldn't it happen to her, at the exact time she most needed it?

A fortunate accident. A mishap, even. As soon as she adjusted to the idea, everything would be fine.

My stomach knotted. Between her and me, anyway.

Rodney was another story.

I couldn't bring myself to actually call Mom for a ride; she might hear the ache in my voice and drag the truth out of me over the phone. So I texted her instead. She texted back immediately: *On my way.*

I sat down on the planter in front of the school while I waited. My hands shook, whether from exhaustion or hunger or anticipation of the conversation to come, I wasn't sure.

It must have been written on my face as well, because Mom took one look at me as I was climbing in the car, and started with the questions.

"What's wrong?" she asked. "Did you skip lunch?"

"Yeah," I said. "But that's not it."

Mom started the car and pulled away from the curb. "What is it?"

"I have some good news, and some bad news," I said. "Actually, they're both the same news."

Mom didn't look pleased about that. "And?"

Deep breath. "I'm pregnant."

Mom blew right through a stop sign.

"Um," I said.

Mom's voice was shrill. "You're pregnant?"

I winced. "Yeah."

Mom looked at me, taking her eyes off the road for a dangerously long moment. "How can you be pregnant?"

"Um," I said again.

She turned back to the road. "Not *how*," Mom said. "I know *how*. How could you be having sex, is what I mean. Didn't your dad talk to you about that?"

"Uh," I said. "I, uh . . ."

"You and Rodney haven't been together that long." Mom pressed her hand to her forehead and shut her eyes, ignoring the road again. I squeezed the armrest. She was doing the math in her head—math she'd done for herself a million times.

"Stop sign," I said.

She swore and stepped on the brake. "That day I saw you two kissing in the car," she said. "*That day.*"

"No," I said. "Jeez."

"When then?"

I flailed my arms around. "Before that. But that's not the point—"

"Before that? Before that you said you weren't even together!"

I did. Crap.

"No," Mom said. "Here's the point. Did you even try to use protection? Do we need to have you tested for diseases?"

I could not answer that. "Mom," I said. "It's Rodney. He doesn't have diseases."

Mom gave me a look like I was the biggest idiot in the world. Which I was, but still.

"Are you absolutely sure you're pregnant?" she asked.

"I had a positive test."

"A home test."

"Yeah."

"Could be a false positive."

"I took two of them in the bathroom at school. They were both positive."

Mom missed the turn for our street, and swore again as she drove around the block. "What were you thinking? Your father talked to you about being careful. But it was too late because you and Rodney were already—"

"Mom!" I said. "Can we focus for a second?"

Mom gave me a warning look, her forehead wrinkling as her eyebrows rose. "Focus on what?"

"The positive side of this," I said. "The good news part."

Mom looked incredulous. "And this is good news *why?*"

I sighed. "It's good news because you can finally adopt a baby."

Mom drove down the exact center of our street, parked cars

ticking by on either side.

"Mom?" I asked.

She turned wide into our driveway, slammed on the brake, and turned off the key.

"That," my mother said, "is the single most twisted sentence you have ever said in your life."

I sat back in my seat, stunned. Yelling, I'd expected. Hyperventilating. Maybe even crying.

Not being called twisted.

Never that.

"Um," I said again. "I'm still pregnant. And you want a baby, so . . ."

"Penelope Overman," Mom said. "Do not even try to pin this on me."

Pin this on her? I was trying to *give* it to her. "But—"

"No," Mom said. "There is no way in hell I am adopting my daughter's baby. Do you not see how ridiculous that is?"

My body seized up. She could *not* be saying that. I'd thought so long about what I was going to say to Rodney, but clearly this was the conversation I should have been rehearsing. She had to take this baby. She had to. I'd turned Rodney away for her. That's why I was in this mess in the first place.

I struggled for air. I just needed to pitch it in the right way. Then she'd see. "People do this all the time, don't they?" I asked. "Grandparents take care of babies when teen moms can't. This will just be more . . . official."

Official, yes. Her baby, not mine. That was the plan.

But my arm tingled, like I could still feel Rodney's hand holding on. Offering to marry me. Offering to raise our child. I'd only thought I'd be giving up a baby, not a whole alternate future.

I looked over at Mom, and found her shaking her head angrily at the steering wheel. When she spoke, her voice was a low growl. "Do you know what people will think? They'll think I asked you to do this. No one will believe that my own daughter

112

would make a mistake this stupid on accident."

For the first time in my life, I wanted to punch my mother in the face. "*That's* what you care about?" I asked. "What people will *think*?"

"No," Mom said. "I just meant—" She shoved the tips of her fingers into her mouth and bit down on them.

I stared at our front door. She said that because part of her knew what I'd done, and she just didn't want to believe it. "I didn't hear you tell Lily she was stupid," I said quietly. "You told her she was *brave*, and *selfless* and—"

Mom gave me a dark look. "I didn't mean for you to take that as *advice*."

I gripped the door handle. "So you'll accept help from a girl who burns you, but not from me."

Mom held up her hands. "STOP."

My mouth watered and my stomach rose. I cracked open the door, but my body didn't retch. She had to take this baby. She had to.

I'd given up everything for her.

But Mom didn't see it that way. And I couldn't tell her the whole truth. She already thought people would think I'd done this on purpose. How much more angry would she be if she knew that I had? Would she refuse to take the baby, just to punish me? If she did, what would I do then?

"I'm calling your father," Mom said. And she got out of the car and stalked away.

I shook myself, trying to loosen my locked muscles. Calling Dad was probably a good move. Maybe he could talk some sense into her.

I trudged into the house. Mom had gone up to her room, so I sat at the kitchen table, my backpack slumping on the floor. Mom spoke so loudly that I could hear every word, even from downstairs.

"Come home right now," she said. "You need to talk to your daughter. Yes, right now. I don't care what you're doing."

She must have hung up on him after that, because she yelled down to me from the top of the stairs: "You're telling him. Not me." And then she slammed her door.

I rested my head on my arms. She sure wasn't winning any awards for parental maturity today. I understood why she was upset, but couldn't she see that I'd done this for *her*? Couldn't she see all that I'd given up so that she could be happy?

My heart sank as I thought about Rodney walking away from me. What was he doing, now? I checked my phone, but of course he hadn't texted me. I wondered if he'd gone straight home, or if he was out somewhere, wandering around, hating me.

I'm sorry, I texted. But I deleted it without sending. He knew I was sorry. It didn't change how I'd hurt him.

Dad's work truck flew into the driveway fifteen minutes later. I heard him slam on his squeaky brakes, and stomp up the front steps in his heavy boots.

He opened the front door and rushed to the stairwell. When he spotted me sitting at the dining room table, he stopped. "Are you okay?" Dad asked. "Where's your mother?"

"She's upstairs," I said. "You have to talk to her."

He looked me up and down, as if counting my limbs. "That's what she said about you."

Things weren't going to get better from here. "I'm pregnant," I said. "And she says she won't take the baby."

Dad's knees literally buckled. He dropped into the chair across from me.

"Sorry," I said. "I guess I should have told you to sit first." At least he wasn't driving.

Dad gave me an exhausted look. "Back up. You're pregnant?"

I buried my face in my arms. "Yeah."

Dad sounded like he wanted to kill someone. "Who's the father? Rodney?"

My stomach dropped. How could he need to ask that? "Of course it's Rodney."

Dad's eyes flicked up the stairs. "I think we should call your mother down for this."

I rested my cheek on my forearm. "She didn't want to talk about it. She said there was no way she was going to adopt her daughter's baby. But you'll talk her into it, won't you?"

Dad pressed both of his hands over his face, and he didn't answer.

"Dad?" I said. "Seriously. Why doesn't anyone see what a good thing this could be? This is your baby we're talking about."

Dad dropped his hands to his knees, his eyes meeting mine. "No, Penny," he said. "*You* are my baby."

My body deflated. *Oh.*

Dad shook his head. "Where is Rodney?"

Maybe gone forever. "I don't know," I said. "I told him earlier today."

Dad's hands balled into fists. "And then he left you to face your parents on your own?"

Ugh. Now, on top of everything, I was making Rodney look like a jerk. "No," I said. "It's not like that. He said he needed time to think."

Dad sat back in his chair. "Time to think about what? Did he push you into this?"

My eyes widened. "No," I said. "Never. It's my fault, okay?"

Dad crossed his arms. "It takes two."

But only one of us was the liar. "Please," I said. "Things are complicated enough with him right now."

Dad glared at the empty chair next to me, where presumably Rodney should have been sitting. "Seems pretty simple to me," he said.

I sighed. At least I'd spared Rodney this. "Can we talk about what's going to happen now?"

Dad settled back into his chair. "Okay," Dad said. "You want your mom and me to adopt the baby."

My voice came out as a plea. "That's the obvious thing to do, right?"

"Maybe," Dad said. "What about Rodney? What does he want?"

Blood filled my cheeks. By now he must have rethought his proposal. It had been a knee-jerk thing. Hadn't it?

"I don't know," I said.

Dad gave a sharp nod. "We'll have to talk to him. And his parents."

My stomach dropped. "His parents?" I hadn't even thought about the conversation that he had ahead of him. They didn't care much about what Rodney did, as long as he kept his grades up. He said all they really wanted was for him to stay out of their way.

How could I not have thought about this? I told him I loved him, but I *still* wasn't anticipating his feelings. "Do we really have to bother them about it?"

"Of course," Dad said. "They should all be involved in these decisions."

I closed my eyes. The least I could do for Rodney was leave him out of awkward conversations with my family. I ran my nails around the under edge of the table. "Does he?" I asked. "Lily's boyfriend wasn't involved."

Dad raised one eyebrow. "Lily's boyfriend made her get out of the car on the highway when he found out she was pregnant."

Jeez. Poor Lily. "Rodney's not like that," I said.

"I know," Dad said. "That's my point." He stood up from the table. "I better go talk to your mother."

I stood along with him. By now, maybe Mom had calmed down enough to be reasonable. "Can I come?"

"From the way she sounded on the phone," he said, "I'd say you'd better not."

My shoulders sank. "You have to convince her."

Dad shook his head at me. "You know how sensitive your mom is about these things," he said. "She never wanted this for you."

My vision blurred. She never wanted my life to be like hers, having kids so young. But it *wasn't*. I was having a pregnancy, not a baby.

Unless she refused to take it. And Rodney refused to forgive me.

Where would that leave me then?

When my vision returned, my eyes focused on a picture in a photo collage on the dining room wall. Mom couldn't be much older than me, and she held a one-year-old Athena in her arms.

I sank back into a chair. Mom had to get over this. If she didn't I'd be just your average pregnant teenager, with no real options except bad ones.

Dad trudged up the stairs, leaving me sitting at the dining room table. Clouds passed over the sun outside the kitchen window, and the room grew dim.

I pulled out my phone. Still no word from Rodney. He said he needed time, but how much time? Hours? Weeks? Months?

No. He couldn't possibly let this hang between us that long. He had to be going as crazy as I was.

I brought up another text message. There must be something I could say to make things better. But everything I could think of was something I'd already said. Rodney wouldn't talk to me, and Mom wouldn't talk to me, and Dad needed to be there for Mom.

So instead I dialed Athena. She would freak out, but at this point, that was preferable to the ringing silence of the empty downstairs. I needed to tell her before she heard it from Mom or Dad, but more than that, I just wanted to talk to someone who wouldn't walk away.

The phone rang twice before she picked it up. The blunt approach hadn't worked well with anyone else, but with Athena, it was the only way to go. She had no patience for beating around the bush.

"Hey, Penny," she said.

Rip off the Band-Aid. "I'm pregnant," I said back.

Athena was silent for a long moment. "Where are you?" she asked.

"Home," I said. "Mom and Dad know."

She swore. "Are you grounded?"

"Um," I said. "I don't know. They're not really talking to me."

"Typical," Athena said. "I'm coming to get you, okay?"

I looked up the stairs. Mom and Dad had their door closed. "Do you think they'll let me leave?"

"Convince them."

"Okay," I said.

As we hung up, I stood up straight, rolling my shoulders back. Finally. A response I could get behind.

I went upstairs and knocked on Mom and Dad's door. Their voices hushed inside. Dad opened the door; Mom sprawled on the bed behind him with a washcloth over her eyes.

"I'm going to Athena's," I said.

"No, you're not," Mom shouted from the bed.

Dad lowered his voice. "It might be a good idea for you to go," he said.

"Tony!" Mom said. "If you're going to undermine me, at least do it where I can't hear."

He looked over his shoulder at Mom, who peeked from underneath the washcloth. He spoke to her in his reasonable voice. "I think you two could both use some space from each other."

"If it's up to me," Mom said, "she's never leaving the house again."

"That," Dad said, "is exactly what I mean."

Dad and Mom looked at each other, having one of those moments where they communicated only with their eyes. "Fine," Mom said. "It's not like she's going to have fun breaking *this* news."

Athena was probably already preparing her speech about what an idiot I was. But at least *she* would stick around to yell it at me.

Probably for hours.

I sat on the porch swing, under the awning, waiting for

Athena. A drizzle of rain floated onto the lawn and grew gradually thicker until a stream of water pumped through the drainpipe at the edge of the porch. Rodney loved the rain, mostly because droplets of water were so much fun to photograph on almost anything.

Was he out shooting in it now, without me?

Athena had her headlights on when she pulled into the driveway, windshield wipers still thumping away. She pushed the side door open and waited while I sprinted through the rain to the car.

I sat down, wiping the rain from my arms, and Athena pulled backward out of the driveway again, looking up toward the house for Mom and Dad. "We had a fuzzy connection, right?" Athena said. "You're perfect. Or paraplegic. Not pregnant."

"Pregnant," I said. "Unfortunately."

"Okay," Athena said, holding a palm up to me. "I'm going to say this out loud, and then you're going to tell me I'm wrong. Ready?"

My nails dug into the armrests. "Ready," I said.

"Tell me you didn't do this on purpose."

The windshield wiper blades squelched across the window. Swish, swash.

Athena focused intently on the road. "Tell me," she said, "that you weren't planning this when we had that conversation about sex."

Swish, swash. Swish, swash.

Athena pulled up to a stop sign and put her hand on my arm. Her voice softened with a kindness I rarely heard from her. "*Penny*," she said. "You know how psychotic that is, right?"

I tore my arm away. "Mom needed help," I said. "Why am I the only one who sees that?"

Athena waved a finger at me. "Mom is crazy," Athena said. "She'll do anything to have a baby. She's sacrificed all of our happiness over it. She needs *professional* help. She—"

"She won't take my baby," I said.

Athena's mouth fell open mid-rant. "What?"

I collapsed against the car door. "She said she can't adopt my baby. It would be too weird. Twisted, was her word."

Athena actually looked impressed. "I . . . didn't see that coming."

My voice pitched upward into a whine. "You say that like it's a good thing."

Athena wobbled her head from side to side. "Maybe it is," she said. "I didn't think there was anything as important to Mom in this world as a baby."

I threw up my hands. "But I'm still *pregnant*," I said. "What am I supposed to do? Give the baby to someone else?"

"You could get rid of it," Athena said.

My heart stopped. An abortion. That was still an option.

Athena spoke with a steadiness I hadn't heard from anyone all day. "Seriously," she said. "I can drive you to a clinic in the morning. I'd take you now, but I'm sure they're closed."

My limbs went cold. "Do you think Mom would ever forgive me?"

Athena rubbed her temple. "Maybe what Mom thinks shouldn't be your first priority."

I sat back, letting that sink in.

Athena punched the steering wheel with the heel of her hand. "I knew I shouldn't have left you alone with her."

"What?" I asked.

"When I moved to school. I knew I shouldn't do it. I couldn't deal with Mom anymore, but you didn't have a choice. And without me there to keep you sane—"

"Mom didn't ask me to do this," I said. "It was my decision."

"It was a bad decision," Athena said. "Really bad."

"Well, congratulations," I said. "For once you and Mom agree."

Athena stared at the road, in a mixture of frustration and shock.

"That's not supposed to be the surprising part," I said.

"No," Athena said. "The shocker is that I was too stupid to see this is what you were getting at when you brought it up before."

I slouched and pulled up my knees, resting my heels on the edge of my seat. "You're not going to tell Mom I did this on purpose, are you?"

Athena's eyes widened. "Are you kidding? I'm not going to breathe your name around Mom for the next nine months. You think I want to deal with the drama?" She was quiet for a moment. "Seriously, though, she didn't guess?"

I shook my head. "Only Rodney knows."

Athena glanced up at the ceiling. "Oh, jeez. Rodney. How'd you talk him into this?"

Raindrops blew across the passenger window in quivering streams.

Athena's eyes flicked to me. "You told him," she said. "Tell me you told him."

"I didn't tell him," I said quietly. "Until after."

Athena swore.

I knocked my temple against the glass of the window. "I know," I said.

Athena stared at the road, stunned. "Okay, that *does* surprise me. You've always been the one to do whatever you think Mom wants. But Rodney? I didn't think you'd give him up for her. He's been in love with you for years."

The glass chilled my skin. How was I the only person on earth who didn't know this? "I didn't know I was giving him up," I said. "You said sex didn't matter to guys."

She held up a hand. "Oh, no," Athena said. "You didn't get this idea from me."

"No," I said. "I'm just saying."

Athena's voice grew quiet. "I knew I botched that conversation, but damn."

"You said sex didn't change things, so I thought—"

Her finger stabbed the air. "I said be careful, or you'll get hurt."

"Well, congratulations. You were right. Again."

Athena was quiet for a moment. "Are you okay?"

"No," I said.

She spoke carefully, like she didn't want to make it worse. Not that she could. "So, Rodney broke up with you?"

I closed my eyes. "He said he needed some time to think."

Athena leaned forward. "He'd probably be relieved if you got rid of it, right?"

I thought about the way Rodney looked at me when he asked me to marry him. If I aborted the baby, it would be like telling him he didn't matter. He didn't get a say. Again.

"I'm not going to get rid of it," I said. "Mom will come around."

Athena sighed. "She probably will. But think about it, because that might make things worse, rather than better."

"Mom isn't a monster," I said.

"Maybe not," Athena said. "I hope you still feel that way in nine months."

Chapter Eleven
Week Five

I slept on Athena's floor that night, wearing one of her t-shirts and some gym shorts. Athena texted Dad to let him know I wasn't coming home, and he responded saying he'd pick me up before school in the morning.

"He's going to kill me," I told Athena.

"Ha," Athena said. "You wish you could get out of this that easily."

Sleep wasn't fast coming, though. I lay between two layers of fleece blanket with Athena's extra pillow stuffed under my head. I watched my phone, waiting. I wondered if Rodney was doing the same.

An hour passed as I listened to Athena and her roommate breathing. Then, finally, I grabbed Athena's laptop from her desk.

I checked my email, and then logged into Rodney and my on-line storage account. I half-expected to discover he'd deleted the thing. Instead, I found a brand-new set of photos with today's date. Rodney always kept the originals on his computer—he wasn't set up to automatically upload them. That meant he'd dumped them into the folder on purpose, and there was no reason to do that unless he wanted me to see them.

I opened the first one. It was a picture of the Golden Gate Bridge, taken standing on the walkway, looking up at one of the towers. The sky behind the tower churned with angry clouds. I immediately wanted to shift it into black and white.

The images traveled across the bridge. Here was one of the San Francisco cityscape, here was another of a tourist leaning over the railing, looking down at the water. There was Alcatraz across the bay, and several of cars with red cable lines towering above. Rodney must have been lying on the sidewalk for those.

He'd walked the bridge—photographed it from every angle. He must have driven up after school, maybe directly after talking to me. It was only a forty-five minute drive, but the walk was miles. He couldn't have gotten home before dark. He must have gotten caught in the rain on the way back.

I scrolled through the folder. I wasn't sure what the message was supposed to be. Was I supposed to feel left out? I'd have given anything to have gone with him. But also, here was a folder of carefully selected images that he wanted me to have. Like a gift—a glimmer of the friendship we used to have.

Maybe a suggestion that it wasn't quite over.

I checked Athena's software. She had an image editing program—not a great one, but one that would do in a pinch. I responded to Rodney in the only way I knew how; I imported that first image and went to work.

When Athena shook me awake in the morning, I was running on four hours of sleep, but I'd edited the first ten images in the folder. Rodney would be able to see the time stamp on the saved images. He'd know I'd stayed up working on them.

I hoped he got the message I intended to send. I still wanted to try, if he did.

Athena waved my cell phone in front of my face. "Morning, sunshine," she said. "Dad's waiting for you out front."

I looked up. Athena's roommate was still passed out on her bed, oblivious. And as I left Athena's dorm, yesterday's jeans sticking to my legs, fuzzy hair sticking out walk-of-shame style,

I couldn't help but wish that were me.

Dad sat in his car in the pull-through next to Athena's building. As I walked toward it, I slowed my pace: there in the passenger seat sat Mom, her hair pulled back in a tight pony tail, her eyes safely shielded behind sunglasses. It was her uniform for the days after the disappointments, the days after her periods or miscarriages or, worst of all, lost children.

I took a deep breath, sucking air down into the tips of my toes. She might yell at me, but today, I wasn't going to yell back. Today, I was going to stay calm. She could scream like a banshee all she wanted, but it wouldn't change the facts. I had a baby; she needed one. Objectively, this should be easy.

Dad waved to me as I climbed into the backseat. But Mom didn't even turn to acknowledge my presence.

"Morning," Dad said. "Where would you like to go to breakfast?"

My stomach squirmed. Preferably somewhere where they didn't serve, you know, food. That answer wasn't going to fly, though, and if Dad wasn't taking me straight home, he must have taken the morning off from work.

At least we were going somewhere public. Mom couldn't yell at me in public. As much.

"Mom can choose where we go," I said.

"Hmph," Mom said.

Dad gave me a look in the rearview. "Waffles?"

Waffles were edible, and therefore disgusting. But a waffle place would have a menu, and a menu might have something I could nibble on without my stomach rebelling. "Whatever you want," I said.

Dad drove us to a corner restaurant with a checkered tile floor. The hostess took us to a booth by the window where the back of the vinyl seats shone with layers of oil from other people's hair.

The hostess handed us menus. I flipped through mine, trying to avoid looking at the links of greasy sausage and thick, heavy pancakes. I'd eaten food all my life. This would have looked delicious last week, especially after the nothing I'd eaten the last few days. I thought morning sickness was just supposed to make you puke, not turn you against all that was good and edible in the world.

I caught Mom staring at me over the top of her menu, and I tried to smile, but it came out stiff.

She didn't smile back.

The waitress had frizzy hair that escaped from her tight bun in puffs around her face. She smiled at each of us in turn. "What would you like to drink?"

"Water," I said, even though I wanted coffee. I already knew the fit Mom would have over that—she nearly crawled out of her skin when Lily came over drinking a frappuccino. Both Mom and Dad *did* order coffee, which meant I was going to have to smell it the entire meal, when it was, in fact, the only non-water substance that sounded okay to put into my mouth.

When the waitress brought my water, Mom held her hand out to me. In her palm was a pill the size of a cough drop.

"What's that?" I asked.

"Prenatal vitamin," she said. "I still had a bottle that I bought for Lily. Take one every day."

I picked the thing up and looked at it. I'd never liked swallowing pills, and this one was seriously enormous. "Okay," I said. I set it down on my napkin. If I drank a whole pitcher of water, maybe I could swallow the thing without gagging. At least I wouldn't have to chew it—only swallow.

"Are you ready to order?" the waitress asked.

"I am," Dad said.

Mom looked meaningfully at me.

I glanced down at my menu. "I'm actually not hungry," I said.

Mom looked at me over her sunglasses. "You are *not* just having water."

I set down my menu. "Food is disgusting, okay? I can't help it."

"I'll give you a minute," the waitress said, and she hurried away. No doubt she thought I was anorexic. Nope. Just pregnant.

Mom opened the menu to the breakfast page and skimmed over it. "Pick an omelet. You need some protein."

My throat closed up. "No," I said. "I could probably drink something. Maybe a grape juice."

Dad looked at the back of his menu. "They have orange and apple."

Ew. "It's not my fault," I said. "Whose idea was it for your body to reject food when it needs it?" Evolution was supposed to ensure the survival of the fittest, not the most obnoxious. It was a wonder that every woman genetically predisposed to morning sickness hadn't died before she could pass on that particular trait.

"At least get a salad," Mom said.

"Fine," I said. At least that sounded less disgusting than eggs. Even the idea of them felt heavy in my mouth. "Can we talk about the baby now?"

Dad gave me a warning look, and I rolled my shoulders back, readjusting my attitude. I was going to be chill. I'd be so reasonable, Mom wouldn't be able to argue.

Dad waved the waitress over, and Mom ordered a Caesar salad for me. If that contained anchovies I wasn't going to be able to look at it.

The waitress gave me a concerned look as she left, no doubt sizing me up. I didn't look anorexic, but I knew from health class that you didn't have to be underweight to have an eating disorder. I wondered if the waitress knew that, too.

"So your mom and I talked over your options," Dad said. "It sounded yesterday like you've already decided what you want to do."

"Yeah," I said, trying not to let my tone say, *duh*.

"So let's talk about that," Dad said. "Calmly and rationally." He looked pointedly at Mom, and she pulled off her sunglasses and nodded. "Obviously," Dad went on, "we need to sit down with Rodney and his parents. I'd like to ask them over so we can all talk."

My heart sank. Bad enough Rodney was going to have to tell his parents, I really didn't want to subject him to a sit down with mine as well. "Is that necessary?"

Mom cleared her throat. "If you want us to take the baby, we need to come to a legal arrangement."

Oh. Right. "Sure," I said. "But do we have to do it all together?"

Mom gave Dad a look.

"We'd just . . ." Dad said, "we'd feel better if we heard from Rodney's mouth that he's willing to give up all rights to the child."

I sighed. That's what this was about. "Okay," I said. "So we'll meet and you'll ask him to, what? Sign something?"

Mom stirred her straw around in her water glass. "We'll ask him to cut off contact with you until after the adoption is finalized."

Ice ran through my veins. "What?"

Dad took my hand across the table. "It's not fair to him, if he's not going to be involved after the baby is born."

Not going to be involved? "Wait," I said. "So Lily was a perfect stranger, and you were happy to invite her into our family, and you've known Rodney for *years*—"

"Penny," Mom said. "Try to be reasonable."

That knocked the wind out of me. "I am," I said. "You guys are the ones trying to push Rodney out of my life like he's nothing."

"Think about it," Mom said. "Lily was different. She didn't have a relationship with any of us before."

Or after. "You're just mad that I slept with him," I said.

Dad leaned his elbows on the table. "It's not about that. Think about how hard this will be on everyone if Rodney is there with you while you go through this pregnancy."

"What about open adoption?" I said. "That's what you were going to do with Lily."

"Right," Mom said. "And you'll have basically that same arrangement with us, because you'll be in the baby's life regardless. But it's one thing for you. It's another to pretend like you and Rodney can just be together and then place your baby with us like it's no big deal. He'll get attached."

I frowned. Attached, like Lily. "You're afraid if he's around, he'll take the baby from you."

"If he's around," Mom said, "legally, he can."

I took a deep breath, looking at Dad. "Is that true?"

Dad wobbled a hand. "California law says that the father has rights if he demonstrates a commitment during your pregnancy. And if he exercises those rights, you won't be able to place the baby for adoption."

My stomach sank. A commitment. Like offering to marry me.

Even though the baby was mine, they were still afraid. And they were going to drive Rodney from my life rather than live in that fear.

And given Rodney's history of reactions, I couldn't be sure they were wrong.

"So what do you want me to do?" I asked.

"We'll all meet together," Dad said. "And we'll offer to adopt the baby, and explain to Rodney that this means he'll have to back off. If you run into each other at school, fine. But other than that, he needs to be out of your life until the adoption is finished."

Mom gave me a wary look. I got the message. She'd agree to take the baby, but only on this condition: that I push Rodney even farther away than I already had.

"What if Rodney won't agree to that?" I asked.

Mom's fingernails tapped her water glass. "He's more likely to if you tell him it's what you want."

The blood drained from my face. Tell Rodney I wanted him to leave me alone? "And if I don't?"

Mom sighed. "Are you ready to be a parent with him?"

Oh, heavens. This had all seemed so much simpler before I got pregnant. At this point, I just wanted my boyfriend back. "No," I said quietly.

Dad spoke softly. I recognized the tone—it was the same voice he'd used when I was eight, and he had to tell me that my cat had been run over by a car. "Only you can decide what you want to do," he said. "But if you want your mother and me to adopt the baby, this is the way it has to be."

Mom took Dad's hand on top of the table. I looked at them, their fingers clasped together.

They were parents. Rodney and I weren't even close to ready to take care of a baby.

The waitress brought the tray over and propped it up next to our table. "One Caesar salad," the waitress said, putting it down in front of me. It didn't have anchovies on it, but one look at the lettuce told me that this was clearly not food. It was some plastic impostor, some cardboard stage prop. Surely not something my mother expected me to put in my mouth.

But she seemed to have given up on the food. As she watched me, I could tell she was only waiting for my answer.

"We'll have to talk to Rodney about it," I said.

Mom and Dad both nodded.

I breathed in deep. That would buy me time to be honest with Rodney, to be sure that he knew exactly what he was doing if he let my parents eject him from our lives.

Chapter Twelve
Week Five

After school, I sat in Dad's office, looking at Rodney's photos. I'd checked the chess room at lunch; he hadn't been at school. Instead, in the folder, I found a set of photos of high rises, and some candids at an outdoor café. I paused on one of a couple holding hands across a bistro table with a big salad between them. I wanted to say that it should have been Rodney and me, but he didn't like salad.

Not only had he gone shooting without me, he'd skipped school to do it. Rodney wasn't much for ditching; he said he was too lazy for make-up work.

So today, he'd been avoiding me.

I wasn't sure where Rodney had taken the pictures, but I guessed it was somewhere in San Jose. I wondered if he'd told his parents he was sick and then left after they went to work, or if he'd just left for school at the normal time and gone shooting instead.

Either way, I had to talk to him. In person would have been better, but I couldn't exactly show up on his doorstep when he was asking for space and clearly going to great trouble to avoid me.

I returned to the folder with Rodney's bridge pictures. He hadn't left me a note, but I could tell from the work history that he'd opened each of the ones that I'd edited between eight and nine AM this morning.

He might be avoiding me, but he was paying attention.

I pulled out my phone. *You weren't at school today*, I texted. *Are you okay?* Stupid question. I deleted the last part without sending it, and replaced it with *I need to talk to you*.

After I hit send, I cringed. Now I sounded self-centered. I sent a quick follow-up text. *I'm sorry.*

I leaned back in Dad's chair. Needy *and* self-centered. There was just no good way to talk to Rodney without showcasing what a total ass I was.

It took a few minutes, but finally he texted back. *Give me a couple of days, okay?*

I sighed. The only way I was going to get to talk to him was if I confronted him with the ugly truth.

Again.

My parents want to talk to your parents, I said. *Have you told them?*

No, he answered. *I'll do it tonight. Or is that too late?*

It's fine. I'll tell my parents not to call until after that. I have some information for you though. About your rights.

K, Rodney replied.

I held my breath. *So can I call you?*

Rodney took an eternity to answer. As he did, I saw one of the photos in our folder update, and I scrolled through to see which one it was.

The couple with the salad. Rodney had put a filter over it that blurred the edges, leaving only the space between them in focus.

No, he answered, finally. *Not yet.*

I hesitated, my finger on the reply button. I wanted to tell him it couldn't wait. But he'd asked for space—the same thing he'd given me for years. I couldn't push it.

It was Rodney who taught me that.

The next morning, Mom made me toast and eggs for breakfast, and presented me with a prenatal vitamin. "Every day," she said.

132

I took it and pointed to the food. "I can't eat that."

"Try," Mom said. Mom went into her bedroom and came back with a book with a baby on the cover. "Read this," she said. "It's got lots of information about what to expect from your body, and what kind of nutrition you need to give to the baby."

I flipped through the first few chapters as I took microscopic bites of my toast. There was a section about morning sickness. *Eat what you can during your first trimester*, it said, *but don't stress too much.*

I rolled my eyes. Mom was the one who should read this book. Though there was a big box in the third chapter singing the praises of the prenatal vitamin, so I gagged that down, along with a huge glass of water.

"Rodney's dad called last night," Mom said.

I swallowed. "What did he say?"

Mom sat down next to me at the table. "They agreed to come over to meet with us tonight." She folded her hands, her fingers knotting together. "Did you talk to Rodney about what we discussed?"

"Not yet," I said.

"Well, you have today at school," she said.

I nodded, and dropped the rest of my toast back on the plate. My body quivered. If Rodney wasn't talking to me, then I couldn't quiz him about what he was going to say to my parents, or tell him about what they did and didn't know. Asking him to keep secrets for me might further convince him he should stay away from me.

What would my parents say when *he* told them the pregnancy was all my idea to begin with?

Rodney wasn't in the chess room again, so I holed up in the library to finish up some homework that was due fifth period. I'd missed a couple of assignments and a lot of study time the last few weeks. We had another test coming up in physiology, and I'd memorized next to nothing. My brain felt like a brick wall—the information just bounced off. Still, I tried to focus, if only to have something to think about besides the imminent disaster.

I stayed buried in homework until six o'clock. I had my physiology charts spread across the table in front of me, with a copy of the practice test in hand. We were labeling respiratory anatomy. Maybe understanding the process would help me learn how to breathe again.

The doorbell rang, and my stomach turned. My mouth watered, and I thought about ducking into the bathroom and spending the meeting in front of the toilet. But no. I had to be there to convince my parents that there was a happy medium between refusing the child and driving Rodney even further out of my life. As much as I didn't want to, I had to face them when Rodney revealed my secret.

At least their reaction would be tempered with Rodney and his parents in the room.

Mom answered the door. I closed my eyes and breathed slowly in and out, trying to label my own lungs as I filled them with air. All I could come up with was the diaphragm, which was so obvious it probably wouldn't get me even a full point of credit.

"Penny?"

I looked up to see Dad standing in the doorway between the dining room and the living room. He'd changed out of his work clothes, but he'd missed a spider web in his hair—a sure sign he'd been crawling under a building today. Past him, Rodney and his parents were choosing seats in the living room.

Dad held a hand out to me. "Come on," he said.

I swallowed. Did I look as bad as I felt? I let him help me up, and joined him on his way into the living room.

Rodney sat on the far side of the love seat by the door, as far from his parents as possible. They'd taken the two arm chairs, leaving my parents the couch. When he looked at me, the corners of his mouth turned up ever so slightly, forming the most understated smile in history. My heart responded in opposite fashion—pounding in my chest, my nausea replaced by breath-lessness.

Rodney's parents looked like they'd arrived straight from work; his dad in khakis and a pressed polo shirt that might have been casual if he wasn't trying so hard. His mother wore a blazer and skirt combination, her hair bobbed above her jawline.

Rodney once told me that his life's ambition was to have a job where he could wear the same thing to work that he wore on weekends, and looking at his parents, I couldn't blame him. Rodney didn't own anything but jeans.

The only seat left in the room was the other half of the love seat, next to Rodney. They'd all left it for me, no doubt so they could direct their disapproval at both of us at once.

As I walked across the room, Rodney's mom got up to give me a hug. I nearly cried into her shoulder, not because she cared, but because she wouldn't have hugged me if she knew I'd tricked her son into fathering a child.

He couldn't have told them. Was he going to lie to my parents about it, too? This was the difference between us: Rodney lied to protect me, and I lied because I couldn't stand for my parents to know the truth.

When I sat down next to him on the love seat, Rodney re-fused to look at me. His eyes had gone bloodshot at the corners; I wondered if he'd been sleeping. I put my hand over his on the cushion between us, and he didn't respond, but he also didn't pull away.

Dad looked at our hands, then shot me a look. I was supposed to be alienating Rodney, not reaching out to him. I sent him what I hoped was a pleading look, and he sighed.

There was an awkward silence, then, as everyone waited for someone else to speak.

"Well," Dad said. "Aren't we all excited to be here?"

My mom and Rodney's both laughed nervously.

Rodney's dad cleared his throat. "Kids sure do make messes for themselves."

135

My face burned. He talked like we were toddlers who'd spilled flour all over the floor.

I looked at Rodney, but he was giving his dad such a look of contempt that he didn't notice.

"I just want to say upfront," his dad went on, "that I think it's important that Rodney take responsibility."

I looked sideways at Rodney, wishing he'd let me call him the day before. He had a free pass to blame this all on me, and clearly he should have.

Rodney's dad kept talking—to my parents, not to us. "So often in these situations the boy is so disconnected from the consequences, and I want you to know we don't support that."

My mom picked at the arm of the chair. That wasn't what she wanted to hear at all, and at least we agreed on that, if not for the same reasons.

"So what are you saying?" I asked. "You want us to get married?"

All four of them looked at me.

"No," Rodney's dad said. "That's not what I—"

"You're not ready for that," Mom said.

My dad shook his head, and Rodney's mom added, "Absolutely not."

I looked at Rodney, but he stared at the floor. My heart ached. Everyone thought marriage was a bad idea—everyone but him.

"I just meant," Rodney's dad said, "that this is just as much his problem as yours." Rodney's dad finally looked at him, and as their eyes met, I could see the contempt was mutual. Some of that predated the pregnancy, but some of it was new.

My fingers tightened over Rodney's. Much as I didn't want to announce what I'd done, I couldn't let him take the fall for me. I had to choose my words carefully, if I didn't want to embarrass Rodney. "He already offered to take responsibility," I said. "That was his first reaction."

Mom gripped the arm of the couch, while Rodney looked at me warily.

"Oh," Rodney's dad said. "Well, good."

I looked at Mom, who was still picking at the upholstery in exactly the way she always told us not to do. I should have told her the truth before, so she wouldn't have to hear it in front of everyone.

But I couldn't let everyone treat Rodney like he was anything but the victim. And for once, I was going to put him first. "But it's not really fair to him, because—"

Rodney's hand clamped down on my arm, and I stumbled over my words.

"What I don't understand," Rodney said, "is why we're talking about whose fault it is. There's nothing any of us can do about the situation. So shouldn't we focus on what happens now?"

I choked on the lump in my throat. Rodney reached out to save me from what I'd done, like it was nothing. But I'd been trying to save *him*. Why couldn't he let me?

Why couldn't I ever manage to put his needs first?

Both Rodney's parents stared at him, while my mom nodded vigorously. But my eyes were on my dad, who looked from me, to Rodney, and then finally back to me. His cheeks tensed slightly, like he was settling things in his mind.

Like he saw what Rodney had just done for me.

Like he was putting all the pieces together.

I bit down hard on my lip. Would *he* out me?

"I think that's a good idea," Mom said, turning to Rodney's parents. "Don't you?"

Rodney's mom nodded. "I think part of what John was trying to say was that if it's a question of money, we'd of course be willing to pay for a solution."

Rodney closed his eyes, rubbing his forehead with one hand. Smart of him. He didn't have to see the horrified look on my mother's face when his mom's meaning sunk in.

"No," my mother said, at the same time that my father said, "Well—"

My parents looked at each other, and Mom nodded, letting

Dad fall on the grenade.

"We've been trying to adopt anyway," Dad said. "So we're not just able, but willing to care for the baby." He cleared his throat. "And, it's . . . *customary* for the adoptive parents to pay for the medical expenses."

Rodney's mom's mouth dropped open. "Oh," Rodney's mom said. "Oh, of course."

She and Rodney's dad exchanged looks. We were having a very different conversation than they thought we'd be having. Which meant that Rodney didn't tell her about the adoption, either. But at least Dad had given her the out. She could pretend she was talking about my childbirth expenses all along, and not about abortion.

So maybe Rodney had cut the conversation short for his own reasons, as well.

Rodney's mom turned to me. "And adoption is what you want?" she asked.

"I think," I said, looking sideways at Rodney, "I think that would be best."

Jeez. I sounded like a commercial. But I really did believe that. Mom and Dad would be way more capable as parents than I would be. I'd never intended to parent this baby. The whole point was for Mom to be, well, the mom.

But I still felt like I was sinking farther and farther into my own trap, and no matter how hard I clawed, I wasn't gaining ground.

In Rodney's earshot, it all sounded like betrayal.

My dad leaned toward Rodney. "And you?" he asked.

Rodney shrugged. "We can talk all we want about responsibility, but ultimately, this is Penny's call, isn't it?"

Rodney's mom gave him a frustrated look. "He's asking for your opinion."

Rodney looked at me. And I saw his opinion loud and clear. It was written all over his face.

He wanted this not to be happening at all.

"It's fine," he said. "It's not like I was planning to be a father."

My face turned red, and all four of our parents found something else to look at. I was sure they were thinking about the two of us having sex, which was bad enough, but since Rodney had covered for me, none of them heard what he really meant to say.

I was the planner. Not him.

Dad's eyes were boring into my skull, and if I looked at him, I was going to cry. "I'm sorry," I said. I aimed the comment at the room, because really, it applied to everyone.

Mom straightened, and I wished I could end the conversation right there. Adoption, check. Problem solved. No need for her to tell Rodney she wanted him gone.

But Rodney loved me. He said he needed time, not to break up. He wouldn't listen to her. He wouldn't.

Mom charged ahead, into the part of the conversation she'd been planning. "If Rodney isn't going to be involved in the baby's life," she said, "it's probably best to limit the amount of time they spend together. Starting now."

She looked at Rodney's parents. Not Rodney. Not me. Dad kept looking from Rodney to me, and shifted uncomfortably. And I could swear that for a second, I saw something in his eyes.

Guilt.

Like he knew how much it hurt me to drive Rodney away.

But still his hand stayed locked into Mom's.

Rodney was the one who responded to Mom. "I understand," he said. Now he was looking Mom straight in the eye, like he wasn't afraid of anything. "I'll stay away."

Roaring filled my ears, so loud I was sure I hadn't heard right. "What?" I said.

And Rodney finally looked at me, and I thought the pain that was buried in them would swallow me whole. "That's how adoption goes, right? I'm not a part of it."

Mom gave a sharp nod. And I opened my mouth to tell Rodney that he had rights, that he could demonstrate a commitment, but really, what would I be saying? That I wanted him to fight my mother for this baby?

I didn't want that. I wanted him to stay a part of my life. Mine, not the baby's.

Why didn't anyone else want that but me?

Dad clapped his hands together. "So we all agree, then?"

Rodney's dad gave a sharp nod and stood, reaching to shake Dad's hand. "Thanks for making the best of a bad situation," he said to my mother.

My body felt numb. On what planet was *this* the best outcome for this situation?

Mom nodded, and shook his hand after Dad did. And then Rodney's parents ushered him up and toward the front door. He walked away with them, like that was it. Like he was just going to leave without a word.

I stood and took involuntary steps toward him. Once Rodney walked out the door, was he gone forever? My hands shook. I couldn't let that happen.

As Rodney moved for the door, I touched his arm. "Wait," I said. "Can I talk to you for a minute? Before you go?"

Rodney's mother gave me a wary look, and his father squirmed. But Rodney nodded. "Sure," he said. He looked at his mother. "I'll catch up in a minute."

Mom opened her mouth to protest, but Dad put a hand on her arm, holding her back, and as I stepped out the door, she didn't stop me. I went with Rodney onto the porch, and shut the door behind me. Rodney's parents filed off to the car, and his mother only looked over her shoulder at us twice. I was pretty sure that was a show of great restraint.

Rodney stood inches away. The porch was dark, but as we stood there, Mom flipped on the light, which reflected in his eyes. "What is it?" Rodney asked.

I waved my arms at him. "Why'd you stop me from telling them?" I asked. "You can blame all this on me. It's my *fault*."

Rodney rolled his eyes. "I don't want to hear it," he said. "From my parents, I mean. I don't want to listen to them badmouth you."

My mouth filled with taffy. He had every right to trash talk me, maybe not to our friends, but at least to his parents. And he didn't want to? "I—um—I," I said.

"Don't read into it too deeply," he said.

But how could I not? "Thank you," I said finally.

Rodney sighed. "You're welcome." He turned to go.

Terror clawed at my chest. I couldn't let him walk away without knowing that he had rights. I didn't want him to fight me, but I also didn't want to manipulate him anymore. I'd told him I loved him, and love meant putting him first. Even if I was irredeemably bad at it, I had to try.

I put a hand on his arm.

"You don't have to do this, you know," I said. "If you demonstrate a commitment now, you have a right to the baby."

Rodney took a step back. "A commitment," he said.

"Yeah," I said. I couldn't believe I was bringing this up, but it had to be said. "Like when you asked me to marry you."

Rodney shook his head, and in a low voice, he said, "Don't worry. I'm not going to fight you."

He took another step closer to the driveway. Closer to walking out of my life, maybe forever.

I could feel my life crashing down around me. "Is this really what you want?" I asked. "No contact? You didn't say. You just let our parents decide."

He looked up at the sky. An airplane flew overhead, like an overly-bright, migrating star. "I think they're right," he said. "If I'm not going to be part of this baby's life, it makes sense for me to be out of yours."

I felt a stabbing sensation in my gut, as sure as if I'd been knifed. "You can't really want that," I said.

He looked at me, and I could see that he'd made up his mind, maybe before he even came over tonight. "I do," he said.

My traitor eyes welled up. Before, he'd said that he needed time. Time to think was a stay of execution, but now I could feel the guillotine falling.

Could he mean it? This was the end?

I looked down at his shoes, waiting for him to turn to go, but instead his hand reached under my chin, bringing my face up to look at him.

My chin trembled. Tears leaked from the corner of my eye, ran down to my jaw, and soaked his hand. He looked at me, and I was certain of this: he still cared.

Without warning, he pulled me into a hug. I crushed against him, wiping my eyes on his shoulder. And I waited for him to tell me that he didn't mean it. He'd only said it to hurt me. He would never leave me alone. He couldn't.

His breath was warm on my ear. "Penny," he said, "you're going to be fine."

My chest cracked open as Rodney pulled away and walked down my front steps. He went with purpose, not turning to look behind him.

I stood on the porch, swallowed up by the sudden emptiness of being fully, truly alone, and it was all I could do not to chase after him and beg him not to go.

Chapter Thirteen
Weeks Five through Seven

I sat alone on the porch swing, numb to the cold and the darkness. I tucked my legs underneath me, so the swing held entirely still. I'd almost bawled in front of Rodney, but now that I was alone, my eyes were empty, as if he'd taken all my tears with him.

Did he really believe I'd be okay? Because I didn't believe him. Not one bit. And the more I thought about it, the more it seemed like he had been trying to convince himself, as well.

The front door opened, and Dad stepped out onto the porch. "Can I join you?" he asked.

I leaned my head against the back of the swing. "Okay," I said. If he figured out what I'd done to Rodney, he was going to confront me with it sooner or later. Might as well do it now, when I had no energy left to fight back. "Shouldn't you be with Mom?" I asked.

He shook his head. "She went to lie down."

I nodded. The conversation with Rodney's parents had been stressful for her, too.

Dad sat down next to me on the swing, his feet planted on the ground. His mouth set in a firm line, like he was getting ready to say something.

I let him bring it up first. Maybe he hadn't really picked up on anything. Maybe I'd imagined it.

"You did this on purpose," Dad said. "You got pregnant for your mother." His tone was even. He wasn't even really asking me, just stating a fact.

But he also didn't sound angry. Not yet.

"I'm sorry," I said.

"When did Rodney know?" he asked.

I cringed, tears threatening me again. Maybe I wasn't entirely empty. "Not until after."

Dad leaned his head back on the swing, and turned to look at me. "I don't have to tell you how unfair that was to him."

Another statement. I waited for the lecture about what a horrible person I was, but it didn't come. Maybe Dad didn't just realize what I'd done. Maybe he saw how I felt about it, too.

"Why didn't you say something?" I asked, "when Rodney didn't?"

Dad looked up at the moon cresting over the edge of the roof. "He was protecting my daughter," he said. "I wasn't going to argue with that."

My nose began to run. "I don't deserve protecting," I said.

"You're stuck with it," Dad said. "From me, at least."

From both of them, it seemed. If only I could convince Rodney that protecting me didn't mean walking out of my life. "Does Mom know?" I asked.

Dad shook his head. "She hasn't put it together."

"But you're going to tell her," I said.

Dad shook his head again. I waited for him to tell me that I was the one who had to tell her. I had to march upstairs this minute and do the right thing. But instead, he just sighed the sigh of a man exhausted to his core. "I think your mother feels bad enough as it is."

I turned to face Dad. "She does?"

"Of course she does," Dad said. "She's your mother. She'll feel responsible for everything you do, whether it's actually about her or not."

Ugh. And in this case, it was, which would only make it worse. "I get it," I said. "I won't tell her."

"Not tonight," Dad said. "But you can't leave the secret between you forever."

I nodded. "Okay," I said. "I'll wait for the right moment." Once Mom had a baby in her arms, she wouldn't care how that child got there.

Then, I'd tell her. Only then.

The next morning, I woke up to a gag reflex that pumped my stomach bile into the toilet for ten minutes straight. If I couldn't eat before, I certainly wasn't going to try now. I'd turned my phone off last night and shoved it in the bottom of my desk drawer, so I wouldn't keep expecting it to ring, expecting Rodney to call and tell me he'd changed his mind. Turning the phone off only helped until I fell asleep. Then I dreamed on repeat about the phone ringing deep in the bottom of the drawer, and no matter how fast I emptied it, I could never dig it out.

When I hauled myself off my knees, I dug it out and turned it on, checking for texts from Rodney that I already knew wouldn't be there.

I went downstairs with dread. But when I arrived, there was a tall glass with a straw where the eggs had been yesterday.

Mom looked up from her stool at the counter. "I made you a smoothie," she said. "I thought you could drink your calories, if you can't eat them."

I love smoothies. I love the way the fruits tang together; I love knowing I'm drinking something good for me even though it tastes like candy. But today all I could think of was the way it would burn coming up.

"I think I'll just have some water," I said.

Mom gave me a look, and to appease her, I picked up the vitamin she'd left on the counter and stuck it under my tongue while I poured myself a glass.

Mom sighed. "Penny. You have to eat."

I closed my eyes. The baby book said I didn't need to push it. Could that be right? Pregnant women had to eat for two, didn't they? How on earth did babies survive, if their mothers' bodies told them to starve themselves?

I picked up the smoothie. When it was still a foot from my nose, I could smell the banana, and it might as well have been bruised black for all I wanted to put it in my mouth.

"That bad?" Mom asked.

I nodded miserably.

She gave me a sad look. "I remember being pregnant with Athena. Everything I ate came up for two months. But you just have to keep eating. Something will stay down, even if it's only a little."

Mom stared out the window, like she was longing for something far away. She used to look at Lily the same way, like she'd give anything to be in her place.

My stomach tightened at the thought of putting the smoothie into my mouth. But Mom would do it, wouldn't she? If this was her baby, she'd drink.

I put the straw to my lips, and sucked some smoothie into my mouth. The tang met my tongue, and tasted fine. But despite the sweetness, my throat constricted.

Swallow, I told myself.

But my body wouldn't.

I set the smoothie down on the counter with a clang and spit into the sink. "I can't," I said. "I'm sorry."

Mom turned her sad, longing look on me. Jeez. She was going to look at me like that for months, wasn't she? It was bad enough watching her do that to Lily.

My skin crawled. The receiving end of Mom's sad looks was so much worse.

I marched back up the stairs, intending to hide until it was time for Mom to drive me to school.

But Mom followed me into the stairwell. "Penny," Mom said.

146

"We need to talk."

I didn't turn around. She couldn't see the look on my face, the way I wanted to glare at her and stomp away like I was a little kid. That couldn't be about the smoothie, could it?

No. That was totally stupid. So either I was completely soaked with irrational hormones, or this was really about Rodney.

I got that she wanted to feel safe about the baby being hers. But did she really have to drive him away?

"Penny," Mom said again.

She was waiting for me to turn around. I tried to wipe the anger from my face. Why was I feeling this way? I did this for Mom. *For Mom*. She should come first.

I sucked in my cheeks. I might not be able to make myself eat, but I could make myself relax and treat Mom nicely. However hard this was on me, it had to be harder on her.

I turned slowly around, keeping my face blank, but I still didn't trust myself to speak.

Mom apparently didn't need me to. "Pregnant women really need to watch their diet, to make sure they get enough nutrition."

I took a deep breath. I could do this. I could speak to my mother like a reasonable person. I wasn't Athena, who yelled.

It was just two little words.

I spoke softly, keeping my tone even.

"I'm trying," I said.

"I know," Mom said. "But you need to try harder. It doesn't seem that way, but if you eat, you'll feel better."

Better? Food was not going to make me feel better about having lost my best friend.

Stop it, I told myself. She was talking about the nausea. Though I tried to keep it out, an edge crept into my voice. "I want to eat," I said. "Trust me. I do. It's not my fault that I can't."

Mom folded her arms. "If you feel this bad without food," she said, "think about how the baby will suffer."

My hands trembled. "I'm not starving your child," I said. "I'll eat something for lunch at school." Probably a Snickers, but I wasn't going to say that to her.

"Penny," Mom said. "You're shaking."

I clapped my arms to my sides, but still my fingers quaked. She thought it was from lack of food, but that was only part of it.

Mom spoke slowly, in the voice she might have used to calm a toddler. "Come into the kitchen," Mom said. "See if you can stomach some crackers."

I took a step backward up the stairs. I couldn't do it. I couldn't sit there while Mom gave me that sad look, as if she hadn't torn my life apart by suggesting that Rodney leave.

Tears burned my eyes again. Didn't she get that I was just trying to help her? Couldn't she look around and see that I was the only one who was? "I'm going to get ready for school."

Mom let out an exasperated sigh, like she'd had enough of me. "Penelope," she said. "You are *not* the only one having a hard time."

Something in my brain exploded, and I nearly yelled: *I did this for you.* But I swallowed the words before they could escape. I should have eaten the smoothie. I should have downed it and lost it and come back for more. Because between the nausea and the low blood sugar, and the things Rodney had said, I really didn't have a chance of holding this next thought in. "I get it," I said. "You wish it was you who was pregnant. Well, trust me. So do I."

If she'd yelled at me, I might have felt justified, but instead her face fell, like I'd slapped her. She deflated, stepping backward away from the stairs.

"Mom," I said. "I didn't mean that." My anger crumbled. That sounded like something Athena would have said to her. Not me.

Damn it.

Why couldn't I keep my mouth shut?

If I'd thought Mom looked sad before, it was nothing compared to the way she withered before me now. "I'm going to go lie down," she said, and she walked away in the direction of the family room. Not her bedroom, which would have required her to come closer to me.

"Mom," I called after her. "I'm sorry."

But she was already gone.

She showed up at my bedroom door a half hour later with a brown bag lunch, and I didn't say one word about not wanting to eat it. She drove me to school in silence, but I could see the things I said hanging like bags around her eyes.

At lunch I bought myself a Snickers and an apple juice, and then looked inside the brown bag. Mom had made me a sprout sandwich—another thing I usually liked to eat. And though I logically knew I'd eaten tons of those in my life, I couldn't imagine how I'd ever gotten over the physical impossibility of swallowing bread.

I called Athena. "You were right," I said. "Mom *is* making me her pet birth mom."

"Um," Athena said, "did I say that?"

"You did."

"Hush," she said. "I'm trying to be gracious."

"Just tell me you told me so."

"What's going on?"

I told her about the smoothie, with emphasis on how hurtful I'd been.

"Well, you're pregnant," Athena said. "I'm sure it's normal to be hormonal."

I rolled my eyes. This went way beyond hormones. "She was all concerned about what I was eating, and I get that, but the baby book says I don't need to worry about nutrition until my second trimester, when I'll be able to eat again."

Theoretically.

"Okay," Athena said. "Now I *will* say I told you so."

149

"Thanks," I said. Though, predictably, that didn't make me feel better.

When I got off the phone, I found Kara waving at me in the quad. I sat down next to her, drinking my miraculously delicious apple juice. The bottle claimed to contain ten different vitamins and minerals.

Take that, morning sickness.

Then I opened the bag lunch and pulled out the sandwich. As I peeled apart the bread, tiny green sprouts spilled onto the table.

"What is that?" Kara asked.

"Lunacy," I said. "How do people eat?"

Kara wrinkled her nose. "You mean how do they eat *that*? Because I don't."

I tucked a single sprout into my mouth. It didn't make my throat constrict, so I tried another. The bread, though, was not coming anywhere near my face. I opened up the sandwich on the table and poured the sprouts into the baggie, so I could eat them without having to look at their spongy companion.

"I take it you didn't make that," Kara said.

I looked over at her tater tots and soda. The thought of grease and carbonation nearly made me choke. "No," I said. "My mom did."

Kara squinted at me. "Does she want you to diet? Because you look fine."

Give it a few months. "She's just on a health kick."

"And you're eating the sprouts," Kara said, "but not the bread."

I shrugged.

"Hey," she said, glancing over my shoulder. "There's your boy."

I forced myself not to look. There was only one person who Kara would refer to as *my boy*, and he wasn't anymore. I picked up another sprout and twirled it between my fingers.

Kara didn't notice my lack of enthusiasm. "They're coming

this way," Kara said. She turned and waved. "Hi, Rodney," she said.

At that point, I had to turn around. And when I did, I found Rodney passing our table with Ryan, Kara's ex-boyfriend.

Was she trying to get *his* attention?

"Hey," Rodney said. He might have been responding to Kara, but he was looking at me. Our eyes met. My heart hammered and my breath left me. As he passed our table, Rodney's hand drifted within inches of my shoulders. I thought he might touch me, but he didn't.

"Um, uh, hi," I said, when they had already passed by. Rodney must have heard me, because he turned around and gave me half a smile. My cheeks turned pink as he and Ryan headed off through the back doors, toward the science wing.

Kara planted her elbows on the table. "Okay. What was that?"

"What was what?" I asked.

She raised one eyebrow at me. "You dropped a sprout down your shirt."

I looked down. It was hanging at the edge of my v-neck like a drowning man clinging to the edge of a boat. I flicked it off. Had Rodney seen that?

Probably.

"I did not see that coming," Kara said.

I looked up at her. "What?"

She grinned. "After all these years, you have a *crush* on him."

"I do *not*," I said.

"You *do*. You were practically drooling! How do you do that? I'd have thought all the years of *friendship*"—Kara tagged air quotes—"would have worn all the magic off."

Now my cheeks were burning. I crossed my arms over the table top and buried my face in them.

"Wow," Kara said. "You are adorable."

I groaned. "Cut it out."

She giggled. "Has Rodney witnessed this? Because he'll tease you more than I will. You know it's true."

151

I put a hand to my forehead. "We're not . . . we're not really talking right now."

Kara set down her soda. "What?"

I sniffed. "Things are complicated, okay?"

Kara was quiet. I peered up to see her contemplating my dis-assembled sandwich. "Holy crap," she said. "Are you pregnant?"

I moaned into my arms.

Kara swore. "And he's not *talking* to you?"

I snapped up to look at her. "Why does everyone think that Rodney is being a jerk to me? He's not, okay?"

Kara looked at me wide-eyed. "Yeah," she said. "Okay."

The people at the other end of the table stared at me. I didn't look around, but I was pretty sure they weren't alone.

At least Rodney had disappeared toward the science wing. If he'd witnessed that little display, I would have curled up into a little nauseous ball.

Who was I kidding? Enough people heard. *Someone* was going to tell him.

"So what are you going to do?" Kara asked.

I rolled my eyes. "Die of starvation, probably."

But Athena was right.

There was no way I was getting out of this that easily.

I slept through the next week and a half. I'd zombie-walk through school in a daze, and then come home and crash in the afternoon. Rodney nodded at me whenever I passed him in the hall, but he never stopped to talk. In my lethargy, I managed not to stalk him.

I did, however, stalk his photography. I guess without me bugging him to study, he had a lot of time on his hands. He sent new ones every day—plants dying from the sudden arrival of the winter chill, toys the neighborhood kids abandoned in the street. One cold gray day, Rodney took a series of photos of light bulbs shattering on black tile. I recognized the floor—he took those pictures in his hall bathroom. I wondered if his mother knew he was smashing glass in the house.

I couldn't keep up with him, so I picked his best shots from each set to crop and color correct. Rodney didn't comment on my work, but I could tell from the history that he looked at the photos almost as often as I did.

At the end of the second week, I was able to eat more, but I could only stomach simple things: chicken nuggets, grapes, carrot sticks. I was going to have a child, and apparently I was going to eat like one, too. I focused on each bite individually. Place in mouth. Chew. Swallow.

I learned from the baby book that I wasn't supposed to see a doctor until twelve weeks, counting from the start date of my last period. "It's stupid," I told Kara one morning before school. "That means when I was one week pregnant, Rodney and I were both virgins."

She shook her head. "You have terrible luck, getting pregnant the first time."

Ouch. I nodded, so she'd think I thought so, too.

"Of course," she said, "I'm surprised you guys didn't do it years ago. You circled each other for long enough."

I wanted to melt right through the floor. If I'd realized that at the time, things would have gone differently. "That's just how it worked out, I guess," I said.

"Seriously," Kara said. "Worst. Luck. Ever."

She wasn't kidding.

I stopped by my locker on the way to first period, and Kara paused, leaning against it. Rodney had cleared his books out, but he still knew the combination. Every time I opened it, I felt a spark of hope that he'd have been there, and left something behind. A book. An old test. Hell, a banana peel. Anything.

But I always found it just as I'd left it.

As I knelt down this time, though, white spots dotted my vision. I paused with a hand on my books, waiting for them to fade, but instead they intensified.

I squeezed my eyes shut. *Don't pass out*, I thought. *Do not.*

"Are you okay?" Kara asked.

A rush of cold spread over my face. I sat down on the floor and rested my forehead on my knees.

A loud rushing roared in my ears, and my mouth watered. "Penny?" Kara said again.

Then I felt the back of a water bottle on my neck—still cold from the vending machine. Kara brushed my forehead, wiping away beaded sweat. I wanted to look up at her, but my clenched eyelids felt like the only things anchoring me to consciousness.

"What's wrong with her?" Kara asked. Her voice sounded far away. Too far. Definitely not in my ear.

I pried open my eyes. My vision cleared enough that I could see Rodney standing over me, one hand on my knee, the other on the water bottle on the back of my neck.

I squirmed away from him. Why couldn't I have just passed out? He'd wanted out of my life, and now here I was falling apart in the hall where he could see me. It probably looked like I was *trying* to get his attention. "I'm fine," I said, even though I could feel sweat breaking out on my forehead. "You can go."

But he didn't. "I'm going to take you to the office," Rodney said. "Can you walk?"

I swallowed. I *would* walk, because if I didn't, he might try to carry me, and then I would have to commit ritual suicide, possibly by clubbing myself over the head with my physiology book.

"I'll walk," I said. And I took a deep breath and straightened to a stand. I didn't want to lean on Rodney, but I couldn't help it.

"Come on," Rodney said. "I've got you."

My heart beat so fast I thought I might pass out again, but my mind actually cleared a little.

"I can go by myself," I said. But I was still leaning on him, which ruined my argument so thoroughly that Rodney didn't even bother responding.

The bell rang. I looked up, and Kara was gone. Had Rodney waved her off, or had she decided to leave us alone to work things out?

She probably thought she was doing me a favor.

Rodney led me down the empty hall toward the office, and I shuffled along, feeling as if we were treading uphill. My mouth started to water again, and as we passed the bathroom I peeled myself off Rodney and ducked in, barely making it to the toilet before I retched.

I knelt on the cold tile with my eyes closed. I didn't want to see what state the floor was in. It would just make me puke again. I counted the seconds, my head clearing. How long would I have to wait before Rodney gave up and left me alone?

Then I heard water running. Wet paper towels pressed on the back of my neck. I twisted around, squinting up at Rodney.

"What are you doing in here?" I asked. "This is the girl's room."

"I'm not going to leave you like this," he said.

My stomach retched again, and I leaned over the toilet, salivating, as Rodney stood behind me, wet towels on the back of my neck.

I'd been wrong. Things could get worse.

He put a hand on my elbow. "Think you can walk to the office now?"

I would, if only to end the humiliation. "Yeah," I said. I stood up and leaned against the wall of the stall. The world seemed to tilt back to normal again, though I still felt sweaty and off-kilter as we made our way down the hall. When we got to the office I sank immediately into a chair.

"You can go now," I said. But Rodney ignored me. He marched up to the receptionist.

"Penny's sick," he said. "She needs to call home."

I must have looked like I felt, because the receptionist didn't argue. Instead, she brought me a cup of water. "Do you want to call your parents?"

"Yeah," I said.

Rodney still hovered over me, but the receptionist shooed

him away. "Go back to class," she said.

He hesitated. "Is she going to be okay?"

"I'm fine," I said. But my voice came out hoarse.

Rodney looked down at me. "I just," he said, "I think—"

"You've done enough," I said. Though this time it came out as a whine. I hunched down in the chair, and wished for this moment to be over.

Rodney leaned over to the receptionist, and said in a low voice. "She's pregnant. Is this . . . normal?"

My hands went cold. If I could have stood, I would have shoved him out of the office.

"We'll take care of her," the receptionist said. And then she ushered Rodney to the door.

I thought I'd feel better once he left, but I didn't. I just stared off into space, hoping no one else in the office had heard. Though, what was the point of hiding? Everyone would know in a couple months, anyway.

The receptionist came back and knelt next to me. "Do your parents know you're pregnant?" she asked.

I nodded.

"I'll bring the phone over," she said. "And you can call your mom."

"It's okay," I said. "I have my cell phone." I rooted it out of my backpack pocket. "I'll ask her to come get me."

The receptionist nodded. "Just make sure she signs you out."

Because I was old enough to have a child, but not old enough to sign myself out of school. As I pulled out my phone to ask the other person I'd wronged to come save me, I couldn't help but think that my life was irrevocably messed up.

And I had absolutely no idea how to make it right.

Chapter Fourteen
Week Seven

The next day, when I arrived at school, Kara was waiting for me at my locker.

"Feel better today?" she asked.

"Yeah," I said. Physically, at least.

She walked backward down the hall toward our first period class, hugging a notebook to her chest. "So, what happened with Rodney?" she asked.

I rolled my eyes. "He walked me to the office. Thanks for leaving me alone with him, by the way."

Kara's eyes went innocently wide. "What? He was helping you. I wasn't going to stop him."

"Yeah, well," I said. "I could have used you when he followed me into the girls' bathroom while I was puking."

Kara clapped a hand to her mouth. "He didn't."

"He did," I said.

Kara looked guilty. "Hey," she said. "Why don't you guys make up? I mean, it's obvious the guy is still in love with you. Ryan said—"

"*Ryan* said?" I asked. "You were talking to *Ryan* about me?"

Kara ducked into class, and I ran after her, plopping into my desk next to hers.

"Why were you talking to Ryan at all?" I asked. "You're broken up, aren't you?"

Kara got a sly look on her face, and slid down in her seat. "You've got to be kidding me," I said. "Have you forgotten the text message?"

"No," Kara said. "I haven't *forgiven* him. We're just *talking.*"

"About *me.*"

From the way Kara smothered her smile, I could tell that wasn't all she was thinking about doing. I pulled out my phone. "Hang on," I said. "I think you quoted that text message to me. I can refresh your memory."

Kara reached for my phone, but I moved it away just in time. "If you rub that in my face," she said. "I won't tell you what Ryan said about you."

I groaned and jammed my phone into my front pocket. "I'm pretty sure I don't want to know," I said.

Kara leaned toward me conspiratorially. "He said that Rodney has been in a bad mood for weeks. Rodney's crushing them all in chess games, and he wanted to know how he could get you two back together so that the beat down could end."

I sank lower in my seat. "Fantastic," I said. "So now I'm responsible for Ryan's losing streak."

"Hey," Kara said. "If Rodney slams Ryan at chess, more power to him. But if Ryan is noticing, then Rodney's funk must be ultra obvious, because no one is more oblivious than Ryan." She wagged a finger in the air. "Trust me. I know."

"I'm not doubting you on that," I said. And I buried my head in my arms.

Halfway through first period, the phone rang. "Penny," Ms. Flannagan said, "you're wanted in the office."

I swallowed. "Should I take my stuff?"

Ms. Flannagan shrugged. "I'd guess yes."

I slung my backpack over my shoulder, and shrugged at Kara's questioning look as I headed down to the office. When I got there, I found a slouching aide behind the desk. "I'm Penelope Overman," I told her. "Who am I supposed to see?"

"Ms. Aston," the aide said. "Don't ask me why, because they

don't tell me anything."

Ms. Aston. She was the Vice Principal in charge of discipline. Going to see Principal Adams might mean something good, but no good came from a trip to Ms. Aston's office. For an awful moment, I wondered if someone had discovered the pregnancy test in my locker.

Then I remembered. No one had to find the test. Rodney had already told them I was pregnant.

I should have expected that to slap me in the face.

Ms. Aston had stringy gray hair that hung limply across the shoulders of her lavender blazer. When I arrived in her doorway, she smiled sympathetically at me. I wondered if she did that for everyone who was in trouble, or just the girls who she expected to be hormonal.

"Hi, Penny," she said. "How are you feeling?"

Starving, I thought. But I said, "Better." And really, feeling hunger was up from where I'd been.

"I understand that you're pregnant?"

I nodded. No point in denying it now.

She handed me a piece of paper across the desk. "We recommend that our pregnant students transfer to Valley, where they can receive support tailored to their situation."

I gripped the flier. Valley was the district alternative school. Potheads went to Valley. Gang bangers went to Valley. People who failed all their classes went to Valley.

"You're kicking me out?" I asked.

Ms. Aston managed to keep up the smile. "Don't think of it like that. At Valley, you'll be able to get support from counselors who specialize in your problem, and have a flexible schedule for your medical needs."

"My medical needs," I said. "Is this because I was sick yesterday? I'm fine. I won't miss any more school." Really. People with the flu missed more school than I had.

Ms. Aston's smile faded into a firm line. "At Valley, you'll also be able to receive group counseling with other girls in similar circumstances."

Jeez. Group counseling with other pregnant girls. I could imagine the dagger looks if I admitted to *them* that I did this on purpose. "Shouldn't you be talking to my parents about this?" I asked.

She nodded. "Would you like to call them?"

To tell them I'd been kicked out of school? Sure, I was dying to. "Um, yeah," I said. I pulled my cell phone out of my pocket.

"Is your mom at work?" Ms. Aston asked.

I shook my head. "She should be home."

"Why don't you sit in the hall," Ms. Aston said. "Ask her to come in and we can continue this conversation."

I nodded and wandered into the hall. I'd actually thought the string of conversations I didn't want to have with my mother had come to an end.

Wrong again.

When I turned on my phone, I had a text from Kara. *What's going on?*

I sat down on the bench outside Ms. Aston's door, and texted her back. *They're sending me to Valley.*

That would give Kara something to flip out over, besides trying to hook me back up with the boy I'd stabbed in the back.

Then I dialed Mom. She answered on the fourth ring. "Penny?" she asked. "Are you sick again?"

"No," I said. "But the vice principal wants to talk to you." I swallowed. This wasn't going to go well. "They want to send me to an alternative school."

Mom was silent.

"Because they know I'm pregnant," I said. "They found out yesterday when I was sick."

Mom's voice was firm and even. "Are you in the office now?" she asked.

"Yes," I said.

"Don't agree to anything," Mom said. "I'm on my way."

She hung up the phone.

160

When I lowered the phone I found another text from Kara.
Crap.

I spit out a laugh. I'd have used a stronger word, myself.

I leaned back on Ms. Aston's bench, staring at the Safe Sex flier on the bulletin board across the hall. *Knowledge is power*, it said. And then in smaller letters, *Power over your body, and your future.*

For the first time in my life, I wished I was a smoker. If I'd had a lighter, I'd have set fire to the bottom of that flier and watched it burn.

They were sending me to Valley anyway.

Mom arrived before I committed arson. She was wearing sunglasses and jeans with stray threads clinging to the knees. She'd been quilting already this morning, which was a sure sign she was stressed.

She stood above me and pulled off her sunglasses. "Which office?" she asked.

I pointed into Ms. Aston's room, and Mom marched in without waiting to be invited. I scrambled off my bench and followed her.

Ms. Aston was on the phone. She looked up at Mom and smiled as I wandered in behind her. Mom plopped down into a chair across from Ms. Aston and waited for Ms. Aston's phone call to end.

I wilted into the seat next to Mom, glad, at least, that she wasn't yelling at me.

Ms. Aston wrote something down on a notepad. "I have someone in my office," she said. "I'll call you back." Then she hung up the phone.

Mom didn't even let her say hello. "Are you aware," Mom said, "that according to federal law, you cannot discriminate against a pregnant student?"

Ms. Aston's eyes went wide. "I—" she said. "Well—"

Mom went on. "Are you aware that this means you are re-quired to allow my daughter to continue in her regular classes, and any other school activities that were available to her before?"

I raised my eyebrows. *I* hadn't been aware of that.

Ms. Aston recovered. "We aren't kicking her out," she said. "We only *recommend* that our pregnant students go to Valley, for the increased support."

Mom looked at me. *Recommend.* I was pretty sure that was the word Ms. Aston had used with me, but a recommendation from the vice principal in charge of discipline sounded a lot like an order to me. "I thought it was a euphemism," I said. When I was the only one here, it probably had been.

Mom gave a sharp nod. "So you brought my daughter in here to scare her out of school, without informing her of her rights. Is that correct?"

Ms. Aston hesitated. Then she handed across the same flier she'd passed me about Valley. "If you look, I think you'll see that—"

"No," Mom said. "Do you know what year the law that protects pregnant students was passed?"

Ms. Aston looked stunned.

Mom cleared her throat. "It was 1972. That's before I sat in an office much like this, in Penny's exact position, and was told I couldn't go to school anymore." Mom set the flier back on Ms. Aston's desk. "I didn't know the law then, but I know it now, and you're not going to do to my daughter what was done to me."

My jaw dropped. *Go, Mom,* I thought.

Ms. Aston looked from Mom to me, and I saw her doing the math. Teen pregnant mom, teen pregnant child. Like mother, like daughter.

I bit my lip to keep from explaining. This was *so* not the time.

Mom dipped her head to the side. "If you'd like, I can get legal counsel."

Ms. Aston's voice was clipped. "No," she said. "Penny can stay in school. I only thought you might want to know about the resources available to her at Valley."

I sniffed. Sure she did.

"There are resources available," Mom said, "*only* if she's at Valley?"

Ms. Aston shuffled some papers. She wouldn't meet Mom's eyes. "No," she said reluctantly. "There's a support group that meets in the evening. It's district funded, but she could potentially—"

"So give me that information," Mom said, "and let my daughter get back to class."

Ms. Aston looked up at Mom, who stared her down with her very best don't-mess-with-my-child glare. Ms. Aston didn't have a clue what she'd brought on herself. Lily had been going to night school. The birth mom before that had dropped out. Mom was defending not just me, but all the birth moms she'd worked with who should have had better support.

Ms. Aston gave me a forced smile. "Get a pass from the front desk so you can go back to class."

Mom actually smirked at her as I got up and walked back through the hall to the front of the office for the pass, and I thought too late that I should have paused to give her a high five.

That would have made Ms. Aston's day.

I smiled all the way down the hall, until I passed Principal Adam's door, and heard Rodney's voice coming from inside.

I paused, putting a hand on the principal's door frame.

"I'm not leaving," he said. "I deserve to be kicked out as much as she does."

My heart dropped. *Kara.* She'd told Rodney about this *already*?

Ugh. No doubt she'd told Ryan, and Ryan told Rodney. The rumor train traveled at the speed of text.

I kept listening.

Mr. Adam's voice was sharp. "Our policy is to give support for pregnant students at Valley. Are you pregnant?"

"That's discrimination. What do I have to do to be treated

163

the same way as her?" Rodney paused. "I could bring a weapon to school. Would that do it?"

I took a sharp breath, and put my hand on the doorknob.

Mr. Adams spoke slowly. "Is that a threat?"

Rodney actually sounded proud of himself. "That'd do it, right? You have a zero tolerance policy for threats."

I had this picture of Rodney getting himself thrown out of school and working at a gas station for the rest of his life. And it would all be my fault. I pushed the door open.

Principal Adams raised a hand to protest, but when he saw me there, he lowered it. Rodney looked over his shoulder at me and sighed.

"Rodney," I said. "What the hell are you doing?"

He shook his head. "Nothing."

My ass. "I'm fine," I said. "Go back to class."

Principal Adams nodded. "She's a smart girl. You should listen to her."

Rodney crossed his arms. "I'm responsible for this, too."

I wondered if telling his parents that had caused him to start believing it. He was obviously out of his mind.

I could see Mr. Adams sizing up the two of us. Of the two of them, he was obviously the more reasonable one. I pointed at Rodney. "Can I talk to him? Outside?"

Mr. Adams waved a hand at me. "If you can get him to stop acting like a lunatic in my office, be my guest."

Rodney glared, and I grabbed him by the wrist and hauled him out. I wanted to shake him by the shoulders and tell him to be grateful that the principal had decided to ignore his threat, but instead I just pulled him to the back door of the building and onto the lawn.

My mom's car was still in the parking lot, so I walked around the side of the building, where she wouldn't see us talking when she left.

When I turned around, Rodney's jaw was set like he was ready for a fight.

164

At least fighting was better than being ignored. "You're trying to get kicked out of school now?" I asked. "What is *wrong* with you?"

Rodney gave me an agonized look. "It's my fault they're kicking you out. I told the lady in the office you were pregnant. That was stupid, but I was worried about you. You looked awful."

My glare softened. He was worried about me?

Ugh. This was so not the point. "You don't just get yourself kicked out of school because you feel bad. They would have noticed anyway. It's going to get pretty hard to hide."

Rodney took a step back. "So, what? You're just going to go to Valley, and I'm going to stay here? Like I had no part in this?"

I leaned against the pointed stucco of the building, staring at him. I knew I should tell him I wasn't leaving, but really. This was ridiculous. "You are the one who wanted no part in my life, remember? You are the one who agreed with our parents that this was the best thing."

Rodney looked at me like *I* was the one who was being ridiculous. "Yes," he said. "I'm the one who decided to have a child and exclude *you*."

I felt like I'd been punched in the gut. He was right. I wasn't the victim here. "I'm sorry," I said. "But you told me that you wanted space, and then I find you yelling at the principal about how you want to be kicked out of school. They'd probably let *me* come back after I had the baby, you know? You'd never be able to come back."

Rodney looked miserable. Obviously, he hadn't thought through all the implications. Though I guessed I couldn't blame him for that. He'd probably caught it from me.

"Still," he said. "It's not fair for them to make you go alone."

My heart cracked open. Why couldn't he have just acted like a jerk, and yelled at me? That was clearly what I deserved. "I'm not going to Valley," I said.

Rodney's face washed blank. "What?"

I bit my lip. "My mom chewed them out. Apparently kicking

me out is illegal, but they conveniently leave that out of the pregnant student orientation."

I wondered how many girls the district had sent to Valley without informing them of their rights. How many of their parents didn't know the law, or didn't come in at all to fight for them?

So many things about this were messed up.

Rodney looked down at the ground. "Oh," he said. "You could have said that to begin with."

I should have. Obviously. "So, what now?" I asked. "You want to be a part of my life if I'm being kicked out, but if I'm not, you're just going to ignore me?"

"I'm not supposed to *see* you anymore, remember?"

"Yeah," I said. "And who agreed to that?"

Rodney opened his mouth, then closed it again. "Come on," he said. "You can't expect me to know how to handle this."

My voice rose. "No one knows how to handle it!" I said. "But you could at least *talk* to me."

"Yeah," Rodney said. "Like I'm talking to you now? This conversation is going *great*."

I felt like he'd shoved me. No doubt this was exactly what he was trying to avoid: a shouting match. "Fine," I said. "Have some more silence." I turned on my heels. Rodney's hand grabbed my shoulder, but I twisted away from him. This time, I didn't wait for Rodney to walk away from me. This time, I walked away from him. I only looked back once. He leaned against the side of the building, catching his breath.

When I turned to walk back into school, I caught sight of someone watching me, near the curb in the parking lot.

My mother. She met my eyes and raised her eyebrows, and I got the message.

We'd been yelling loud enough. She'd heard every word.

Chapter Fifteen
Weeks Seven through Twelve

When I got home from school, I shut myself in Dad's office and opened the photography folder. Rodney hadn't added any new photos, but there were still plenty in the folder I hadn't edited.

This time, though, I didn't open any of them. Instead, I slumped in my seat. I'd been working on Rodney's pictures, but I hadn't taken a single shot of my own in weeks. Sure, I was just emerging from a serious case of brain fuzz, but still. Why was *I* editing all of *his* work?

I shut down the computer. I was doing it because I felt guilty, that's why. Because I was begging him to still communicate with me.

I rested my forehead on the edge of the desk. Today, that was going to change. Today, I was going to send a message of my own.

I'd get right on that. Just as soon as I figured out what on earth I wanted to say.

For the next few weeks, I settled into a pattern. Mom drove me to school, and I tried to concentrate on schoolwork and not look for Rodney in the halls. We ran into each other occasionally, of course, and every time we did, he'd nod, and I'd nod back. I didn't want to push him, but since I'd been the one who'd run away from *him*, I tried standing nearer to him a couple of times, so he'd know that I wasn't avoiding him. Each time, I'd hesitate, wondering if this was the time he'd talk to me. But he'd just look away and keep walking, like I wasn't the girl he was sending all his pictures to.

I heard from Kara that he'd won another chess tournament. Maybe he was doing better without me around to distract him. Maybe he was glad I was out of his life.

I might have believed that, if it weren't for the photos.

The most recent set had been of the trees at the park—the same ones where we'd taken the pictures of the fallen leaves. Rodney had photographed the bare branches in black and white, layering over each other against the gray sky. There were so many branches in each shot, and yet they ached of loneliness.

I wished I'd thought of that. So, in the afternoons, between sleep and homework and more sleep, I tried to take pictures. I wanted to find something bright and growing to send. Flower buds about to blossom. New plants breaking the earth. But in December, things like that were scarce. I even checked the flower section of the grocery store, but their stock was low, and the leftover stragglers were turning brown at the edges.

I bought some wilting daisies, arranged them on a windowsill in the sun, sprayed them with a spray bottle to get some fresh dew drops, and tried to cut the brown parts out of the shot.

No luck. The pictures looked like a sad memory of something that used to be beautiful. I could edit them, of course, but Rodney would notice.

As Christmas approached, my brain fog began to clear, and I scrambled through school work, trying to catch up before my teachers started calling home. Mom hovered around me, like she was trying desperately not to micromanage my life. And in return, I tried not to snap at her when she assigned me meals and ordered me to bed.

It's fine, I told myself. An uneasy peace was better than no peace at all.

The day of my first doctor's appointment was two days before Christmas break. I felt better than I had in weeks. I ate toast and fruit for breakfast, without the slightest urge to gag. My body hadn't changed yet—I could still button my jeans with ease. The doctor finally wanted to see me, and now I could almost pretend that there was nothing I needed to be seen *for*.

No, the point of the doctor's appointment was for Mom to hear the heartbeat. Once she saw that everything was fine—that I wasn't destroying her baby's life with my inability to eat a perfect diet—then she'd relax.

Please, I thought in the car on the way there. *Please let her relax.*

But she sat hunched over the steering wheel, gripping it with both hands. She even *drove* nervously. I could hardly blame her. I was digging my nails into the armrest myself.

When we arrived, Mom went up to the receptionist to check in as if she was the one with the appointment. I didn't mind, though. It saved me from trying to stammer out my situation to the receptionist, when obviously all she wanted was the information Mom gave her: my name. Mom returned with a clipboard that asked for everything else.

A woman with an enormous belly came into the office with a toddler trailing behind her. The girl looked like she was about two—probably the age Athena was when Mom was that pregnant with me.

"Come on," the mom said. "Hurry up."

Her little girl ran immediately over to the pile of magazines and pulled out a copy of *High Five* with a jack-o-lantern on the front. The mom leaned over, scooping the girl up and resting her on her hip. How the girl fit there with the Mom's belly being so big was beyond me.

I sucked in my stomach. Would *my* body be able to do things like that, or did it come from having an older child already? One point I was clear on: I was *not* doing this again in the even remotely near future. Maybe when Rodney and I were much,

much older.

I squeezed my eyes shut. When was I going to stop envisioning my future only with him in it?

"Are you okay?" Mom asked. She paused with her pen halfway down a medical history form. I glanced down at the little row of check marks she'd put in the "no" column next to depression, diabetes, heart disease, and headaches.

"Yeah," I said. "Fine. Let me finish that."

If I was old enough to see an obstetrician, I was old enough to fill out my own medical forms.

But Mom shook her head. "I'm almost done. It's easy. You've always been healthy."

But when she checked no next to "other mental illness," I had to wonder. There had to be something wrong with me, right? Otherwise, how the hell did we end up here?

"Penelope?" a nurse called. She smiled at me, and then at Mom, who followed with the clipboard. "Would you like your mother to stay in the waiting room while we do your intake?" she asked. "I can call her back before we check for the heartbeat."

I shook my head. "It's fine," I said. "She can be here for everything." I smiled at Mom, trying to let her know that I wasn't going to exclude her, and she smiled back, like she was trying to reassure me.

Yes. There was definitely something wrong with the both of us.

The nurse led me into an exam room that might have been at my regular doctor's office. I'd expected the walls to be covered in those development pictures where the babies look all squished and uncomfortable, like in the fetal anatomy section of my textbook. But instead we were led into a small room with an exam table and a computer desk. I perched on the table while Mom settled herself into one of the padded plastic chairs off to the side.

The nurse pulled up my chart on the computer and typed in

the information from Mom's clipboard.

"How long have you been sexually active?" she asked me.

My cheeks burned. *That's* why she wanted to start with me alone. I should have listened. "I got pregnant the first time."

Mom resettled in her chair, but I refused to look at her. The nurse nodded and typed something into the computer. She didn't even look up at me as she asked the next question. "And were you using birth control?"

I stole a side glance at Mom, but she busied herself by digging through her purse. "No," I said. I forced myself not to cringe. The nurse wasn't going to ask if I got pregnant on purpose, but it was obvious, wasn't it? If Mom wanted to know, she'd put two and two together in a heartbeat.

The nurse typed something into the computer, and I forced a laugh, reaching for a distraction. "Do you have a button for stupid teenage girls who don't know their actions have consequences?"

The nurse gave me a sad smile. "Fortunately," she said, "our software is non-judgmental."

Mom finally gave up on whatever she was looking for in her purse. She looked up at me, biting her lip.

Did she believe it?

I shook myself. Jeez. Did it matter?

I shifted on the exam table, paper cover crumpling beneath my legs. Yes, it did matter to me what my mother thought. That's why I still hadn't told her the truth.

The nurse took my pulse and my blood pressure, and then stood to leave. "The doctor will be just a minute," she said. "We'll bring in a monitor and take a look. You'll have the big ultrasound in a few months, but he likes to get a look at this stage, just to make sure everything's normal."

Mom's shoulders tensed. I gave her what I hoped was a re-assuring smile. That's what we were here for. To make sure everything was normal. And when it was, hopefully we'd both be able to relax.

The nurse looked from me to Mom, then left, closing the door behind her.

I wondered how many girls like me she saw in a week. Were all their mothers nervous wrecks?

After a long silence, Mom said, "I talked to our adoption agency."

I nodded. We needed to get things squared away. "What did they say?"

Mom fiddled with the strap of her purse. "They said that with adoptions within a family, sometimes the process is easier. But we've already done all the background checks and home inspections, so either way, we're covered."

That was good. Simple and easy. We all needed more of that. "So what do I need to do?"

"You'll meet with one of their counselors, who will talk to you about your rights. Other than that, we don't do much until the baby is born. Then we sign an adoption agreement, and thirty days later, it becomes legal."

We signed. That meant Mom and Dad and me. Not Rodney. "That's it?"

Mom dug her fingernails into the strap so hard that the stitching began to give. "The counselor will probably ask you if you're under pressure to give up the baby."

Ah. That's what she was worried about. "Oh," I said. "No problem there."

Mom nodded, staring down at the floor. "And they want you to give a statement that the father hasn't demonstrated any commitment to you or the baby."

My face flushed. To me *or* the baby. "That's what I have to say?" I asked. "That he's never demonstrated a commitment to me?"

"Not since you've been pregnant," Mom said. She narrowed her eyes. "He hasn't, right?"

"Um," I said. Mom sank back in her chair, and I searched wildly around the office, like one of the signs posted in here

172

would tell me the right thing to say.

Mom closed her eyes. "What happened?" she asked.

Crap. I'd covered when the nurse nearly gave things away, but now here I was, telling Mom things that were even less of her business. But if I didn't tell her, and Rodney brought it up later . . . "He offered to marry me."

Mom's eyes bugged out. "What? When?"

I flailed my arms at her. "When I first told him. Way before you said we shouldn't talk to each other."

Mom dropped her hands onto the chair's armrests with a united thud. "You can't get married," Mom said. "Do you have any idea how hard it is to make it as a married couple when you're just teenagers?"

I glared at her. "I said *no*."

Mom settled back into her chair, but she didn't look happy.

And I had to admit, that feeling was mutual.

There was a knock on the door, and then it swung open. The doctor stepped into the room, with his nurse trailing behind him.

Doctor Kauffman had thick brown hair that grew past his shoulders, pulled back in a low ponytail. He smiled at Mom, and shook her hand. Then he turned to me.

"You must be Penelope," he said.

"Penny," I said.

He took my hand as well. "Penny," he said. "Do you mind if your mom waits outside for a minute while I talk to you?"

He directed the question at me, but he was clearly asking both of us.

"That's fine," I said quickly. I'd learned that lesson from the nurse; if the medical professionals want to talk to you alone, let them.

But he didn't ask me any more embarrassing questions about my sexual history. Instead he said, "Your blood pressure looks good. It looks like you haven't had a pap smear before—do you mind if we check your cervix today?"

Oh. I had a painfully accurate idea of where my cervix was. "No problem," I said. "Whatever you need to do."

Dr. Kauffman opened the exam room door, but he invited the nurse back in instead of my mother. I got that she was there for legal reasons, but the only thing worse than stirruping my heels and being prodded with a cold, hard tool was the awkwardness of being *watched* while it happened.

Rodney didn't need to worry about my nose labeling failures. I had absolutely no desire to go into medicine. For what I expected to be the first of many times in this pregnancy, I was just glad when the procedure was over.

Dr. Kauffman excused the nurse, and my mother came back in, glancing nervously from me to him.

My stomach tightened. I really hoped she was worried about the health of the baby, and not about the adoption itself. I was supposed to be the birth mom she *didn't* have to be nervous about.

"Let's take a look at the baby," Dr. Kauffman said. The nurse wheeled in a monitor attached to a round stick that looked just like the back end of a turkey baster. "We'll do a big ultrasound at twenty weeks," Dr. Kauffman said. "But I like to take a look at your first visit, just to be sure everything's okay."

I pulled my shirt around my ribs and Dr. Kauffman smeared my stomach with a warm gel. Mom watched, cheeks crinkling anxiously. Dr. Kauffman pressed the rounded stick to my stomach, pushing against my abdomen and rubbing it around. A steady pulse came from the speakers.

"That's your heartbeat," he said. "The baby's will be much faster."

He pushed against the space between my hip bone and the fleshy part of my belly. Gray shapes shifted on the monitor. As he slid the probe toward my belly button, another beat ticked from the speakers. The noise pulsed quickly, like a sonar sound effect from a submarine movie. As the doctor pushed the stick under my belly button, the noise grew softer, then louder, then softer again. "We've got movement in there," he said.

My heartbeat quickened, and with it the slower thumping noise. "It's moving already?" I asked.

The doctor nodded, and the beating became softer again, then faded away. I supposed that made sense—lots of living things were tiny. Ants moved. Mites. Bacteria. But a person that small, already able to squirm around—I couldn't picture it.

It turned out I didn't need to. Dr. Kauffman ran the probe against my hip bone, drawing a line down toward my pubic bone, and the fast pulsing was back. He touched the monitor, pointing to a dark gray blur in the center. As he tapped the screen, a measurement appeared around it.

"Looks like twelve weeks," he said. "Is that what we were expecting?"

I nodded, my eyes glued to the screen. Dr. Kauffman angled the stick to the side, and the blur flitted away, disappearing again in the sea of gray fuzz.

"Is it . . ." I squinted at the screen. "Is it *reacting* to you?"

Dr. Kauffman nodded. "Maybe just the change in pressure. But at this age, they definitely squirm when you poke them."

I held my breath, trying to feel that wiggling mass swimming around inside me. But all I felt was the pressure of the stick as Dr. Kauffman searched out the quick little heartbeat again, measuring it.

"Everything looks good," he said.

I heard Mom let out a breath of relief, but I still couldn't bear to look away from the screen. It looked good? There was a *person* in there. How could he talk about it as if it were ordinary?

He pulled the stick away, and turned off the monitor. And only then did I look up at Mom and find her looking straight at me.

Blood drained from my face. I was supposed to be watching *her*. This was *her* baby, not mine. And how must she feel, having to look at someone else's ultrasound, wishing she were the one who was pregnant? She must feel so stupid—her idiot daughter can get pregnant, but she can't.

But as I looked into her eyes, I didn't see embarrassment, or sadness, or frustration. I saw something else—something infinitely more painful.

I saw fear.

A pit hardened in my stomach. The baby was fine. Things looked good. The freaking *doctor* thought so. Mom should be happy, shouldn't she?

But when Mom looked back at the now-blank monitor, her face softened, like what she'd seen there was a comfort.

It wasn't the information on the monitor that made her afraid. It was *me*.

Did she think I wouldn't be able to part with the baby? That I'd make the choice Lily did, and the others before her, and keep it?

I forced a smile. "Good, then," I said. "Everything's good."

The doctor nodded. Mom nodded. But I was pretty sure that Dr. Kauffman was the only one who believed it.

"We'll see you back here in a month. If you experience any bleeding, cramping, or severe pain, I want a call about it, okay?"

I nodded, trying to look at him, but in my mind, all I could see was that little, shifting blur.

A child. Mine and Rodney's.

A living, moving, feeling person that, for the next several months, no one could care for but me.

Chapter Sixteen
Weeks Fourteen through Seventeen

few weeks later, in January, I stood in the center of the street with my camera lens pointed at a lake-like puddle. Last winter, Rodney and I had taken tons of pictures of street puddles—always with one of us spotting cars for the other.

Today, I was alone. Drizzles of rain misted down, and even though I was using a lens hood, I kept having to stop to clean drops off the glass.

Still, the shot I was working on was going to be worth it. When the puddle stopped sloshing from a passing car, I framed the curb against the reflection of two street lights; a red arrow, and a green circle. As the sky sprinkled droplets onto the puddle, the light fractured in rippled patterns. I pressed my shutter down, snapping away.

One of these pictures was going to be perfect. It was the sort of picture Rodney would think of—equal parts *I can do this without you* and *don't you miss doing this with me?*

I checked my lens, and rolled my eyes, trudging to the curb to clean it. Again.

My phone vibrated in my pocket. I stood safely on the curb, protecting my camera from the rain beneath my jacket, and checked it.

The text was from Athena. We were supposed to meet up for lunch.

On my way, she said.

I'm out taking pictures, I texted back. *Can you pick me up? Sure,* she said. *Where?*

I gave her directions to the park down the street, and walked down to the empty playground while I waited.

Thick drops of water collected on the bar above the swing set, falling down onto the seats. I walked across the wet wood chips and snapped some pictures of the water collecting there. I knelt at the base of the swing set, taking shots of the dripping swings in the foreground, set against the backdrop of the bar, and the stormy sky beyond.

When I was done, I pulled my jacket down over my butt and sat on the wet seat. I held my camera in my lap, protecting it from the rain with my body, and flipped through the pictures.

I'd caught one of a particularly fat drop, stretching downward, top thinning against the seat, about to fall. Above it, the swing set loomed, dark against the dim sky. Only the raindrop had any shine to it. It was the best picture I'd taken in months—maybe all year.

"I win," I said. But of course there was no competition without Rodney around to care.

I tucked my camera under my jacket, where it wouldn't get any wetter than it already had, and kicked out my legs. A shower of drops fell down on me as my swing shook the bar, and I turned my face up into them, letting them drench me.

I put my hand on my stomach.

I tried to imagine the person the baby would be, my brother or sister, the sibling my parents always meant for me to have. Maybe in a few years I'd push him or her on a swing just like this, the way Athena used to do for me when I was three and she was five.

What would that baby think of me?

I opened my eyes again; the sky remained drab.

"I'll be the best sister ever," I said aloud. But that was wrong. If I was too good a sister, the child would wish that I were its mother. I'd be a good sister, but not as good a sister as Mom was a mother, so this baby would never have a reason to wish this had happened any other way.

And Rodney. Oh, goodness, Rodney. Would he be the child's brother-in-law?

I squeezed my eyes shut. Only if he forgave me. And that was a big, improbable if. I focused on breathing, in and out. In and out. I'd find a way to explain him, whatever we turned out to be.

What would my baby look like? Some cross between me and Rodney?

No, I thought. Not my baby. Mom's. *Mom's*. I had better not slip like that in front of her.

Athena pulled into the parking lot a few minutes later and honked the horn.

"What are you doing?" she shouted out the window at me. "You're soaked!"

I was, and as I ran through the rain to reach the car, my shoes kicked up water from a pothole puddle, spraying my jeans even more.

Athena turned the heater up full blast. "Mom will kill you if she sees you like that," she said. She eyed my camera as I pulled it out of my jacket. "Get anything good?"

"The best," I said. "Totally worth it."

Athena shrugged down inside her own fleece jacket. "Just make sure your hair's dry before you go home. Where do you want to eat?"

"Carrows," I said. Rodney and I used to go there after shooting all the time, to compare spoils. "I want cheese sticks."

"Done," Athena said. And she drove out of the parking lot, water spraying behind the car. I was glad she didn't ask why. Taking Athena to do things that Rodney and I used to do together made me officially pathetic. But it was a rainy, lonely kind of day. When the sun came out, I'd try to do better.

Athena parked in the back parking lot, and we walked along the row of windows that faced into the seating area. As I turned to look in, I caught sight of Rodney, sitting at a table across the restaurant.

I froze, staring at the sleek brown hair of the girl sitting across the table from him.

Kara.

I couldn't breathe. As I watched, Rodney waved his arms in the air, in the way that he always did when he was venting about something.

To me. He vented his problems to *me*. I grabbed Athena's arm and pulled her to a stop.

Kara nodded and took a sip of her drink. She put her hand on the table as she spoke. But she didn't touch him. She just rested her hand near his as he rolled his head onto the back of the booth seat, and stared at the ceiling.

"What?" Athena said, following my gaze. "Wait, is that . . . ?"

"Rodney," I said. My chest ached. Rodney and Kara weren't going out, were they? No. Kara kept trying to get me to hook back up with him. She wouldn't do that if she wanted him herself. Besides, she had Ryan. Maybe.

Rodney rubbed his temples, stretching his eyes wide like he was trying to figure out an unsolvable problem.

Oh, no.

He was talking to her about *me*.

I came to my senses. Rodney could look up at any time and see me *spying* on him. I squeaked as I ducked down below the glass and rushed to the end of the row of windows, dragging Athena with me by the arm. I stood again, leaning against the building. Athena stumbled next to me, standing under the eaves of the building. Drops of water smacked the sidewalk in front of us.

I breathed.

Athena looked over at me like she wasn't sure what to say. "Do you want to go somewhere else?"

"Um," I said. We'd have to walk back by the windows, and if Rodney saw me, he'd know I was here, and that I ran away from him. I was getting more pathetic by the second.

I sank onto my butt on the strip of dry concrete beneath the eaves. My jeans were still wet from the swing, and they clung to my thighs. My vision went bleary.

I squeezed my eyes closed. I was *not* going to pass out here. There was *no way* I would come even *close* to letting Rodney save me from that again.

Athena sat down next to me, tucking her feet under her so the rain wouldn't drip on her shoes. "So, are they . . ."

"No," I said. They were just friends. They had to be, right? I mean, Kara was still all googly over Ryan, and she'd been trying to convince me to get back together with Rodney.

But that was last *month*. How much time had they been spending together? Had Rodney been taking her *shooting*?

My stomach turned. Even if they weren't together, Rodney wouldn't talk to me, but he was apparently just fine talking to Kara. He was cheating on me as his friend. *Friend* cheating. It was totally a thing.

I clenched my jaw. "Go ahead," I said. "Say it."

Athena squeezed my hand. "Say what?"

I sighed. "You told me sex would change everything. You warned me."

Athena's arm wrapped around my shoulders, and I leaned into her, the dampness of my jacket soaking into her fleece. I looked at the car. We were going to have to crawl past the windows on our knees if we didn't want Rodney to see us. I didn't even have to ask. I already knew that Athena would do it for me.

"I'm sorry," she said.

I looked up at her. "For warning me?"

She shook her head, sadly. "I'm sorry that you can't go back to being just friends."

I lowered my head onto her shoulder. "Yeah, well," I said. "I'm ninety-nine percent sure we never were."

For the next three weeks, I stalked the hallways and the quad, watching for Rodney and Kara. I saw Kara in class, of course, but she'd stopped talking about Rodney and Ryan, which was exactly what she would do if she didn't want to tell me she was dating my ex-boyfriend. I saw her with Rodney in the halls a couple times a week, always with their hands hanging at their sides, or shoved into their pockets. Not touching. Not yet. But how long had Rodney been interested in me, without holding my hand at school?

Years. That's how long.

Whenever he saw me watching them, Rodney gave me a nod, and I searched his face for traces of guilt, for some sign that he was totally over me. But his nods didn't seem to change, for the better or the worse.

If there was something going on, he wasn't going to give it up that easily.

I managed not to outright stalk them until the end of the third week, when I not-so-casually walked by the chess room at lunch, just to see if they were there.

They were. In the quick glance I got as I walked past, I saw Rodney and Ryan sitting across a chess board from each other, Kara perched cross-legged on the desk behind them.

Was she there for Rodney, or for Ryan? I shook my head. It shouldn't matter. Rodney was free to do whatever he wanted. I should be hoping that Kara would treat him better than I had. If I really cared about Rodney, I should be wishing him the best.

That day after school, I was pulling some books out of my locker when Rodney slapped a piece of paper against the metal door of the locker next to mine.

"Behold," he said.

I stared at the paper. I'm not sure if I was more surprised that he was talking to me, or by the big seventy-five written at the top. "You got a C?"

Rodney nodded calmly. I didn't know how he could do

that—just stand there like talking to me was the most natural thing in the world. My heart pounded just thinking about all the ways I might screw this conversation up.

Chief among them was demanding to know if he was dating somebody else.

I stayed focused on the test. "I got an eighty one," I said. "I thought that was bad."

Rodney raised one eyebrow. "See? You finally beat me."

"I guess," I said. That had always been the goal—a friendly competition that he always won. If I'd scored higher than him before, I would have rubbed it in for hours. Days. Weeks even.

But now?

It didn't seem right to be happy.

"What happened?" I asked.

He rolled his eyes. "I guess all that studying you made me do had an effect after all."

I smiled. "You didn't really study with me. You mostly played video games."

Rodney crushed the test in his fist. "Yeah, well. Auditory learning for the win."

I swung my locker closed. It had never occurred to me that I might have been helping Rodney just by announcing stuff at him while he played. I always thought he picked up all the information in class. He never seemed to pay much attention to the material when we studied together.

"Thanks for telling me," I said. "I know you didn't have to."

Rodney shrugged. "Thought you should know."

I held my breath. If he and Kara were together, would he think *that* was something I should know? I busied myself with my backpack, shoving some papers in it at random. I expected Rodney to walk away, then, but he kept standing there, looking down at his wadded paper, like there was something else he wanted to say.

My heart skipped faster. I zipped up my backpack, stalling, giving him time. I wanted to know. Didn't I?

Finally, Rodney looked at me, staring straight into my eyes. "So this thing where we're not talking? I hate it."

My chest fluttered. He hated it? "That makes two of us."

Rodney looked down at my backpack. His voice was almost reluctant. "I miss you."

The world fell silent, as if nothing existed in it but him and me. I held perfectly still, when what I truly wanted to do was tackle him in a giant hug and make him promise never to avoid me again.

I held my breath. If I spoke, I'd say the wrong thing. This moment would devolve into a fight, which was the last thing I wanted. I could tell from the wary look he gave me that this thought, too, was mutual.

Rodney gripped his backpack strap. "So, what are you doing now?" he asked. "I mean, for the next couple of hours?"

Anything you want, I thought. But I bit my tongue. Just because I *was* desperate didn't mean I had to announce it to him. I shrugged. "Going home, I guess. What about you?"

Rodney shuffled his feet. "I was thinking of studying in the quad. Want to join me?"

He didn't have to make it sound *painful*. But I guess it was painful to be around me, after what I did to him. If he was willing to try, even after everything, I couldn't blame him if it still hurt.

I kept my voice even. The last thing I wanted to do was scare him off. "Yeah," I said. "Sure. Of course." I pulled out my phone. "Let me text my mom, so she doesn't wait for me."

Rodney stiffened. "Is she going to be mad?"

I cradled my phone. This felt like a trick question, and I wanted to answer it perfectly. "I'll tell her I'm studying," I said. "We're allowed to run into each other at school. And we're still at school, right?"

Rodney sighed. "Sure."

That didn't seem like it had been the right answer, but it hadn't sent him running, either. I sent the text as quickly as I could. I didn't love lying to my mother, but this tender truce with Rodney was as delicate as a bubble. If I breathed too hard, it would pop.

We walked to the quad in silence, and not the comfortable kind. And I thought for a terrible moment that this was how things might be with Rodney from now on. Awkward. Uncomfortable. Like strangers—no, worse. Like people who used to be friends.

But Rodney just sat down at one of the lunch tables and pulled out his physiology book.

"Here," he said, flipping his book over. "Why don't you quiz me?"

I couldn't tell if that was a gesture to help me feel better, or a brush off. I turned my book to the nearest practice chart in the exercise section at the back of the chapter. The side-view of the penis stared up at me.

New unit. Reproductive anatomy.

Fabulous timing.

"Maybe we should just study on our own," I said.

Rodney glanced down at the chapter and his face went pale. He nodded quickly, and pulled his book back in front of him.

I tried to imagine how this study session would have gone before. Could we have labeled the foreskin without feeling awkward? Would we have laughed our way through? I wasn't sure, now. That old relationship felt fuzzy—like a thing I might have dreamed. Especially since I was sure now we'd never really been just friends.

"Okay," Rodney said. He pulled some papers out of the back of the book—blank copies of the exercise charts. "Let's each fill these out from memory, and we'll see how much we already know."

I pulled out my own book. Truthfully, I hadn't even looked at this unit yet. Mr. Moore wouldn't start going over it in class until the end of the week. So I opened my book and glanced at the chart, trying to learn the names.

I squirmed on the hard bench. Rodney had taken a risk asking to study with me. It was my turn to take a risk back, to open communication with him again. I thought about asking him what he thought of my pictures, but I bit my tongue. If I brought that up, and things went wrong, he might stop posting them. I didn't want to talk about the baby, because that was too close to the heart of things, too tender and uncertain. I needed something around the edges of the problem. Something like letting him know I knew he was hanging out with Kara.

"I saw you at Carrows," I said. "A couple weeks ago."

Rodney looked up, his face entirely blank, like he was waiting for the rest of my statement.

"What?" I said. "I was with Athena."

Rodney nodded slowly. "You didn't say hi."

"Um," I said. "Right. We weren't talking."

He smiled sadly. "Touché."

My pen hovered over my notebook paper. I looked sideways at Rodney, but he squinted at his book. I'd tried to open the conversation up, so that him hanging out with Kara wouldn't be a secret. But if he didn't talk about it, that was even more uncomfortable than if I hadn't mentioned it at all.

Finally, Rodney sighed. "I didn't tell Kara," he said, "if that's what you're worried about."

I sat up straighter. That *wasn't* what I was worried about, but maybe it should have been. "She knows I'm pregnant."

"Yeah." He spoke sharply. "And she knows that your parents are adopting the baby. So I left it at that."

I'd seen the frustrated look on his face as he waved his hands across the table at her. He'd told her *something* else. I put my pencil down. Or maybe not. Maybe those two facts were enough to justify that reaction. The only difference was, he told her how he *felt* about it. "I get it," I said. "You need someone to talk to." Someone not me, apparently.

Then Athena's voice came back to me, loud and clear. *I'm sorry that you can't go back to being just friends.* I might never

186

be the one he talked to again.

I wiped my palms on my jeans. "So," I said. "Are you and Kara . . ."

Rodney turned fully toward me, his eyes widening. "No!" he said, with so much force that I knew he meant it. He rubbed his forehead. "Jeez, Penny."

"What?" I asked. "It was a legitimate question."

He cupped his hand, and looked at it as if he expected to find in it the answers that he needed. "It's not really on my mind," he said. "I'm not going to go after someone else while my girlfriend is pregnant, you know?"

My heart did a cartwheel, and I stiffened, trying not to out-wardly react. His girlfriend? Still?

Really?

Rodney squeezed his eyes shut, like he'd said something he wished he could take back. I picked up my pencil, breathing carefully, evenly.

I waited one breath. Two. Three. Four.

He didn't open his mouth. He didn't take it back.

He still thought of me as his girlfriend. I let myself smile. This didn't have to be awkward. I reached over and took his physiology book. "Here," I said. "Let me quiz you."

Rodney gave me a half-smile, looking down at the book. "I may have forgotten what unit was next," he said. "I guess I should have asked you to study last week, when we were still in the lungs."

I forced myself to laugh. "Yeah, well. Time to grow up, I guess."

Rodney's face grew serious. He looked at me, his chin tucked close to his shoulder. I turned toward him, our noses inches apart. His eyes met mine; I wasn't ready for what I saw in them: the pain, or the longing.

Rodney still loved me.

He held my gaze for a long moment, neither of us breathing. And I tried to answer back with my eyes what I saw in his—I still wanted him, too. He had to know that. He *had* to.

But that's the thing about looks—you never can tell if your message is being received the way you mean it to be. So instead I tilted my chin to the side, leaning closer.

Rodney looked down at my mouth, his teeth barely grazing his bottom lip. Our shoulders bumped together, and I closed my eyes.

A cold rush of air breezed between us, and I opened them again to see that Rodney had turned away, staring at his hands in front of him on the table. His shoulders were angled away from me, and that message I did get, loud and clear.

No.

I clamped my teeth down on the inside of my cheek.

So much for things not having to be awkward.

Rodney ran his fingernail over a groove in the table. "I'm sorry," he said.

"No," I said. "No, you have *nothing* to apologize for. It's me. I'm the one who sucks at this."

He didn't deny it.

I sighed. "It would help, though," I said, "if you could tell me how to make it better. It's hard, not knowing what you want."

Rodney sucked his lips in, and I kicked myself. There I went again, picking at the wound, when it had only barely begun to heal.

Rodney sighed. He looked up at the sky, and down at the ground, and then finally, finally at me.

He cleared his throat before he spoke. "I think it's probably best," he said, slowly, "if we go back to being just friends."

I gripped the edge of the bench. I wanted to point out that we kissed all the time when we were "friends." But that wasn't what he meant, obviously.

What if Athena was right? If there was no going back, and he couldn't bring himself to be with me again, what would that make us?

Nothing.

I tried not to let that eviscerate me. I should count myself lucky that he still believed we could give friendship a chance. "Are you sure that's what you want?"

He took a deep breath, his back straight. "Yeah. I am."

I felt a stabbing sensation, starting in my heart, and angling down through my chest. Maybe I was having a heart attack; maybe I could just die right here, and have it over with.

Shut up, I thought. *Pull it together.*

The groove in the table was growing deeper. It was a wonder he wasn't wearing a hole in his finger, as well.

I got it. He still loved me, but he didn't trust me. We were too much of a mess; regardless of how he felt, he didn't want me back.

I could walk away from him now. But Rodney's friendship was worth something, even if he couldn't bring himself to be with me. Whatever we felt for each other, I was still going to have this baby, and I was still going to give it to my mother. Much as I hated it, Mom was right; Rodney couldn't afford to get attached. Besides which, he'd promised my parents he'd stay away. Under the circumstances, I was spectacularly lucky he was offering me friendship at all.

And though I couldn't see it now, I had to believe that there was some way for the two of us to survive this—to work out our relationship, even if it had to be after the baby was born.

"I can respect that," I said. "Just don't stop talking to me again."

Rodney nodded, and pointed toward the physiology book. "So, quiz me?" he asked.

I handed him a practice sheet and pulled the book between us.

I'd quiz him all day. Tomorrow. The next day. Whenever. Forever. And somewhere along the line, I'd learn to stop feeling like dying, because we used to be so much more than friends. Somehow, I'd learn to be grateful that I still got to have him in my life at all.

But telling myself that didn't stop me from worrying about the future.

And no amount of just-friendship from Rodney would keep me from wanting to curl up and cry.

Chapter Seventeen
Week Seventeen

That weekend, I barely got out of bed. Mom came in to check on me several times, but I sent her away, telling her I was tired. "That book says fatigue is normal," I told her. "So I'm just going to sleep."

Sleep didn't help, though. Eyes open, eyes closed, asleep or awake—I just kept hearing Rodney's words echo through my mind. *I think it's probably best if we go back to being just friends.*

He still loved me. I knew he did. But, like the decent guy that he was, he was trying to do the right thing and respect my parents' wishes. He was trying to be what I needed him to be, even if it wasn't what I wanted.

The more I thought about it, though, the more impossible it seemed that we'd ever be able to work it out. It wasn't like I was going to give the baby to a stranger. The child would still be in my life, but not really in his. How long would that make my mother nervous? How long would it bother him that my brother or sister was biologically his child?

Oh, man.

Probably forever.

If it did, where did that leave us? I believed him about Kara, but how long would it be before he wanted to date someone else? And then what would I be? The friend he asked for advice?

I buried my face in my pillow, trying to shut out the noise, as if it wasn't coming from inside my own head.

Friends or nothing. Those were my choices. I had to figure out how to be friends in a way that didn't tear us both apart. If I could do that, maybe it would prove to him that I could be trusted.

Maybe it would convince him to change his mind.

I curled up tighter on my bed, as if I could will myself back into the womb. This baby might have a lot of problems coming, but it didn't know about them yet.

I wished I could be as blissfully ignorant.

On Sunday night, Mom sat down on the foot of my bed. "That bad, huh?" she asked.

I groaned.

Mom shook her head. "I'd have thought you'd be moving out of the morning sickness. If it's getting worse, maybe you should see the doctor."

I shook my head. "I'm sure it'll pass," I said. "The book said it's normal." As normal as a depressed girl who screwed over her boyfriend could be. I scrunched down on my pillow. I couldn't look like this for Rodney. I had to be happy the next time I saw him, so he'd get that I respected his wishes. I looked up at Mom. "Can I stay home from school tomorrow?"

Mom pursed her lips. "Are you sure there's nothing you want to talk about?"

I couldn't tell her the truth. I wasn't even supposed to be *talking* to Rodney. "No," I said. "I just want to sleep."

"Okay," Mom said. "If you feel the same in the morning, I'll call you in."

But I already knew that I would.

Mom did call the school on Monday morning, and then she stood in my doorway, making a sympathetic face. "I'm going grocery shopping," she said. "What can I bring you?"

I lay back on my pillow. "Corn flakes?"

Mom smiled. "You want the kind with the frosting?"

She knew me too well. "Yeah. But not if it'll hurt the baby."

"I think you'll be fine," Mom said. "You're eating much better these days."

Since my nausea had subsided, I'd been trying to eat every-thing Mom offered me—smoothies and whole wheat bread and all. I still couldn't stomach eggs, though. I didn't want to even *think* about eggs.

"Try to take a shower before I get back, okay?" Mom said. "You'll feel better." And then she shut the door again.

I wondered if that was a subtle hint that I smelled. I'd been lounging in the same set of pajamas for the last forty-eight hours, so I probably did.

When I heard Mom leave the house, I dragged myself out from under the covers and into the bathroom. I stared at myself in the mirror, at my ratty bun, and my wrinkled PJs. I turned on the shower, inhaling the steam. I ran my hand over my ab-domen—my pants still fit fine, even my jeans, but my abs felt firm where they'd once been soft.

I left my hand there, hoping for that moment you see in mov-ies, where suddenly the baby kicks and the mother jumps, all surprised at the movement inside her. But I didn't feel anything, except the slightest twinge of a cramp in my back, no doubt from spending all weekend in bed.

I turned, stretching my arms up to outline the slightest hint of a bump across my belly. I hadn't felt the baby move at all yet, but I had to admit I was looking forward to that part. And as I stood there, looking at the crazy thing my body was doing on behalf of my mother, I couldn't help but feel like I'd done this one little thing right.

There was a little kid growing inside of me. A child Mom had always wanted but never got to have. Soon, Mom wouldn't have any reason to freak out anymore, and I could work on getting things with Rodney back to where they used to be.

Things would work out. I just needed to hold on a little longer.

I pulled off my shirt. My whole body felt achy, like I'd been still for too long. I stripped off the rest of my clothes, but as I took off my underwear, I froze.

They were soaked through with watery red dots.

Blood.

More dripped down my thigh, spotting the white tile. My stomach turned. I couldn't be starting my period. I hadn't had one of those in four months.

Miscarriage. My mom had had several. One day, she'd be fine, and then she'd start bleeding and wouldn't stop. Incompetent cervix, they called it, as if her very anatomy needed to be fired.

I closed my eyes. Was that *genetic*?

No. I'd read about this in the baby book. Spotting was normal. But how much was a spot? How many spots were okay?

I changed into a pad and new underwear and searched for the baby book. This was probably nothing. But the number of times I had to repeat that over to myself told me I didn't believe it.

I found the page where I'd read about spotting—the book listed the signs that meant bleeding was serious—abdominal pain, back pain, gushing blood, dizziness, fever.

See, I thought. *I'm fine.*

I'd just finish my shower and by the time I was done, the bleeding would stop. I went back in the bathroom, the mirror now fully fogged, and undressed again, stepping under the hot water. It poured through my hair, and I closed my eyes, drawing the steamy air deep into my lungs.

Then I scrubbed my legs, washing away all traces of blood.

It would stop. It *would*.

I was rinsing the conditioner from my hair when the back pain began. It was subtle at first, just an ache deep in my spine like I might have had if I'd been standing too long in a line, or contorting too much to get a perfect shot. I held my breath, standing beneath the spray, letting the hot water hit my back where it hurt. Heat was good for cramps. My body would relax. The pain would ease.

Except that it didn't. The next wave felt like a sharp stabbing. The pain shot up my spine.

I stepped out of the shower, hands shaking. If I had pain or bleeding, the doctor had said, he wanted to hear about it.

I dried my hands on a towel.

More watery drops of blood splashed across the floor. My back throbbed. I pulled on my underwear and pad, wrapped another towel around myself, and headed for my room.

Under a pile of notes on my desk I found the paperwork from the doctor's office, including the number I was supposed to call. With fumbling hands, I found my cell phone and dialed.

A recording answered. "If this is a medical emergency," it said, "please call 911, or go to the nearest emergency room."

I swallowed. *Was* this an emergency? That's what I was calling to ask *them*.

"If you have a question for the nurse, please leave your name and number, and we will get back to you as soon as possible."

I pinched the paper with the phone number on it between my fingers. "This is Penny Overman," I said after the beep. "I'm bleeding, and I . . . don't know if that's a problem or not."

I left my number and hung up.

My back throbbed again, and I fumbled through the rest of the papers, hoping there was something more helpful in them. There, on one of the papers, was the list of miscarriage symptoms: back pain, cramping, bleeding.

I read the words over once, twice, three times. I had two symptoms out of three. Unless the back pain *counted* as cramping, in which case I had all three. I collapsed onto my bed.

If I wanted to know exactly what a miscarriage was like in all its graphic detail, I could ask Mom. But unless I wanted to terrify her, I couldn't tell her. I'd just wait for the doctor to call back. And they'd tell me it was nothing.

I grabbed a water bottle from my nightstand—I kept them there now, because I was constantly parched. I woke up dying of thirst at least once every night. Now I sipped my water, and took deep breaths. If I had a miscarriage, did that make me exactly like Mom? Would I cry for weeks? Would I crumble to pieces?

It only took five minutes for the phone to ring, but it felt like forty.

"I'm calling for Penny," the nurse said.

I fought to keep my voice from shaking. They probably got calls from panicked girls all the time. All the time. And it was probably usually nothing. "That's me."

"Penny, this is Dr. Kauffman's nurse. How are you doing?"

"Okay, I guess."

"Tell me about the bleeding. How heavy is it?"

"I don't know," I said. "Medium?"

"Is it gushing or dripping?"

"Dripping," I said. "Is that bad?"

"It's probably fine," she said. "But I think we should have the doctor look at you, just to be sure. Can you come in?"

That wasn't what I wanted to hear. If it was fine, I didn't need to be seen. "Do I have to?"

"I think you should to be on the safe side."

Safe. That's exactly what I wanted to be. "Okay. What time?"

"We'll fit you in as soon as you get here. I'll let the front desk know you're coming."

I closed my eyes. Not right now. Right now was urgent. I wanted to come in leisurely sometime in the next few days. That's what you did when you saw the doctor for probably nothing.

"Okay," I said. "I'll see what I can do."

Mom had gone out with the car, so I couldn't drive myself. She'd answer her cell phone if I called, but then I'd have to explain. To Mom. That the person carrying her baby was bleeding.

I wasn't going to do that for probably nothing.

I immediately dialed Athena. Her phone rang five times and then went to voice mail. I swore, hung up, and then dialed again.

This time it hit voice mail after two rings.

She was probably in class. Like everyone else in the world I knew.

I hung up again and shook my phone. I could leave Athena a message, but then I'd have to deal with her later, after everything turned out to be all right.

I still needed to make it to the doctor, and I needed someone to drive me. There was only one other obvious choice. But he was at school.

Wasn't he? What if he'd decided to stay home to avoid me, the way I'd done to him? Then he might be around. He might answer his phone. I wasn't supposed to see him outside school. But this was . . . maybe not an emergency . . . but definitely an extenuating circumstance. Giving rides was totally something that *friends* did.

I dialed Rodney before I could second guess myself. Again.

The phone rang. And rang. And rang.

And then went to voice mail.

I swore again. He had to be at school. I put the phone down and scrunched down on my bed, which, now that I was clean, I could tell definitely smelled like unwashed Penny.

I had to call Mom. I had to. I'd just tell her I changed my mind. I thought I should be seen by the doctor. Like, now. But it wasn't serious. Nothing serious.

And of course, she would totally believe me.

I cringed with my finger over the button to dial.

And then the phone rang. I looked down at Rodney's name. Rodney was calling me back.

"Hey," I said, trying to sound casual.

"Hey," he said back. "You just called?"

"Yeah," I said. "Aren't you at school?"

"I just got out of first period," he said. "Didn't you?"

I took a deep breath. "No." *Casual*, I thought. Like I was asking him for a ride to the store.

In the middle of the freaking school day. "I need a favor."

"What's that?"

"I need you to drive me to the doctor's office."

Rodney paused. "Right now?"

"Yeah," I said. "Can you leave school?"

Rodney's voice was strained. "What's wrong?"

"Nothing," I said. "The doctor just wants to check some things. Can you come get me?"

"Your mom can't take you?"

I squeezed my eyes shut. I could lie to him, but I could already feel the cracked door of our friendship beginning to edge shut. This was a stupid idea. A terrible idea. He couldn't leave school for me. Obviously he couldn't. His parents would find out. *My* parents would find out. "Never mind," I said. "Sorry to bother you."

I heard a loud bang on Rodney's end, like a door shutting. "This is serious."

"I don't know," I said. "I mean, no. It's fine. I don't want to worry anyone." I cringed. Anyone but him, apparently.

"I'm on my way," Rodney said.

"No," I said. "You don't have to—" But Rodney had already hung up the phone.

The drive from school to my house should have been fifteen minutes, *if* no one stopped him on his way to the parking lot. Instead, it took him five.

"I'm not dying," I said as I opened the door. And, as if to make a liar out of me, my tail bone ached viciously.

"Right," Rodney said. "But you need to go to the doctor badly enough that you called me out of school."

I bit my lower lip, hard.

Rodney steered me toward the car. He'd left it running. He opened the passenger door for me and then ran around the car to climb in the other side.

As he backed out of the driveway, he glanced at me. "Is your mother going to meet you there?"

"Um." Hadn't I told him that I didn't call her? Probably not. I'd probably dodged the issue. I chewed my lip. Why couldn't I stop lying to him?

"Um?" Rodney said. "You didn't call her?"

I floundered for an explanation. "I didn't want to worry her." That, at least, was the truth.

Rodney's mouth dropped open. "She doesn't know you called me? Because I'm not even supposed to *be* with you."

I smashed my palm into my forehead. "I won't tell her, okay?"

"She's your mother," he said. "She's going to ask how you got to the hospital."

I shivered. "The *doctor*," I said. "Not the same."

Rodney rolled his eyes. "Penny," he said. "This is really messed up."

I slumped in my seat. He was right. Of course I had to tell her. But if Rodney insisted that he was just my friend, that wasn't a commitment, right? It wouldn't interfere with her adoption. It ought to be okay for us to be just friends. "I'll tell her," I said quietly. "Once I'm sure I'm okay."

Rodney raised his eyebrows at me. "And if you're not?"

I took a deep breath. "I'm sure I am. Don't argue with a pregnant woman. She has intuition." Though, if that was true, I was pretty sure my intuition receptors were entirely clogged.

I gave Rodney directions to the doctor's office. He drove like a maniac, and I was half convinced we were going to crash into a pole and die.

At least then I wouldn't have to talk to my mother.

We arrived at the doctor's office, and I climbed out of the car, moving with purpose so that Rodney couldn't come over and try to help me.

"Thanks," I said without looking at him. "That was really nice of you."

Rodney climbed out of the car, following me inside.

"You could go back to school," I said. "Then you'll just get marked tardy in one class and it won't be a big deal and your parents won't—"

"Penny." Rodney put his hand on my arm, which had apparently been violently shaking.

Crap. I should be putting up a brave front for him. I should be making him believe that he was okay to go.

"I'll stay in the waiting room," he said. "At least until your mom gets here."

I stared straight ahead. Until Mom got here. And saw him in

the waiting room. And totally murdered me, birth mom or not.

"You don't have to," I said.

Rodney rolled his eyes. "Obviously," he said. And he took me by the arm and guided me into the office, as if I couldn't walk in on my own.

I would have argued more, except that I wasn't actually sure that I could have.

"Thanks," I said.

"Sure," Rodney said. "Of course."

But I could tell from his tone that he was as unsure of all this as I was.

There was no *of course* in a situation like ours.

In the doctor's office, Rodney took the seat as near to the door as possible.

It wasn't fair of me to leave him here like that for long. I pulled out my phone. "I'll text my mom," I said. That was clearly what I should have done to begin with. I sent her one line: *I'm okay, but at the doctor's. Meet me here?*

But, like a coward, I still turned off my phone so I wouldn't have to see her reaction.

When I approached the receptionist's desk, I expected to be asked to take a seat. But instead, the nurse came right out and ushered me into a room they had waiting for me.

Now more than just my hands were shaking. If they really wanted me to think that this was no big deal, they should have let me wait for twenty minutes, at least.

The nurse did take the time to check my pulse and blood pressure. I told myself that meant they weren't really in a rush— they probably wouldn't do that if they thought I was going to have to go into immediate surgery or something.

But then a worse thought cut through, one I wished I hadn't thought of at all: if miscarriage was a thing that could be fixed by surgery, Mom would have been under that knife. If I was miscarrying, there was nothing they'd be able to do.

I clutched the edge of the exam table while the blood pressure cuff tightened around my arm. Mom had been caught in a whirlpool of grief for years. I'd been trying to reach for her, to save her. But what if in doing so, all I'd done was caused myself to fall in?

"Relax," the nurse said.

Fat. Chance.

I breathed deep. The pain in my back had subsided, for the moment at least. *See,* I thought. *Nothing wrong. False alarm. I've terrified Mom for nothing.* When she was done with my vitals, the nurse had me describe the problem. How long had I been bleeding? How much? Then she handed me a drape. "Undress from the waist down. Put this across your lap. The doctor will be just a minute."

I held the drape in front of me. It was just a piece of soft fabric that looked like it had been washed many, many times. "Should I leave my underwear on?" I asked. "I'm wearing a pad."

She reached into a drawer and handed me a thick pad of gauze. "Sit on this," she said.

What if I soaked through? Did that mean the baby was going to die?

Dr. Kauffman came in almost immediately after I sat down under the drape. *It's just because they squeezed you in,* I told myself. *It's just because he's trying to get to his next patient on time.*

"Penny," he said, "I hear you're experiencing some bleeding."

"Yeah," I said. "That's normal, right?"

"Sometimes," he said. "Let's have a look."

The nurse stood in the corner of the room while he stretched on a plastic glove and helped me lie back on the table. He poked at my abdomen first, then at the bleeding area. I chanted the anatomy in my head as he went over it. Uterus, ovaries, labia, vagina, cervix. I didn't need to learn those from a physiology book. I'd heard them in health lectures since I was ten.

"All right," Dr. Kauffman said. "I'm going to send you over to the ultrasound room. That way we can get a better look at what's going on."

A stabbing pain shot up my spine again, though I couldn't tell if it was cramping or panic. He was supposed to take one look and tell me it was fine. There wasn't supposed to be anything to look closer *at*. "You can't just use that cart thing again?" I asked.

Dr. Kauffman actually had the nerve to smile. "I just want to make sure we don't miss anything," he said.

They left me alone to dress. And before I knew it, the nurse was helping me into a wheel chair. *I can walk!* I wanted to shout. *I'm fine!*

But with my shaking knees, I'd probably trip and fall and break open my head, and then Mom would show up to find me bleeding from both ends and she'd have an aneurysm and die.

I sat quietly in the wheel chair as they rolled me down the hall.

The nurse must have noticed my panic, because she bent down and spoke softly in my ear. "Did you bring anyone with you today?"

Rodney. He was probably still here, wasn't he? Mom couldn't have gotten here that fast. "Yeah," I said. "A friend."

The nurse's voice was kind. "Would you like me to ask her to come in with you?"

She didn't tell me that everything was going to be okay. And if she saw that I was distressed and wanted to comfort me, she would have said that, if she could.

Mom was probably driving straight from the grocery store. Maybe milk would spoil in the trunk. Maybe she'd left her groceries in the aisle. But when she arrived, Mom would come in with me, and grip the arms of chairs and bite her nails and generally look like she wanted to climb the walls.

Just like me.

And more than anything, I just wanted Rodney to sit next to me and *not* radiate fear. I wanted to be with someone who wouldn't fall to pieces on me.

An ultrasound was just a stick on my belly. It wouldn't be too embarrassing, for me or for him. I wanted to let him be strong for me. I wanted to let him in.

That's what he'd wanted all along, wasn't it?

"Yes," I said. "Can you go get him?"

The nurse hesitated, probably because she hadn't realized my friend was a guy. But as she wheeled me into the ultrasound room, she whispered, "Sure."

By the time the soft knock came on the door, I was already on the ultrasound table, belly lubed, with the waistband of my jeans pushed down to my hip bones. The tech opened the door, and Rodney stood there, his hands jammed in his pockets.

"Hey," I said, pointing to the chair next to me. "Sit with me for a minute?"

The tech stepped aside and got her probe ready while Rodney shuffled into the room and lowered himself into the chair.

"Are you okay?" he asked.

No, I wanted to say. But if he meant physically, I didn't want to scare him. "They're checking to see," I said.

Rodney took a deep breath and nodded. He pulled his phone out of his pocket and fiddled with it. As he sat down in the chair, the nurse poked her head back in.

The tech took her rounded stick and ran it over my belly button. When the doctor did that last time, my belly gave way, still soft. But this time the stick barely dug into the skin; my uterus was firm underneath.

My hand fidgeted at the edge of the exam table, while Rodney played with the edge of his phone case. My fingers still trembled, and I wanted him to take my hand, but even as I thought that, I kicked myself. I was supposed to be his friend. And friends didn't hold hands.

Except when one of them was in the hospital, I thought. Maybe they held hands then?

But Rodney didn't. Instead, he glanced upward to the flatscreen mounted to the wall above us as the gray, blobby picture appeared.

I held my breath. I waited for the tech to tell me that every-thing was fine. There was nothing to worry about. The doctor was just being cautious.

But she didn't say that. She didn't say anything at all, just moved around her probe with one hand and clicked with her mouse with the other, taking still shots of whatever she was looking at. She ran the stick along the side of my belly, and that's when the image became clear.

I'd seen ultrasound photos before, of course. We'd had a march of them across our refrigerator doors—babies that other girls had promised to Mom. This looked just like one of those pictures: the bulbous head, the undersized body. Much clearer than the little squirming blip I'd seen at my twelve-week appointment, here was a full profile shot of the baby's head. Its arms and legs curled together, the ultrasound showing the motion in quick little jerks.

Moving. And until that second, I hadn't articulated what I'd really feared. That the baby was already dead. That there was no hope.

But how bad could things be, if something that tiny was living inside me, and still moving?

As if to reassure me, its body curled tighter, and I could swear that those tiny fingers started playing with its toes.

My skin washed cold as I became aware of Rodney sitting next to me, also looking up at the screen. His mouth hung open just slightly, and I could swear he was holding his breath.

Seeing the baby. Our baby.

The one I was giving away.

Rodney glanced down at my stomach, then over at me, and then quickly, instantly, down at the floor. He shoved his phone hard back into his pocket, and cleared his throat.

A horrible, dark feeling came over me. Shame that I'd brought him in here. Guilt that I'd made him see that.

Most of all, a terrible, painful regret that I'd dragged him into this at all.

Rodney's face grew red as he jammed his hands deep in his pockets, as far from holding mine as they could get.

A knock came at the door, and without a pause, it swung open. Mom stood in the doorway, peering into the room. The tech made to get up, but I held up a hand.

Mom's eyes ran over me, as if checking for missing limbs. "Penny," Mom said. "Are you—"

But before she could finish her question, Rodney was on his feet. He didn't spare a look for either of us, just strode to the door and twisted past her, walking into the hall.

And that's when I knew: Athena *was* right. Rodney and I would never be just friends.

And it was killing him every bit as much as it was killing me.

Chapter Eighteen
Week Seventeen

Mom apparently didn't want to make a scene in front of the ultrasound tech, because she saved her freak-out until we were sitting back in my exam room, waiting for the doctor.

She paced the floor. "Why didn't you call me immediately?"

I covered my face with my hands. "I didn't want to freak you out for nothing."

"The nurse said you were *bleeding*. Are you in pain?"

I shrugged. "Not much." My back throbbed, accentuating the lie. But the baby was moving. The extra pain was probably from stress.

Oh, jeez. Would stress make this even worse? I raised my head, trying to loosen my shoulders. "Really, Mom," I said. "It's nothing. Spotting is normal. The baby is moving. Everything's fine."

Mom took a deep breath and glanced down at her phone. "I called your father. He's on his way."

"Mom," I said. "You didn't have to do that."

I expected her to argue with me, but instead she squinted at me, like she had when I was little and she was trying to decide if I was lying. "Are you sure?" she asked. "Did the doctor say it was okay?"

206

"*Yes*," I said, even though he hadn't. "He just wanted to do an ultrasound to make sure."

Mom's shoulders relaxed. She believed me. But then her eyes hardened. "Then what was Rodney doing here? Shouldn't he be in school?"

I groaned. I should have told her I was dying. If she thought the baby was in danger, she'd have been distracted from him. "He gave me a ride, okay? We've decided to be friends." Even those words hurt to say, but Mom didn't notice. Her arms flailed about.

"You *decided* that? After you both agreed not to see each other?" Her voice grew higher and higher pitched. I was pretty sure they could hear her in the hall.

"Look," I said. "If this is about the baby—"

Mom snapped. "*Of course* it's about the baby! Rodney was sitting in an *ultrasound* with you. He could easily use that to prove that he was committed to—"

"Mom!" I shouted. "He's not committed to me, okay?"

I closed my eyes. I hoped Rodney had taken his car and gone back to school, because I'd shouted loud enough that if he was still in the waiting room, he'd have heard.

Where was Dr. Kauffman, anyway? When I arrived, he was right in. Now that Mom and I were trapped in here together, waiting, he left us to torture each other.

"I'm sorry," I said. "I won't call him again, okay?" *Ever*, I told myself. Except to let him off the hook that I'd flayed him with.

That's what the bleeding was. My wakeup call.

Mom sank into a chair, deflated. "Why didn't you call *me*?" she asked. "My phone was on."

"I know," I said. "But really, I just didn't want to worry you."

Mom gave me an incredulous look.

"I know, I know," I said. "I fail." I curled up on the exam table with my arms around my waist.

Mom sank into a chair. "I'm glad you called the doctor right away," she said. Then she looked up at me. "You did, didn't you?

207

This just started?"

"Yes," I said. "Like an hour ago."

Mom's voice grew quiet then. "Penny," she said. "If you can't go through with this, tell me now."

I sat up straighter. In point of fact, I'd never been more sure that I had to. I couldn't even be a good girlfriend. There was no way I could be a good mother to a helpless little person. "I can," I said. "It's fine."

Mom gave me a look. "What I saw in there with Rodney didn't look fine."

I sucked my lips inward and clamped them closed with my teeth. "Neither of us is ready to be a parent."

Mom nodded, and rolled her shoulders like she was trying to shrug off a burden. But she still hunched forward, bowing under their weight.

As I looked at her, I wondered if *she* could go through this again. It was a horrible thing to ask about a woman with two almost-grown children, but was *she* ready to be a mother? She'd been ready to give up before I dragged us back into this, and maybe that would have been for the best. This baby was alive, but my back still ached. Were we going to be walking on eggshells through the rest of this pregnancy?

Yes. We were. Mom would never relax. Not until she had her own baby at home in her arms, and maybe not even then.

Nothing I could do would make her.

Muscles cramped again in my tail bone, and I held my breath, blinking through the pain. I couldn't fix things with Rodney, and I couldn't make things okay for Mom.

What was wrong with me that I couldn't make anything better?

The door swung open, and Dr. Kauffman stepped in, holding a stack of papers. "Penny," he said. "How are you feeling?"

"Lousy," I said. Mom looked at me in alarm, and I felt the familiar panic fluttering in my chest. I shouldn't have said that. Now she would worry.

Except she'd worry *anyway*. If I couldn't stop it, why did I spend so much energy trying?

Maybe because *I* didn't want to feel panicked. I looked up at Dr. Kauffman. "The baby's okay, though, right? I can go home?"

Dr. Kauffman settled into his chair, studying the papers in front of him. "Are you in any pain?" he asked. "Cramps? Back pain?"

I turned toward him so I wouldn't have to see Mom's face when she realized I'd lied to her. "Yeah," I said. "But that's normal, right? The book said—"

"Have you suffered any physical trauma?" he asked. "Have you been in a car accident? Or fall?"

My skin prickled. "No," I said. "Of course not."

Dr. Kauffman laid one of the papers on his desk so I could see it. I could see the outline of the baby's foot in one corner of the image, but he pointed to another area of the scan, where one dark blob met another. I stared at it, as if this would tell me something.

"This," Dr. Kauffman said, "is your placenta."

Mom took in a sharp breath, like she'd somehow learned something from that, but I refused to look at her. Seeing her reaction would just make me feel worse.

Dr. Kauffman's full attention was on me. "It's supposed to separate from the uterine lining immediately after the baby's born. But sometimes the separation begins early. We call that placental abruption. Yours is small so far, but you can see it here." He pointed again, but to me, the image looked like a gray line next to another gray line.

I leaned back. Understanding the picture wouldn't make it go away.

"Okay," I said. "So how do we fix it?"

I heard Mom stepping away. The chair behind me creaked as she sank into it again.

"Unfortunately," Dr. Kauffman said, "we don't. But sometimes it fixes itself. You don't have any risk factors for this, so that's a good sign. But I want to admit you to the hospital for a few days, so we can monitor you and the baby."

Blood drained from my face. The hospital? *Days?*

"No way," I said. "I can rest at home. I'll be good. I'll stay off my feet. Bed rest is a thing, right? I can do that."

Dr. Kauffman held my gaze. "Penny," he said. "You're bleeding internally. That puts both you and the baby at risk. We need to monitor your blood pressure and the baby's heart beat, because if this gets worse, your life could be in real danger."

Bleeding? I looked down at my stomach, as if I'd suddenly be able to see myself covered in blood. But no. *Internally.* Where no one could see.

Shouldn't I be able to feel that?

I still refused to look at Mom. Listening to the shallow way she was breathing was already making my heart race.

Would that make the bleeding worse?

Mom's hand reached for mine, but I tucked it out of her reach. My eyes burned, but I wasn't going to cry in front of her. I wasn't going to let her see me scared. I wasn't.

Why did I text her? If I hadn't, Rodney could be sitting here with me. He could be the one holding my hand.

I gripped the edge of the exam table. Screw it. If I couldn't make Mom feel better, I was going to do what needed to be done. I'd find out exactly how bad this was, and not try to make excuses. If there was no hope, Mom should know, shouldn't she? She'd just asked me not to string her along. "Tell me the truth," I said. "Is the baby going to die?"

To his credit, the doctor didn't look away. "You're at seventeen weeks," he said. "If I had to deliver today, the baby would have almost no chance of survival. But babies can survive as small as twenty-three, even twenty-two weeks sometimes. Ideally, you'll heal and make it close to full term. But at minimum, we need to buy you more time."

Mom's voice was quiet. "Penny," she said. "Is that what you want to do?"

As opposed to what? Let the baby die? "Yeah," I said. "It's just five weeks. We can do that."

I tried not to think of pictures I'd seen in my physiology book—images of premature babies so tiny they looked like they were only half-formed.

Mom put a hand on my knee, and I held perfectly still. "I need to go call your dad," she said quietly.

I bit down on my lower lip, hard. *She* got to talk to Dad. *She* got to seek comfort from someone she trusted. But I wasn't even supposed to call Rodney and tell him what was going on.

"Do you want to know the gender?" Dr. Kauffman asked.

I froze. *The gender?* They weren't supposed to check that for another few weeks. But I'd had an ultrasound. If he happened to see . . . .

Mom stood, suspended. It took several heartbeats for me to realize she was waiting for *me* to answer. Did *I* want to know? I finally spared her one quick glance.

Big mistake. Nothing Dr. Kauffman had said prepared me for the stricken look on her face or the tears gathering below her eyes.

"Yes," I said.

Dr. Kauffman spoke quietly. "You're having a boy."

A boy. Not a replacement for Anna, or the other babies Mom lost, but a little boy, who'd be a person in his own right. A little boy who might die, even if I did everything in my power to help him get here safely.

Oh, crap. Would he look like Rodney? Would he have his mannerisms? Would my own brother forever remind me of the guy whose heart I broke?

Mom's eyes closed, and a tear welled out of the corner of her eye and hung there, like a little blister. When her eyes opened again, she half smiled at me. I knew it was all she could muster, but for the life of me, I couldn't paste one on in return.

If I lost this baby, was I looking at what I would become? A deep well of sadness, unable to cope?

And if I was, who would support *me*?

Guilt settled in my stomach like bad eggs. That thought was beyond selfish. What was I doing, resenting her? She was the one I was supposed to *help*. "Call Dad," I said.

Mom nodded and turned to go. The door clicked shut behind her like a slap to my face. I'd failed her in every way. I just wanted everyone to be okay—my mom, Rodney, myself, this little boy—*everyone*.

Why was that too much to ask?

Chapter Nineteen
Week Seventeen

The hospital was only across the parking lot from Dr. Kauff-man's office, so the nurse wheeled me there. I didn't feel one stab of pain for the entire trip over, and even though Dr. Kauffman had given me painkillers, I told myself they couldn't have kicked in yet. This was just a precaution. They'd monitor me for a few days, I'd spend some time on bed rest, and then I'd be fine, and the baby would be fine, and we could be on our way and pretend that none of this ever happened.

Unless Mom had a stroke in the meantime.

Mom pulled the car across and she and Dad both met me at the elevator. Mom gripped Dad's hand so tight I was pretty sure they were both going to lose circulation and maybe their limbs. I could see the headline now: *teen pregnancy leads to double amputation.* At least they'd each get to keep one of their arms.

The hospital had crammed more furniture into my tiny room than I would have thought possible. There was the bed, of course, and then a sectional couch big enough for a family member to sleep on, and two uncomfortable-looking plastic chairs. Mom and Dad squeezed onto the couch, with their knees mashed against the side of the bed, while the nurse wheeled in a cart covered in cords and a monitor, crowding the room further.

I hoped we wouldn't be here that long.

Mom and Dad still gripped each other's hands. The nurse

hooked me into a belt with sensors that wrapped over my abdomen and sent data arcing across a monitor to my left. I studied it until I could recognize my slow, steady heartbeat, and the baby's tiny heartbeat, pulsing along with two beats for every one of mine.

I leaned back into my pillow. I just had to hold on. My baby would make it at least five more weeks. Maybe he'd be born as soon as he was old enough to breathe on his own—early, but ready. Mom would have her baby; my baby would have a life.

And then, at last, all of this stress would be over.

After about fifteen minutes, Athena swept into the room, her eyes shooting daggers. She stood at the end of my bed, some of her hair hanging out of her ponytail like she'd been obsessively pulling at it.

"Penny," she said. "What the hell? Are you okay?"

"Yeah," I said. "Sorry, I should have called you. I mean, I tried, but you didn't answer." I shot a look at Mom, hoping she hadn't caught that I'd tried to call Athena before I'd texted *her*. Both my parents had somehow managed to keep their limbs, though Mom was now threatening her circulation by winding her purse strap around and around her wrist.

"I called," Dad said.

"Good," I said. And then, turning back to Athena, "Sorry."

Athena's eyes bugged out. "Why are you apologizing to me?" she asked. "Stop *doing* that."

I held up my palms. "Doing what?"

Athena clamped her hands over her eyes, like this was all just too much to deal with.

"Honey," Dad said to Athena. "Why don't you have a seat."

"Yes," Athena said, her voice crawling with sarcasm. "Let's all sit around and pretend that Penny isn't dying."

My heartbeat quickened. As I looked up at the monitor, the baby's matched pace. "I'm not *dying*," I said.

Athena widened her eyes at me. "Don't be stupid. Placental abruption can kill you."

Mom looked up at her wearily. "Athena," she said. "You're not helping."

"*I'm* not helping?" she said. She drew herself up to her full height. "If you weren't so obsessed with having a baby, this wouldn't even be happening."

The air grew thick, dampening all sound. Mom stood off the couch, her face livid, and Athena glared back with equal force. I wrung my hands, wishing I could step between them. My mouth fumbled for the words that would make them stop, but Mom got there first.

"You," she said quietly, "cannot pin this on me."

Athena waved her arms in the air. "Are you kidding me?" she said. "Are you blind?" I could tell in the way her stance changed that she was getting worked up, like a rubber band stretched near to breaking. I balled my sheet in my hands. This wasn't the time to tell Mom the truth. Not in the hospital. Not with everything she wanted on the line. "You guys," I said. "Stop it."

But Mom didn't even look at me. "What's that supposed to mean?" she snapped.

Dad sank deeper into the couch, looking at the floor. A look of satisfaction crossed Athena's face. Of all of us, she was the only one who didn't mind being the voice to deliver the hard news. But she hesitated, then, her eyes flicking to me.

She wanted to tell Mom. She was burning to tell her. She was looking to me for permission.

But Mom looked over at me, and I could see it was already too late. The pieces she'd been holding at arm's length were finally snapping together like magnets.

She was going to realize the truth. And then, if we said nothing, we'd all know, and we *still* wouldn't have talked about it.

I slipped my hands under my thighs, digging my nails into my skin.

I couldn't let Athena be the one to deliver the news. Mom would take it even worse, coming from her. "Mom," I said. "I got pregnant on purpose. I wanted to have this baby . . . for you."

I huddled down in the bed. If I'd been a magician, maybe I could have disappeared—slipped under the sheets and never surfaced again. But no, magicians did their tricks by misdirection, by distracting the audience into looking at something else.

There'd be no distracting Mom from this now.

Dad covered his eyes with his hand. Mom looked over at him, her face contorting as she noted his lack of shock.

He was no help. Come to think of it, he'd never been any help when Mom was freaking out. He always laid low, waiting for the storm to pass. We used to wait it out together, while Athena battled the winds. Before I put myself directly in that storm's path in a desperate attempt to stop it.

It hadn't worked, but for the first time, I wondered if it wasn't my total failure at fault. Maybe *no one* could have stopped the winds. Maybe it didn't matter how good of a daughter I was. Maybe my family would still be a mess, no matter what.

And if it wasn't my fault, it was no wonder that I couldn't fix it. I was an idiot even to try.

But I still couldn't stop myself. "I'm sorry," I said. "I was just trying to make it better."

Mom closed her eyes, and her face seemed to go gray. "How," she said, but she stopped as her voice lilted higher, and broke. She tried again, lowering her tone. "How could you have ever thought this would be better?"

I looked around at my wilting father, and my shouting sister, and my fading mother. I looked at the beeping monitors, and at myself, strapped in bed, and thought about the poor, unwitting child maybe dying inside me in a soup of my own blood, and I told her the truth. "I thought it was the only way you'd ever be happy. I didn't think you'd ever stop crying unless I found a way to give you a baby."

I waited for her to scream at me about what an idiot I'd been. I deserved it. But Mom's cheeks seemed to collapse in on themselves. Her chin quivered, like she was barely hanging on.

"How could you think that?" she asked. "We're a family. We

would have pulled through."

Athena's voice was flat. "In her defense," she said. "We all thought it. Penny's just the only one crazy enough to do anything about it."

The pain of that seemed to hit Mom square on, and her frame swayed. Dad stood and steadied her from behind, giving Athena a stern look. She wasn't supposed to say things like that to Mom. None of us were.

But wasn't it about time that *somebody* did?

"I'm sorry," I said to Mom. "Things have just been so bad for so long."

And I waited for her to tell me that things hadn't been that bad. That we'd been dealing just fine. That it was all my fault if I thought she'd been having such a terrible time. But instead, her lower lip wobbled, and she pawed at her eyes. Then she turned and paced out of the room, with Dad following right on her heels.

I sank back in the bed, wishing I could meld with the mattress and become it: a soft place for people to rest. But I was the opposite, like a nail to the foot. A thing that only caused pain, and never prevented it.

Athena bit her lip. "I made things worse, didn't I?"

I let my hands fall limply at my sides. "No," I said. "It had to come out eventually."

Athena sat down on the couch, her hands on her knees. "Yeah. But maybe I could have started that fight somewhere other than the hospital."

I squirmed in the bed. I wanted to chase after Mom and apologize, to make sure she was okay.

But who was I kidding? She wasn't okay. If I couldn't make it better, that should mean I didn't have to, shouldn't it? It should absolve me of the responsibility to try.

But instead of feeling comfort from that, my stomach twisted around the pit that just kept growing larger and larger.

If I didn't fix it, maybe no one would.

Chapter Twenty
Week Seventeen

I sent Athena to get herself dinner around seven o'clock. Mom and Dad still hadn't come back, and watching her watch the door with guilt etched all over her face was worse than scrutinizing the baby's heartbeat. I couldn't take it.

When I checked my phone, I found a text from Kara, asking if I'd been sick.

Yeah, I texted back. *I'm in the hospital.*

She texted back almost immediately. *?!?!!*

Not much to tell, I sent back. *They're just observing me to make sure things are okay.* That wasn't exactly true, but it was as much as I was prepared to explain over text message.

Okay, Kara responded. *Keep me posted.*

I appreciated the thought, even though there wasn't anything she'd be able to do.

When a knock came at the door a few minutes later, I assumed it was a nurse. Athena couldn't be back yet, and Mom and Dad wouldn't knock. "Come in," I called.

When the door cracked open, Rodney peered in. "Hey," he said. "Is it safe?"

Never, I thought. I sat up as much as I could without disturbing the sensors. "How did you know I was here?"

"Athena," Rodney said. "She just texted me. I told her your mom didn't want me around, but she said they weren't here right now." Rodney stepped into the room, and I watched him take in the monitor, and the cords running underneath my sheets.

I straightened in bed, tugging at the sheet so it covered my hospital gown up to my armpits. I'd been wishing at the doctor's office that Rodney had stayed, but now I was shocked at how much I wished that Athena had minded her own business for once. "She shouldn't have done that," I said. "You don't need to be here."

Rodney hesitated, but the door snapped shut behind him. "Well," he said. "I am."

I sighed. "Do your parents know you're here?"

"Yeah. My mom called right after Athena texted to find out where I was."

"And?"

Rodney gave me the traces of a smile. "And she told me I didn't need to be here. It's a popular theory. But I told her if I'm old enough to father a child, I'm old enough to be at the hospital with that child and its mother."

"You're not old enough," I said.

Rodney rolled his eyes, his tone dry. "That's what she said. And I said the evidence states otherwise."

I wouldn't have thought it possible, but that actually made me blush. This time, I tried to sound like I meant it. "No, really, though. You should go."

"Because of your mom?" he asked. He studied the monitor, like he was trying to decipher it. "Athena said it's bad." Rodney took a step closer to the monitor. "Is that the heartbeat?" he asked.

I pointed to the blue line. "The fast one," I said. "The slow one is mine."

Rodney's mouth hardened into a thin line. "They have you on a heart monitor." He looked at me, appraising the situation, and I could tell by the hollowness of his eyes that he was coming to the right conclusions.

"I'm—" I said. "It's not that—"

219

He tensed and looked down at me, waiting for the lie.

I shut my mouth. If I told him the truth, he'd worry. If I didn't, he'd know, and then I'd be hurting him by not being honest with him, again.

A scream balled up in my throat and lodged there, and from the look on Rodney's face, I figured he felt the same. Rodney stood there, his whole body tense. What happened to my re-laxed Rodney, the guy who talked me down from my stress?

I happened to him, that's what. I'd dragged him through hell for months, and it was slowly eating away at him from the inside, leaving only a tired, worn-out shell. And he still loved me, so he couldn't walk away. But if I was willing to drag him through this, how could I claim that I loved him back?

I couldn't.

"Rodney," I said. "You don't need to worry about me, okay?" I'd have added this conversation to the list of wrongs that I'd done him, but I was pretty sure the end of that list was in China by now. "Seriously. You can go."

Rodney put his hands in his pockets. "Is that what you want?"

Blood pounded in my ears. Was that what I wanted? No. What I wanted was for him to lie down next to me and hold me and tell me that even though this was all my fault, he still loved me, and that everything would be okay.

My body went numb. I wanted him to take away the pain, to make it easier to bear. To bear it *for* me, so I could keep marching forward with things that hurt him.

I wanted him to do for me what Dad and I did for Mom. I wanted to drag him through hell, the same way Mom dragged me.

If this was love, it was a sick, twisted kind.

"It'll be better for everyone," I said, "if you just go." And it would be. For everyone but me.

Rodney's chest seemed to sink in. He shuffled his feet. His voice was so quiet, I could barely hear him. "Okay," he said. He turned toward the door, but as he did, a sharp pain cut right through the pain killers and tore up my back. I winced, and drew a sharp breath, and Rodney wheeled back around, eyes wide.

"It's fine," I squeaked. But I wasn't fooling anyone, especially him. I shut my eyes, but I heard the legs of the chair next to me scrape against the ground. And then Rodney had my hand in his, his fingers knotting through mine, holding onto me like he thought I was going to slip away. "Should I get a doctor?" Rodney asked.

I eyed the nurse call button. But the cramp began to subside. And there on the monitor was the baby's heartbeat, and the flat line that indicated I wasn't having contractions. They were watching my numbers from outside; they'd know if something really bad was happening.

When I was a child, I'd always been afraid that cuts and bruises would never heal. I'd peel back Band-Aids to peek at them. What if they didn't get better?

But they did. They always did. And this was just an internal cut, a tiny tear, bleeding inside rather than out. I couldn't peek; I couldn't cover it with a Band-Aid. But it would heal.

It *would*. "I'm okay," I said. "Really."

But Rodney put his other hand on my forearm. His face had gone pale.

He didn't believe me.

That's when Mom opened the door. And I had this horrible, selfish thought: *Good*. If I didn't have the courage to make him leave, at least she would. He'd listen to her when she told him to go.

From the red rims of Mom's eyes, I could tell she'd been crying, though now she seemed to be all dried up. Rodney's hand actually shook as he looked at her, and I remembered a moment months ago, when he'd said goodnight to me on my front porch while Mom sat in the swing, just after Lily decided to keep her baby. I'd had this thought about Rodney then: he was never awkward with anyone. And I flattened onto the bed, wishing I could erase the misery I'd put him through since then.

I held my breath, waiting for the blow up. I expected her to scream at me, to scream at Rodney, to get dragged out of the room by hospital security, possibly by her hair. Rodney would leave and never come back. He'd find someone else and be happy, and someday I'd get over that. I'd learn how to breathe again. And even if I didn't, at least I wouldn't have to watch him hurt and know that it was all my fault.

Mom eyed Rodney's hand in mine. She drew a slow, deep breath, and even though I was staring right at her, she refused to look me in the eye. But she and Rodney looked at each other, and I could feel his hand tighten on mine as he, too, braced to be kicked out.

But Mom just sighed, wearily, and her shoulders drooped. She walked across the room to the sectional and sat down. Dad followed behind her and joined her on the couch, but neither of them said a word.

Mom still wouldn't look at me, but after three or four minutes of quiet, she turned to Rodney. "Thank you for being here for Penny," she said.

Rodney and I both let out a breath together. His shoulders dropped in relief. I closed my eyes and lay back on the pillow, hating myself for being glad that he stayed. It meant I was already the same sort of person that Mom was—the kind who took all the support she was offered, without caring who it hurt.

And at that moment I was certain: if I lost this baby, I was going to turn out just like her: sad, sick, and irrevocably broken. I tried not to move. I tried not to breathe.

I had to hang onto this child for all of our sakes.

An hour later, a nurse came in. Rodney had let go of my hand, and sat with his elbows on the bed, twiddling his thumbs like he was playing an imaginary video game. The scant air between us shifted with each flick of his thumb, and I wished he'd reach out and touch me again, but I couldn't reach for his hand. I couldn't deliberately tie him to me any more than I already had.

I'd done enough.

As the nurse approached the bed, he got up and moved to the end of the sectional, next to my mom. And Mom actually reached out and put a hand on Rodney's shoulder, and squeezed.

What planet was she from? I couldn't even watch. The nurse bent over me, adjusting the sensors.

"Did I move too much?" I asked.

"I'm just checking," she said. "The numbers are a little off, so I wanted to make sure."

My skin went cold. I looked up at the monitor. There was my heartbeat, and the baby's. Still no contractions. No alarms, no odd beeps, nothing.

"What's off?" I asked.

"It's probably just the machine. You haven't felt the baby move yet, have you?" she asked.

"No," I said. "Is that bad?"

"Not at all," she said. "I was just asking."

"So did that fix it?"

"I'm going to send the numbers to the doctor," she said. "He'll come by and talk to you."

The nurse put the sheet back over my belly and left. Mom walked over and looked at the monitor, her face stretched thin. I was pretty sure she couldn't read it any better than I could. Still, it looked to me like the blue line representing the baby's heartbeat rippled against mine differently than it had before. I looked for the actual number on the side, and though I found something I thought was it, that value didn't tell me anything more. I had no idea what a normal fetus heart rate was, let alone a sick one.

I put my hands over my belly, careful not to disturb the sensors. The baby had been moving during the ultrasound, so he was okay then, wasn't he?

"What's it feel like when a baby moves?" I asked Mom.

Mom wouldn't meet my eyes, but she did answer. "Hard to describe. Kind of like a fish swimming around inside you."

My hands shook. I focused on my abdomen, trying to feel any changes. How would I distinguish the movement of a baby from the gurgling of my stomach, or the squishing of my other organs? The inside of a body moved as it processed—these weren't sensations I paid a lot of attention to.

But what if I couldn't feel it because it wasn't happening? "If there's no movement, that's bad, right?"

"Don't worry about it," Mom said. But I could tell that she was.

Sure. No problem. Jeez. Was that what I sounded like when I told people everything would be fine?

By the time Dr. Kauffman came in, Mom was pacing again, walking back and forth in the little space at the foot of the bed.

How are you feeling?" the doctor asked me.

"Scared," I said. "Something's wrong, isn't it?"

"The baby's heartbeat has slowed."

My hands and feet went cold. I looked up at the monitor. Which one of those numbers was the heartbeat? I'd known something was different. If an adult's heartbeat slowed, you'd take them to the emergency room. It seemed like a lot could go wrong with a person before their heart started to react. "So what do we do?"

"There's not much we can do," Dr. Kauffman said. "Do you mind if I examine you? Just your stomach this time."

Rodney was already up and by the door. "It's okay," I said to him. "You can stay." But he took the chair farthest from me, and focused on the corner. Doctor Kauffman pulled back the sheets over my abdomen and prodded the flesh over my hip bones. When he pressed to the side, a dull pain spread through my stomach.

"Ouch," I said. As soon as he removed pressure, the physical pain stopped. But the ghosts of it radiated into my limbs. I was supposed to be getting better. I was supposed to be healing, and that meant it should hurt *less*.

His face grew concerned, and he prodded more, asking me to identify the exact spot of the soreness. Then he sat down and put his elbows on the bed next to me. "We can do another ultrasound," he said. "But I'm not sure we'd see anything we haven't already. Your vitals are still okay. Are you having any dizziness? Feeling light headed?"

I took a deep breath. I hadn't been feeling that way until he suggested it. I shook my head.

"This problem may still reverse," he said. "You can have more time if you want. But you're young, and not very far along. I just want to make sure you understand that you have options here. At this stage, complications are a real possibility. If you continue bleeding, you could experience shock, and you run the risk of needing emergency surgery to terminate the pregnancy. You don't have to wait. We can do surgery now, if you'd prefer."

My heart skipped. Terminate now? End the life of a little boy who might be just fine? Seal in stone my fate of becoming a wreck just like my mother?

I put a hand on my belly, just below the sensors, feeling how firm my skin was. A lump formed at the back of my throat. I couldn't swallow. I couldn't breathe. I looked up at Mom, who clung to Dad's arm. She wasn't speaking up. She wasn't telling the doctor that of course I would never terminate. She wasn't speaking on behalf of her unborn child. She just watched me quietly, waiting for me to decide.

Rodney looked at the floor. And I wished I could ask him what he wanted, but I couldn't. Not in front of my mother.

Gah. Why was I *still* trying to spare her feelings?

"Penny?" the doctor asked. "Do you understand?"

"Yes," I said. "We can end this now, and if I don't, there are risks."

He nodded. "Do you know what you want to do?"

I looked up at the monitor, at the large arcs of my heartbeat, and, superimposed, at the tiny, rapid arcs of the baby's. Not as rapid as it had been, apparently, but still there. A boy. Biologically Rodney's son. In the future, my mother and father's son. But right now, definitely mine.

I steeled myself. I wasn't going to give up on him. I wasn't going to let them take away his chance that everything would still be all right. I wasn't going to break my mother's heart again, and I couldn't accept the breaking of mine. Mom's pieces might never come back together, but this baby and I still had a fighting chance.

"No surgery," I said. "I want to wait it out."

From the way Dr. Kauffman's lips curled in, I could tell that wasn't the answer he wanted. But if the risks had been high, he would have insisted, wouldn't he? He was a doctor. He wouldn't let me put my life in terrible danger.

My chest muscles tightened. Except, he needed patient permission for surgery, didn't he? And if my mother wasn't insisting, and I said no . . . . Would he·let me die, rather than interfere?

"That's okay, right?" I asked.

Dr. Kauffman nodded. "If things get worse, we'll have to revisit this."

I pulled in a deep breath, trying to send healing oxygen into every part of my body. Once, I sliced my finger open with a kitchen knife. It had barely hurt at the time, but days later, as it began to heal, pain shot from my knuckle to my fingertip. Sometimes healing can hurt worse than the injury.

I looked at my mother, and I saw in her red-rimmed eyes the consequences for all of us if it didn't.

When Athena came back, Dad told her to go home. "We can't all crowd in here over night," he said. "We'll call you if anything happens."

Fear ran over me like an icy hand. *Anything.* Like what? My death?

Athena stole a glance at me. "If I'm going to go home," she said, "you and Mom have to at least run home for a change of clothes first. You don't want to stay here all night without any kind of a break."

I smiled. Athena was taking care of me, in her own way, by getting Mom out of my face. Was that why she was always the one to confront Mom? I'd always thought it was because she couldn't help herself, but for the first time, I wondered if maybe it was more about protecting me.

My heart sank. That should be a good thing—protecting the ones you love. But in our case that meant Athena was part of our sick, twisted dance. Not the outside observer, but one of the principal players.

How could I not have known that before?

When Mom and Dad left, Athena sat down next to me. "I'll stay if you need me to," she said, "but I think I've done enough damage."

"It's fine," I said. "Don't apologize. I should have said those things to her a long time ago." *Before* I got pregnant, really. I shouldn't have made Athena back me into it, but those were my steps, and I knew them well. What would happen if I took different ones? Things would change, for certain.

But would they get better, or worse?

Athena squeezed my arm. "You want me to stay?" she asked.

I couldn't watch Athena continue to manipulate our parents on my behalf. Not now that I could see that was part of the problem. "No," I said. "Go sleep."

"I'll come back tomorrow," she said. And then she slipped out the door.

Rodney and I sat, alone. He hadn't left once since he'd arrived. I looked over at him. I had to try, one more time, for his sake. "You really can go home," I said. "You must have been miserable sitting here with my mother."

Rodney looked at me like that was the dumbest thing I'd ever said in my life, which, considering our history, must have made this a real winner. "Penny," he said finally. "You're in the *hospital*. Stop trying to make everyone else okay."

I turned my face away. I *should* stop. But maybe I didn't

know how. Already I was trying to find the right words to make him feel like he was doing a good thing, here. To tell him that I needed him, and I was glad he'd stayed, without making it sound like I was pushing him for more. I dug my fingernails into my palms; he'd *just* asked me to stop that.

But what else should I do? Just let everyone be miserable? How would *that* be better?

I leaned back against my pillow when I felt something shift inside me—a tiny flutter against my belly button, like a butterfly flapping its wings. I pressed my hand to my skin, but it was gone. Had I imagined it? Had it just been my stomach settling? Was it the bleeding? I couldn't be sure, but I kept my hand there, in case the fluttering came back.

Rodney inched closer to me. "Are you okay?"

"Yeah," I said. "I think maybe I just felt the baby move."

His eyebrows shot up. "Really? That's a good sign, right?"

The tiny flapping returned, like someone tickling my belly button with a feather from the inside. It was too soft to feel with my hand, but the internal sensation was definitely there.

Rodney hesitated, his hands hovering above the couch arm, like they were trying to decide where to land.

"I don't think you could feel it from the outside," I said.

And he nodded, but even so he stood, moving closer, and settling back in the chair next to me. He hesitated a moment longer, and then he took my free hand in his, like that's where he'd wanted it to be all along.

I didn't move; I didn't twitch; I didn't breathe. I couldn't do anything to let him know how badly I wanted him to hold on. Rodney lifted my hand in his, closing his eyes and pressing my fingers to his forehead. My whole arm tingled. This wasn't a just friend's move. He had to know that we'd never be that. And he was still here, despite my protests.

What had I done to deserve that?

My stomach sank. I didn't deserve it. I couldn't.

After a moment, Rodney let go of my hand and stretched his

arm, like he didn't know what to do with it if it wasn't connected to mine.

Just then the door opened, and a new nurse came in. I resettled on the bed. We must have passed the shift change.

She eyed Rodney. "Are you family?" she asked.

My heart beat faster. If he wasn't, would she send him away?

Gah. Wasn't that what I was supposed to want? For him to go home and get some rest and not suffer here with me?

Rodney sat up straight, and shook his head.

His words from earlier rang in my ears: *the evidence states otherwise.* My heart pounded harder, and as he opened his mouth to say no, I interrupted him.

"Yes," I said. "He's the baby's father."

The nurse checked the monitor and repositioned my sensor belt. She seemed to be totally oblivious to the look of shock on Rodney's face.

For a terrifying moment, I was sure that I'd said the wrong thing. It would be painful for him to attach to a child that wouldn't be his, and I'd gone and pushed him into it. But then his mouth softened into a smile, just barely, and he leaned back into the couch.

The nurse fussed over me for so long, I was sure that my mother was going to come back in before she left. But at last she straightened my sheet, pointed out my call button, and bustled out the door.

I held my breath, looking over at Rodney. I found him watching me. Our eyes met.

"Thank you," he said.

My mouth went dry, so rather than speaking, I nodded. And a realization buzzed through me—this was what Rodney wanted from me all along. Not to be free from responsibility. Not my endless string of apologies. Not to take the baby. Maybe not even to marry me.

He wanted me to recognize his part in all this. He wanted me to quit making excuses, and just say the truth out loud. He was the baby's father. He was involved, whether any of us wanted him to be or not.

And even if it took me forever, at least I'd gotten that one thing right.

Chapter Twenty-one
Week Seventeen

Right after my parents returned, the cramps came back with a vengeance. I arched my back against the mattress as the pain shot up my spine. Rodney's grip tightened on my hand as I shut my eyes. Even beneath my lids, they filled with white spots. My skin went clammy all over, and my feet turned to ice.

I heard Rodney calling my name, and the door opening and my dad's voice shouting down the hall. *There's a call button*, I thought, but I couldn't open my mouth to tell him. A roar in my ears drowned out all sound, and for a long queasy moment, I prayed to lose consciousness.

When my mind finally cleared, I opened my eyes. A nurse was jabbing an IV into my left arm, and Rodney still had hold of my right. My parents stood crowding around the foot of the bed. The door opened again, and Doctor Kauffman came in.

He motioned for my parents to step aside, and they reluctantly did, though Mom never took her eyes off my face. The doctor asked the nurse a question, and she hung a bag of fluid above my bed, attached to my IV. My head started to clear, and I tried to sit up, only to wilt back into the sheets.

"Penny," Dr. Kauffman said, "how are you feeling?"

My voice came out scratchy and weak. "Crappy. Am I okay?"

He shook his head. "Your blood pressure is dropping."

Another wave of nausea washed over me. "That's bad, right?"

"Yes," Dr. Kauffman said. "We're going to need to deliver. Now."

I clawed at the mattress. "No!" The word came out so loud that everyone in the room, nurse included, stared at me. "I mean," I said, "can't we wait longer? Can't we see if it gets better?"

Doctor Kauffman leaned over me. "It's getting worse," he said. "You're bleeding too much. If we don't deliver, you could end up in emergency surgery. You could die."

Rodney's hand clamped down on my arm, like he could anchor me here.

But I shook my head, my hair knotting against the pillow. "If you deliver, the baby *will* die."

"That's right," Dr. Kauffman said. "I'm sorry."

I squeezed my eyes shut. If I didn't give permission, would they go ahead and do it anyway? If Mom insisted, they probably could. I looked up to find her standing at the foot of my bed, looking me in the face at last.

"Mom," I said. "We can't do that. This is your baby we're talking about."

Mom spoke firmly, like there was no doubt in her mind about what should be done. "Penny," Mom said. "I'm looking at my baby, okay? And I don't want your life in danger. Not for anything. Do you understand?"

That should have made me feel better. It should have made me feel like I was loved and wanted. But all I felt was a surge of anger, the strong, forceful kind that I didn't even know I was capable of.

"Not for *anything*?" I shouted. "Not for the child you made us all miserable for?"

"Penny," Dad said sharply. "Your mother is right." I recognized that tone. It was the one he used on Athena, when she went after Mom. My nerves caught on fire. I hadn't changed the dance; I'd just stepped into her shoes.

I glared at him. "Why does Mom always have to be right?" I

yelled. "Why does the whole world have to revolve around *her*?"

Dad put a hand on Mom's arm. "She's hysterical," he said. "She doesn't know what she's—"

But Mom put up a hand, silencing him. She stared at me, but her eyes glazed over, like she wasn't really seeing me.

Or maybe she was seeing, not just me, but the last seven years of our lives. Finally. Clearly. For the very first time.

"I'm sorry," she whispered.

I dropped my head onto the pillow, squeezing my eyes shut. I wished I could block them all out, ignore them, make the whole world go away. Everyone but Rodney, who blessedly still hadn't let go of my hand. I squeezed it, trying to draw strength from him. Strength I didn't deserve, after dragging him through hell for nothing.

"Okay," I said. "If there's nothing else we can do, then let's get it over with."

My ears rang. Get it over with? This was a baby. *My* baby. Whose heart was still beating, at least at the moment.

I fought to catch my breath.

But I knew from Mom's experience how quickly that could change. And she was right. I couldn't kill myself over this. The baby couldn't live without me, not for several more weeks. If I died, we both died. It didn't get much more senseless than that.

The muscles in my pelvis tightened, like menstrual cramps from hell. After everything I'd lost over this, here we were at another failure. It was supposed to be a good thing to sacrifice your own comfort for the people you loved. It was supposed to be the right thing to do, wasn't it? So why the hell didn't anything good come out of it? How did I end up here?

The doctor knelt so his face was level with mine. "Penny," he said. "I need you to listen carefully, okay? You need to make a choice here, and I need you to understand your options."

I spoke through my teeth. "I already told you I don't want to wait any more."

"I know. But you have two options for termination, and I

need to talk about the possible risks with you." He waited.

I pried my eyes open. "Okay," I said. "I'm listening."

He nodded. "We can remove the baby surgically," he said. "It's called a D&C. But if we do that, you won't be able to hold your baby. You won't be able to see him, understand?"

I swallowed. It wasn't until that very second that I realized I could hold a seventeen-week-old baby. My arms ached. "Don't do that."

"Okay," Dr. Kauffman said. "The other option is to induce you. You'll have to go through labor—though we won't let you dilate as far as if you were full term. The contractions might help the bleeding some, or they might make it worse. If you continue to hemorrhage, we'll have to stop and do the surgery anyway."

I closed my eyes, waiting for my parents to cut in, to make my decision for me, but they didn't.

I swallowed. I'd already decided that Mom was right—my life came first. If I went ahead with the induction, was I just putting myself in more danger?

I glanced at Rodney, but he shook his head slightly. He wasn't going to decide this for me. Mom probably would, but I didn't want her to. This was my pregnancy. I could choose.

"Induce me," I said.

"Do you understand that you may still not get to hold him?" the doctor asked.

"I get it," I said. "But you can try."

Dr. Kauffman nodded. "We can."

I looked at Rodney again. "Then do it."

Rodney took a deep breath, and then nodded.

I waited for my parents to argue, but they didn't.

No one did.

The doctor stood up. "Do you want an epidural? The pitocin we use to induce labor produces strong contractions."

"Yes," I said. "Give me drugs." I didn't want to feel anymore. I didn't want to feel anything at all.

When Dr. Kauffman stepped away, Dad came over and put

a hand on Rodney's shoulder. "Why don't you wait with me," he said.

It wasn't a question, but Rodney looked down at me for permission. My throat closed up. I clamped my fingers down on his hand. Dad said me, not us. The implication was clear. I wouldn't be alone in delivery—Mom would come. And I couldn't be alone with Mom when I lost my baby. I didn't want to look into the empty eyes of the person I would become.

"Please," I said to Rodney. "Don't leave."

"Penny," Dad said, "they're going to take you over to labor and delivery now. Your mother will go with you."

"*No*," I said. "I want Rodney to come instead."

Rodney squeezed my hand and looked up at Dad. And like the amazing person he was, he actually said, "I'm not leaving her if she doesn't want me to."

And a part of me reasoned that I should just tell him to go and make everything easier on him, and on Dad, and on everyone in the whole world who would be inconvenienced if I didn't just do as they asked. But that part of me was drowned out by a great tide that threatened to tow me under if Rodney let go, even for a moment. And screw it, in this one moment, I was going to have what I needed.

Rodney had steel in his eyes. "I mean it. I won't leave her."

"Tony," Mom said. "It's fine."

I looked up at her in surprise. She was still watching me, but her expression had turned strong and certain and in that moment, I believed her. In this one moment, I really was her baby. She'd give up what she wanted for what I needed. My tear ducts burned, and I hated that it came as a surprise.

Dad looked back at Mom, and for a moment he hesitated. And then, slowly, he took his hand off Rodney's shoulder. And over the roaring in my ears I heard him say to one of the nurses, "He's the baby's father. He's going to stay with her." And the nurse nodded.

Dad turned to go, but I saw Rodney mouth, *thank you*. Mom

stood next to the bed, watching Rodney and me. For a moment, a flash of pain crossed her face. And then she stepped aside, and followed Dad out of the room.

Rodney held onto my hand while the nurses wheeled me to a larger room and sat me forward on the bed so the anesthesiologist could insert a plastic tube into my back. I thought I'd be scared at the idea of the needle, but I just felt numb, inside and out. I wondered if the drug would compound numbness upon numbness until I couldn't feel anything ever again. I could do circus acts—The Girl Who Cannot Feel. I'd be a cautionary tale. Watch out, girls. Don't be like her.

We watched the monitor as a formerly flat line rose in waves, marking my contractions. They arced endlessly, one after another, marching me forward into the future in which I would be empty and broken, just like Mom. I couldn't feel a thing; my whole lower body felt like it had fallen asleep. I watched as the needle on the clock passed in stop-motion. Midnight. One-fifteen. Three-thirty. Rodney didn't get up. He didn't even shift in a way that would force him to let go of my hand.

At four in the morning, I looked up into Rodney's face. His eyes were bleary from lack of sleep. He sat with his head supported by his free hand, his thumb wearing a hole in his temple. His other hand held mine like it was permanently attached, like he didn't know how to let go of me any better than I knew how to let go of him.

He leaned back in his chair, eyes closed. His whole body seemed to droop, like he'd been carrying too much weight for too long. And I wished more than anything I could take it all back—not just the last few months, but the last several years as well. I wished that I could give him back all the times I jerked him around, all the moments I must have stepped on his heart without realizing. I wished I could go back in time and give him somebody better than me—someone who was really capable of giving him her whole self.

236

And that's when I knew that I loved him. If he wasn't here, I'd have floated away out of my numb body and down the hall and disappeared. His grip kept me grounded, centered. Rodney always did that for me. I was destined to be just like Mom, losing all my babies, swallowed whole by the agony of it. But I knew this one thing, beyond a doubt—if I was going to lose all my children, I didn't want to lose them with anyone but him.

It was this last piece that made me sure of what I had to do: I couldn't stand to drag him through it, not even for the comfort of keeping him. I couldn't keep doing this to him, not for years, not for our whole lives. The price for him was just too high. These hours weren't just the end of my pregnancy. They were the end of us, too. They had to be, because if I hurt Rodney one more time, I was going to dissolve.

I couldn't treat him the way Mom treated us. I had to love him better than that. If he couldn't walk away, then I had to do the right thing.

I had to be the one to cut him free.

And at that exact moment, the rapid beep of the monitor stopped. I looked over, and there, where the sensor had previously been picking up the baby's heartbeat, was a still, flat line. I shifted beneath the belt. Maybe I'd just messed it up. But there was my heartbeat, sure and strong, and the waves of contractions, moving before my eyes.

Only the baby's heartbeat was gone.

I crushed the sheet beneath my hand, sitting up as well as I could when I was unable to feel the lower half of my body. If a fully born person had died, I was sure the room would have been full of all the medical personnel on the floor, pushing out family and rushing in with paddles and syringes to restart the heart. But this baby was still inside me, and he couldn't survive outside. They couldn't get to him to save him without guaranteeing his demise. He was right here, mere feet away from people and machines that could save him—except that they couldn't. No one could do a thing.

"He's gone," I said.

Rodney just watched me, quietly. "Does he have a name?"

I shook my head. I hadn't dared think of a name for Mom's baby. Not after what Lily did with Anna. But I looked up at Rodney, and I wanted to give him this one thing, even as everything we'd been to each other was slipping away. "You could name him," I said.

Rodney's eyes widened in surprise. "No," he said. "You should."

And I wanted to insist that he do it, but really, what I wanted to give to him was a redo of the last few months. I wanted to put him first. A name couldn't do that. Maybe nothing could. "I can't think of one," I said.

He nodded. "There's still time," he said. "You will."

A moment later, a nurse rushed in to check the monitors.

"The baby's heartbeat stopped," I said.

The nurse nodded, checking me. "You're at a six. It's time to push."

And just like that, the waiting was over. I focused on her instructions as she told me which muscles to tense—flattening my tendinous inscriptions back toward my lumbar vertebrae. The whole room seemed to ripple with the waves on the monitor, rising and falling in a relentless march into the future, into the end of everything. Rodney held onto both my hands and pressed his forehead into my cheek, clinging to me like the world was spinning out from under us. And I breathed and sobbed and pushed until the doctor came in at the last moment and the baby slid out of my body.

The nurses wrapped him in a blanket and laid him on a cart to clean him, and I held my breath, willing him to cry, willing him to move, willing him to live despite what I'd already seen.

But the tiny body on the cart lay still. He was already gone, even before he arrived. No bigger than the palm of my hand, it might have been a plastic replica of a baby, if not for the coating of blood.

Grief washed over me in a wave, and I held tight to Rodney's hand, which was warm and soft and *alive*. The nurse wheeled the cart over to Rodney and me. A second nurse was switching around my IV bags. "I'm going to turn off the epidural now," she said. "Some feeling should start to return soon."

And then the first nurse walked over to us. "You wanted to hold him?" she asked. I nodded, and she rested his tiny body in my hands. The baby lay on a bed of flannel cloth, with his head turned to the side as if he were sleeping. He didn't look much like an infant—he was too lean where he should have been soft, and thin where he should have been round. He looked more like a starving alien child, with jutting ribs and a head over-sized for his meatless body.

But he was so human in the details. His hands had little wrinkles at all the joints—tiny knuckles with their skin patterns already formed. His little eyelids folded neatly over his eyes—his toes had already grown tiny toenails. His body might not look ready, but the little bits of him were already fully formed. I wondered if he'd been sucking his tiny thumb in the womb, or folding his little hands against each other to form those wrinkles. Surely, someone already so detailed would have formed detailed habits. I wished I could have felt them. I wished I could have seen them.

As I looked down at him, a tingling returned to my legs and my feet. I could flex them again, like they were waking from a long sleep.

The baby weighed almost nothing. He fit into my palm, his still limbs lifeless and rubbery. I brushed his tiny fingernails, and pushed the tip of my finger into the palm of his hand, letting the fingers spread against it.

Little and unfinished though he was, I wished I had some way to carry him with me.

And then I had a thought.

"Rodney," I said. "Do you have your camera in your car?"

"Yeah," he said. "Are you sure you want—"

"Go get it," I said. "Quick. Before they take him away."

Rodney got up, letting my hand go at last, and hurried to the door. A nurse came in as soon as he left. "Your parents want to come in," she said. "Should I let them?"

The baby's fingers still pressed lightly against my skin, like the hand of a ghost. "No," I said. "Give me a few more minutes."

The nurse nodded, and I held my breath, waiting for Rodney to come back.

When he did, he didn't even have to ask what I wanted. I cupped the baby in my palms, and nestled my hands into the sheets for a soft, white backdrop. Rodney turned on extra lights and stood above us, snapping shots. These weren't photos I would show to anyone. I couldn't stand the thought of someone cringing at them, or thinking his body was gross. Maybe it was, but it was the only one he'd have, the only way I'd ever see him. These were just for me, and for Rodney. Our baby.

The very last thing we would ever share.

I looked at the cart where they'd cleaned him. "Is that tall enough to prop the camera on?" I asked. "Can you get your hands into the picture?"

Rodney looked at me. "Are you sure?" he asked.

I nodded. I wanted one more image—one last piece of Rodney to hold on to.

Rodney propped the camera up and set the timer, and then his warm hands cupped around mine, forming a second circle, supporting our child.

And just for a minute, I could see the family we could have been. Just for a minute, I let myself taste what I'd lost.

Pain clogged my throat. I wanted to say something perfect, something that would make everything seem meaningful, seem better.

But there weren't any such words in the world. Sometimes, language just isn't enough.

"Did you think of a name?" Rodney asked.

I looked down at the baby. This was the only time I could

see him. I could name him later, sure, but it seemed like the sort of thing I should do in his presence, even if he was mostly already gone.

"Gabriel," I said. "That sounds like an angel name."

"It is," Rodney said. "He's in the Bible, in the Christmas story."

I wrinkled my nose at Rodney. "Is it too religious?"

He smiled. "No. I like it."

"I don't like Gabe, though," I said.

"No," Rodney said. "Gabriel. No nicknames."

My nose dripped. My mother always called me Penelope, until I went to kindergarten and the teacher shortened it. I loved being Penny, bright and shiny and worth something. Mom tried to resist the name, but there was no fighting it. Dad met me in first grade; he'd never known me as anybody but Penny.

But Gabriel wouldn't have teachers, or friends. He wouldn't go to school. His name wouldn't be repeated over and over. My eyes began to water, and I said, "It's not like the kids at school are going to shorten it."

If I'd wanted us to hold it together, I should have kept my mouth shut. Rodney held my hands under Gabriel and we cried.

Chapter Twenty-two
After

I held Gabriel until the nurse came and asked to take him away.

"My mom might want to see him," I told her.

She nodded. "Do you want her to come in now?"

I shivered and shook my head. I didn't want to stare into the darkness we now shared. It couldn't be avoided forever, but I also didn't want to watch her hold Gabriel as if he was hers.

Just hours ago, I'd still been planning on giving him to her. Now, I couldn't imagine sharing him with anyone but Rodney. Would I have felt that way no matter when he was born? If I did, I had no idea what I would have done, but I'd have picked any of those possible options over *this*.

"Could she see him somewhere else?" I asked.

"Of course," the nurse said. "We'll ask if she wants to."

I didn't know how I was ever going to talk to my mother again, after the things that I'd said, after the way this had turned out. I was supposed to *fix* everything. How had I ended up broken as well?

The nurse wrapped him up in the blanket like he might catch cold, and I took one last look, knowing I'd never see him again.

I knew I should cry more when he was gone. I wasn't sure if it was the pain meds, or the hormones, or the sheer exhaustion, but I couldn't do anything but stare into empty space. Rodney still held my hand, but his grip was looser. He kept shaking his head, like he was trying to stay awake.

I wasn't the only one who noticed. The first thing my father did when he walked into the room was make Rodney go home. "It's five in the morning," he told him. "Your mother is up. She wants to come get you."

Rodney looked like he hadn't slept in a week, so I nodded. "Go on. We'll talk later." Rodney gave my hand one last squeeze, and my heart split right in half. Next time I saw him, I'd have to tell him it was over. We wouldn't talk anymore, for real. It wouldn't be fair for me to drag this out any longer.

It took a while for Mom to come in, and when she did, her eyes were red and swollen. I looked down at her hands—the ones that had probably held my baby last of all.

She was his *grandmother*, I told myself. Even if the baby wasn't her child, he was still her family. The pain in her eyes was legitimate, and a part of me still wanted to fix it.

But when I reached for the strength to do that, I found nothing but emptiness. I couldn't give her what she needed. I didn't have anything left to give. Since what I'd given so far had only caused more pain, that should have been a good thing. But instead, it made me hurt to my core.

"We named him Gabriel," I said. And I waited for the flash of pain on Mom's face, the reminder that I'd taken Gabriel from her, the way that Lily took Anna, and renamed her Tina.

But Mom just put a hand on my arm. And though her eyes filled with tears, there was something else in them when she looked at me. Not emptiness, or fear, or the deep pain I was used to seeing. She looked at me as if she really *saw* me.

And for a split second, I thought maybe she was proud.

After Rodney left, the world spun in a blur. The doctor examined me, and he and the nurses clucked about how good it was that the hemorrhaging had stopped. *Too late*, I thought.

I nodded along. I was definitely still losing blood and the doctor said I might be for weeks. But the tear that had threatened my life was gone. My body was no longer trying to kill me. It left me sore and empty, like a hollowed out melon, and I wondered if I'd ever feel whole again.

It seemed to take them forever to release me from the hospital. My parents shifted in and out of my room, taking turns crashing on the couch. I wanted to reach out to them, to tell them everything was fine. But Rodney was right. *I* was the one in the hospital. I was the one whose body ached and bled and lost everything and probably always would.

Just like my mother.

And as I watched my mother sleep on the too-short couch, her legs folded to fit, I couldn't help but wonder how she'd survived it this long. She'd been desperate and grasping for years, but now, looking into the face of the gaping emptiness that threatened to swallow me whole, it seemed like a miracle that it hadn't been worse.

I slept, but I kept waking up in fits, my heart pounding. I'd put my hand to my stomach, and wait to feel movement, and then I'd remember. Finally, I started stretching my eyelids open, counting the monotonous ticks of the clock, anything to keep from falling asleep.

Athena came back sometime while I was out, and I woke to find her sitting with Mom, silent for what must have been the first time in her life. When Mom left the room, Athena leaned over to me. "Rodney texted me," she said. "He wanted to come back to be with you, but his parents are pissed and are keeping him home."

Ugh. One more way I was ruining his life. I wondered if they were more angry about him skipping school, or about him being with me.

Probably me. After all, the school hadn't gotten pregnant with his child.

I handed Athena an empty cup from the bedside table. "Would you get me some more ice?" I asked. Really, though, I just wanted to be alone.

But as soon as Athena walked out of the room, my cell phone rang. I picked it up, hoping it was Rodney, but the caller ID flashed with Kara's name.

Oh, jeez. Kara. I'd told her I was in the hospital, but she'd think I was still pregnant. I could ignore her call, but I'd have to go back eventually. I'd have to walk back into the halls at school like I was still a whole, high-school-aged person who cared about things like homework and yearbook and prom.

Then again, maybe Kara had talked to Rodney by now. Maybe she'd already heard.

There was only one way to know.

I answered the phone and put it to my ear. "Hey," I said.

Kara's voice shrieked through the speaker. "Hey!" she said. "Ohmygosh, are you okay?"

I closed my eyes, still not sure what she knew and what she didn't. "No," I said. "No, I lost the baby."

Kara gasped. "Ohmygosh," she said again. "Are you still at the hospital?"

"Yeah," I said. "For now."

Kara's voice dropped low, like she was sharing in some secret. "So," she said. "Are you, like, you know . . . relieved?"

I leaned back like she'd slapped me. *Relieved?* I just lost a *child*. How could I be relieved?

But as Athena walked back in with the cup of ice, I started to remember. I should be relieved because I was a teenage mom, and that was a bad thing. A million other girls in my position probably would have been relieved. This meant they didn't have to deal with the consequences of their actions, right? This meant they were free. So I should be, too, shouldn't I?

"No," I said. "I'm not relieved. Not even a little."

Athena's eyes widened, and she sat down.

"Oh," Kara said. "Sorry, I didn't . . ." She fumbled for words. "Is that because of your mom?"

"No," I said. "It's because . . ." But I already knew there were no words to make Kara understand. "I'll just see you at school, okay?"

"Yeah," Kara said. "Okay. Do you know when you'll be back? Because I can collect your assignments for you. Do you want me to—"

"Yes," I said. When I tried to think about what I must have missed, my mind went blank. Whatever Kara did, it would be better than anything I could direct her to do. "That would be great."

"Okay, well, if you need anything else—"

"I'll let you know," I said. Even though I already knew there was nothing I needed that Kara could possibly provide.

Athena raised her eyebrows at me as I hung up the phone. "Friend from school?" she asked.

"Kara," I said. "She doesn't get it."

Athena gave a slow nod. "I'm not sure I do, either, to be honest."

I pulled the sheets up to my chin and burrowed into the pillow. "I'm glad you're here anyway," I said.

"Okay," Athena said. "I'll stay then, and try not to say anything horrible again."

I nodded. Sometimes, that was the best any of us could do.

They finally released me that evening. I came home to the same house I'd left, but I felt out of step, like I'd lived here in a past life. My aching leg muscles complained as I climbed the stairs, but I pushed them harder. I *should* hurt. I *should* be in pain. They'd sent me home with more drugs, but I already knew I wouldn't take them. If I stayed numb, how would I ever recover?

The door to the empty room that would have been Gabriel's nursery was closed, and as I walked by it, my heart squeezed. It was directly across from my door—closer to my room than Mom and Dad's. How could I have thought that I could listen to him cry at night, and let Mom get up and take care for him as if she was his mother?

I hurried past the door, and into my own room, closing the

246

door behind me. The pile of papers from the doctor still lay on my desk—the one with the miscarriage symptoms on top. I jammed them inside the baby book and threw the whole thing into the trash.

I lay down on my bed, but though my body felt exhausted, my mind kept spinning, focusing on the oddest things. The ticking of my clock. The gurgle of water in the pipes. The rush of the wind in the trees outside. The whole world was alive with motion and sound, and I lay perfectly still, unable to pass into unconsciousness.

Eventually, I got up. My body seemed to ache more the longer I lay still, and the doctors hadn't told me I had to rest. The house was quiet; Mom and Dad's door was closed. I gathered from the silence that they'd both gone to sleep, probably assuming I'd done the same. Instead, I moved down to Dad's office. I turned on his computer and opened Rodney and my photography folder, but Rodney hadn't dropped in the pictures of Gabriel. He hadn't updated the folder in several days. I sighed. His parents might have taken away his computer. Or maybe he was sleeping—he hadn't had much more rest than I had the last few days.

I pulled out my cell phone, trying to figure out the right words to say to Rodney to tell him that I understood he was better off without me. Now I could understand Ryan's decision to break up with Kara over text message. I really didn't want to hear Rodney's reaction, be it pain or relief.

But I'd at least call him, even if I couldn't face him in person. I owed him that.

I found his number in my phone—he was the last person I'd dialed. My finger paused over the call button, but I couldn't press it. I couldn't do this. Not yet. I needed to sink back into my world again, first. When I felt real again, I would tell him. It might be easier while I still felt detached, but this was the last gift I could give him: I would feel the full force of the pain when I finally let him go.

247

And then I knew what I had to do—what would bring me back to my senses. I was never more aware of the world than I was when I was framing it through the lens of my camera. I went back upstairs for my equipment, dug my tripod out of the closet, threw on a hoodie, and headed into the backyard. I might not know who I was now, but I'd always taken pictures, even before I met Rodney. Even if I needed to let him go, I couldn't let that go with him.

Beside Dad's barbecue, I set up my tripod and aimed it up through the branches of our poplar tree, focusing my camera on the sliver of moon peeking through the leaves. Its light was almost blocked by the speckle of leaves—only a few fragments of brilliant white shone through. I set the two-second timer, so the picture wouldn't blur as I jarred the camera while pressing the button, and took several shots.

I considered them in the screen. They were good, but not great.

I could do this after Gabriel. I could do this without Rodney. I *could*. If I didn't, I might disappear, and I didn't want that.

I wanted to matter.

Our sliding glass door opened, and I turned to see Mom standing in the doorway, rubbing her arms. She was still wearing her clothes from the hospital, but her hair stuck up in all directions. "Did you sleep?" she asked.

I shook my head. "I don't want to."

Mom shivered. "Just a minute," she said. "I'm going to get a coat."

I thought about offering to come inside, but the cold air on my cheeks felt crisp, and it felt good to feel anything. Mom closed the door, and came back a few minutes later wearing a jacket and slippers, and carrying two lawn chairs. She set the chairs up on the concrete patio, facing the moon, and I sat down next to her, looking up at the sky. The stars were out—I could see the Big Dipper, and Cassiopeia, which exhausted the sum total of constellation names that I knew. Without a lot of magnification, stars didn't make for very interesting pictures, unless you did a super long exposure and found something fantastic to put in front of them.

The tree did not count as fantastic, yet Mom and I stared up at it, looking at the leaves rather than at each other. Finally, Mom spoke.

"Did you really think you had to do this?" she asked. "Or I would never be happy?"

I wanted to rush to tell her that I'd never thought that, that we'd all just been upset and said things that weren't true, but instead, I breathed in the night air. "I didn't have to be an idiot about it," I said. "That was on me."

I expected Mom to fall apart again, but instead she just looked at the sky with quiet acceptance. "I understand what you were trying to do," Mom said. "I can't believe I didn't see it before."

"Did you want to?" I asked.

Mom snorted. "That's exactly what your father asked me. Did you two talk about this?"

Busted. My cheeks burned. "Just once."

"Ah," Mom said. "So everyone knew that you did this on purpose except me, and no one saw fit to tell me."

"I didn't—" I said. "I mean—"

"You thought if you said anything, I'd break down," Mom said. "You thought I couldn't bear the idea that this was my fault."

I cringed. "Yeah."

"Penny," Mom said. "I'm your mother. I'm not made of eggshells."

I sucked my bottom lip between my teeth.

Mom heaved a great sigh. "I'm sorry that I acted like I was for so long."

I stole a glance at Mom, but her eyes weren't teary, and she wasn't holding back some horrible tide of grief. She just stared calmly up at the sky, like she'd emerged from the dark to remember how big the world was.

I followed her gaze up to the stars. I wanted to remember that, too, but even though the sky was big, to me it still looked dark.

Mom turned to look at me. "Listen," she said. "I was wrong. I let myself get so wrapped up in having a child with your father that I lost sight of the rest of my life. And worse, I taught you to see the world that way. That's what really bothers me, I think. It's not the years I've lost. It's the skewed view of life I've given to you."

A cold breeze picked up, wafting down into the valley from the bay. I slipped my hands inside my hoodie, and pulled the hood up around my face. "Athena handled it differently," I said.

Mom looked up at the sky. "Athena resents it. You *adopted* it. Either way, I'm sorry I made you both live like that for so long."

I kicked the heel of my tennis shoe against the frame of the lawn chair. All my instincts told me to take the blame. The pregnancy had been my choice, not hers. But that was just more excuses, wasn't it? More taking things onto myself, so that other people's lives would be easier.

But it didn't make them easier. Not for them, not for me. It just hurt.

"Penny?" Mom asked. "Are you angry with me?"

"No," I whispered.

Mom shook her head. "You should be."

I was sick of worrying about how I should feel. "Maybe," I said.

Mom sniffed. I wondered if she understood how hard that was for me to admit. Mom had it hard, didn't she? Who was I to be mad at her? But to listen to her tell it, I was the one who had it bad. I was the one who had to live with a mother who rested her happiness only on things she couldn't have. "I love you," I said. "I get that it was screwed up, but that's why I did it."

"I know," Mom said.

I squinted at her. "And you're not mad?"

Mom let out one burst of a laugh. "I was," she said. "At the hospital. I was angry, and heartbroken, and terrified."

I'd been all of those places, too. "And now?"

Mom looked up at the stars, considering. "Now I just want things to be different," she said. "Do you think we can get there?"

I wanted to tell her that of course we could. That it would be easy. That, poof!, we could magically have a functional family. But it wouldn't. There wasn't any easy fix from broken to whole again. Gabriel taught me that.

Still, there had to be some way to get there—some path that would lead us to a happier place. And if I didn't know exactly what that was, at least I could look at my family and have a good idea of what it *wasn't*. "I'll forgive you for being a crappy mother," I said at last. "If you'll forgive me for being a crappy daughter."

Mom laughed, genuinely this time. "Done," she said. "I guess we all have some things to work on."

We did. Dad, too, though I wasn't sure he knew it yet. Given how many times I still wanted to make everything instantly better, I clearly had a long way to go. But I could see the problem now. That seemed like a good place to start.

"What are you going to do?" I asked. "About, I mean . . . about having a baby."

Mom reached over and brushed my hair behind my ear, like she used to do when I was little. "Well, I have a year and a half left with this one before she goes off to college," she said. "So I have some lost time to make up."

I smiled. Most of my friends would be pissed if their parents decided to get more involved in their lives in their last two years of high school. But Mom was right. We did need to make up some time.

I looked down at my picture of the tree behind the moon. "I could teach you how to take pictures," I said.

Mom laughed. "You can try," she said. "But really, I'd just like to look at more of yours."

But then what? Mom was right. In a year and a half, I'd be gone. And Mom would still be in her mid thirties, already an empty nester. "What about after that?"

The moon reflected in Mom's eyes. "I was thinking about foster care," she said. "I never wanted to do it before, because I didn't think it would be fair to you and Athena. Foster kids have been through a lot. You never know what kind of problems you'll be dealing with." Mom looked down at the grass. "But everybody thinks that way, you know? Everybody wants a baby. And your dad and I would be in a position where maybe we could do some good."

I thought about that, about children without parents moving in and out of Mom's home. Not babies, but kids for my mother to love. Family, but a different kind.

And for the first time, I could picture it: a happy future for my parents in which they never had a baby of their own.

But when I tried to picture myself in that future, I couldn't. Logically, I knew I could still go to college. Study photography. Take pictures. Maybe even start up a portrait business myself. But it felt cold and empty, like I'd always wish that I'd done those things with Rodney, not because I couldn't do it without him, but because I wanted to be the girl who didn't screw that future up. The girl he could trust. The one who didn't hurt him. The one he thought I was before all of this happened.

My eyes found their tears again, and my face contorted. I slipped deeper into my hood, hoping Mom wouldn't notice, but she put a hand on my arm. "Penny?" she said. She didn't ask if I was okay. I obviously wasn't. "Talk to me?"

I wanted to hold it all in. Mom was standing on the edge of happy. It wasn't right for me to ruin it.

But I'd *just* agreed that things would be different. And if not talking to my mother was what dug me into the dark, maybe the opposite would pull me out.

I sniffled, and snot collected in my nose. "I've screwed everything up."

Mom held her breath. "Have you talked to Rodney?"

I bit my lip, hard. "What makes you think it's about him?"

Mom scooted her chair closer, resting her arm around my shoulders. "After the way he was with you at the hospital, I'm honestly surprised that he hasn't come pounding on the door."

My nose started to run. "I was thinking about calling him."

"You don't sound happy about it."

"No," I said. "I'm going to tell him that we shouldn't talk to each other any more."

Mom's eyebrows shot up. "That sounds . . . drastic."

"Is it?" I asked. "After everything I put him through? He'd be better off with somebody else."

Mom shook her head. "Penny—"

"You always said it was stupid to get involved young, right? And you were right. All I do is hurt him. That's all I've ever done."

Mom grimaced, probably remembering all the times she had said just that. "I don't think—"

My voice angled up into a wail. "He said I didn't care about his feelings. And he was right. I was selfish. But now that I do care, it's obvious this is what's best for him."

Mom was quiet for a long moment. When she finally spoke, her voice was sincere. "Does Rodney get a say in what's best for him?"

Both my eyes and my nose ran. If I didn't give him a choice, I was doing what I always did: trying to solve the problem by doing what *I* thought was best. But in this one case, couldn't I be right? "Isn't it obvious?"

Mom got up and knelt on the ground beside me, rubbing my back. "Penny," she said. "That boy wants to be around you. He insisted on staying with you when any other guy would have run away."

"Yeah," I said. "Because he's too loyal. I've done nothing but ruin his life for *years*. It's about time I did him a favor."

Mom planted her hands on my shoulders and looked me

straight in the eyes. "You're not ruining Rodney's life. He's in love with you. Anyone can see that."

I scrunched my eyes closed. Of course he was. "That only makes me the person who can hurt him the worst."

Mom nodded. "Like I've hurt you."

I cringed, still honestly surprised that Mom wasn't dissolving in tears along with me. How could she deal with having hurt me without collapsing?

She wasn't trying to fix me, I realized. She was only being honest, and trying to move on.

Why was I still trying to fix things for Rodney?

I sat back in my chair. I was trying to control his pain the same way I'd tried to control Mom's. All I'd done was switch him for her.

I could feel my resolve cracking. But it felt like standing on the surface of a frozen lake. Maybe my resolve was the only thing between me and drowning. "Being with him can't be the right thing, because of how much I've hurt him."

"Penny," Mom said, "what do you want?"

I remembered Rodney's words, from months ago on the bleachers, when I'd asked him the same question.

I want to be with my best friend forever, he'd said. *Take millions of pictures. Be stupidly happy.*

And the words cut me deep, because they were exactly what I wanted, too. I just hadn't believed it was possible.

And now?

I looked over at my mother, whose face was calm, despite the horror of the last few days. She'd survived it, even though I'd forced her into yet another loss. I'd survived the last few years, even though my family was a mess. Mom could smile now, even though we both knew how much we'd hurt each other.

"How do people do this?" I asked. "Wound each other and then just go on as if it never happened?"

Mom was quiet for a long moment. "I think that people forgive each other, because we're all stupid sometimes. I think that we let go of the pain, because we also want to be forgiven ourselves."

I closed my eyes. That's why Mom wasn't yelling at me, now. I'd done stupid things, but now that she knew the whole truth, she could see that she also had a part in it. She'd hurt me, and I'd hurt her, and if we wanted things to be different, we couldn't keep making the same stupid mistakes. We had to live differently.

I hadn't given Mom a say when I decided to give her a baby. I'd kept it secret, because I wanted to decide for her what she would do. I'd done the same to Rodney, and if I broke up with him now, I'd be doing it again—making choices for him, without giving him a say. That was the same old Penny, the same old habits, the same old problems.

I didn't want that anymore. I wanted things to be different. And that meant I had to give Rodney a choice, and really listen to what he wanted.

Hurting each other was what people did. But maybe we made up for it by loving each other, too. Even if sometimes loving meant letting go.

I wasn't going to have that conversation with him over the phone. "Can I borrow the car?"

Mom smiled. "My keys are on the counter," she said. "I'm supposed to tell you not to stay out late while you're recovering."

I nodded. My body was sore, but not broken. Healing was possible. I needed to give it a chance for once, instead of getting in its way.

Rodney's room was upstairs at the front of his house. I could see his light on as I parked Mom's car out front. The only other light in the house came from Rodney's parents' bedroom. I could ring the doorbell, but one of them would answer the door, and if they chewed me out for what I'd done to their son, I'd lose my nerve.

Instead, I slipped through their side gate and into their

backyard. I sat down on a bistro bench at the roots of their huge shade tree, and pulled out my phone.

I'm in your backyard, I texted. *Does that make me a stalker?*

Depends, he replied. *Can you tell me what I'm doing right now?*

I smiled. *Texting.*

Busted. You ARE a stalker.

Among my many talents. I also predict the future.

Oh? And what do you see in mine?

Hmm, I typed. *A bench, a garden, and a girl.*

"I see that in my present," Rodney said from the corner of the yard. I'd left the gate open, and he'd come through so quietly that I hadn't heard.

I turned around to smile at him. "Maybe," I said. "But I saw it first."

Rodney sat down next to me on the bench. He was wearing jeans and a thick hooded sweatshirt. Given the time it had taken him to come down the stairs, he must have still been up and dressed.

"So," Rodney said.

"So," I said back.

He smiled. "I'm glad you're here."

My heart picked up pace. We sat there, side by side, not touching. My head swam with the enormity of all I wanted to say. I didn't know how I'd ever get it out.

Rodney looked at me. "How are you feeling?"

Did he mean physically? Or otherwise? "Crappy," I said. "But I'm surviving."

He nodded slowly. "I think that's going around."

"How are things with your parents?" I asked. "Athena said they were pissed."

"Yeah," Rodney said, drawing the word out. "They yelled. A lot."

I shuddered. "They probably hate me."

"I think they're more mad at me," Rodney said. "I may have

256

told my dad that he only wants me to take responsibility if there's no actual responsibility involved."

Ouch. "That's the truth, isn't it?"

Rodney nodded. "It's also true that I think he's an ass."

I put a hand on his arm. "You didn't say that."

Rodney didn't pull away. "I didn't. But I thought it. A lot."

I sighed. "I haven't exactly been the kind of person they'd want you dating, you know?"

Rodney gave me a sidelong look.

I cringed. "Not that we're dating anymore." I sounded like I was fishing, and maybe I was, but mostly I was drowning. Rodney just sat quietly, refusing to rescue me.

"I almost called you, earlier," I said. "I was going to tell you that obviously you'd be better off without me."

Rodney exhaled loudly. "What changed your mind?"

"My mom, actually," I said. "She told me I was being stupid."

"Thank her for me."

"So you don't want me out of your life?" I asked. "Because you probably should."

He cocked his head. "I tried that. It was awful."

"Yeah, but—" I put my head in my hands, steeling myself for what I had to say. "I don't want to hurt you anymore. I don't want to drag you through hell." I kept my face down. I couldn't look at him and say this to him. "I just think it might be better for you if we were just friends, like you said."

Rodney's hand rested on my shoulder. "Yeah, but that's crap, isn't it? We were never really just friends."

I groaned. "No. We never were. So maybe that means we shouldn't be anything. If I turn out like my mother—"

Rodney's fingertips rested in the groove of my collar bone. "You're not your mother."

He sounded so sure that I wanted to believe him. I looked up. "How do you know? Because if I lost this baby, I might lose them all, you know? I might turn out to be just like—"

"Whoa," Rodney said. "Are you planning our whole lives

already?"

My heart hammered so hard it about broke my ribs. Our lives? His and mine? Together?

"I think," I said. "I think I was trying to tell you that being with me won't be good for you."

Rodney leaned against the back of the bench and let out a long, slow breath. I waited for him to admit I was right. I was, wasn't I? He still loved me, sure, but loving someone and thinking they're good for you are two different things.

"So can I kiss you yet?" he said.

My mouth dropped open. "What?"

His arm shifted around me, warm against my shoulders.

"Um," I said. "Did you hear anything I said?"

"Yeah," Rodney said. "I heard my best friend spouting self-loathing crap about what a terrible person she is. You don't expect me to actually buy into that, do you?"

I smacked him on the shoulder. Hard.

He didn't even wince.

What was *wrong* with him? "Could you consider just for a minute that this is probably not the last time in your life that I'm going to hurt you? That I might make you really miserable? That our lives might be full of pain?"

"Okay," Rodney said.

I kicked my feet at some leaves, waiting, but Rodney was quiet. "Okay, you'll consider it?"

He sighed, and ran his thumb under my jaw, turning me to face him. "Okay," he said. "Sign me up."

A gleam of moonlight ran through his eyes. "Don't be stupid," I said.

The ghost of a smile played across his lips. "Take your own damn advice."

I wanted to ask him why he would do that, but his hand brushed against my cheek, and my breath caught in my throat.

He'd do that because pain wasn't the only thing in my future. It swallowed my mother for a long time, but even she was

258

finding a way past it. She'd held onto her pain, onto her one precious vision of the future, and lived inside it like a moth refusing to emerge from its cocoon.

But now, she was starting to cut her way out.

Maybe I didn't have to build a sack around myself at all. Maybe I could make a different choice than she made. Maybe I could be like Rodney—accept the pain, embrace it as part of what was necessary.

Part of what I wanted, even.

And move on to everything else that would also happen in our future. Take millions of pictures. Be stupidly happy.

Forever.

"Okay," I said.

Rodney's mouth broke out in a full smile. And then I threw myself at him, literally. I buried my face in his shoulder and tossed my arms around his neck, pressing against him so tight that I could barely breathe. He wrapped his arms around my back, the sleeves of his sweatshirt enveloping me like a blanket. I ran my hands up the back of his neck and through his hair, my fingers tingling at the mere thought that they were *allowed* to be there. How? How did I take this for granted for so long?

When I trusted myself not to burst into tears, I whispered into Rodney's neck: "Is this what it feels like to be stupidly happy?"

Rodney laughed. "You wouldn't believe how much I've missed you."

"Mmmm," I said. "I think I have a pretty good idea."

"Oh," Rodney said. He leaned back, digging into his sweat-shirt pocket. "I have something for you."

He reached for my hand, and I felt a cool metal chain coil into it, followed by something smooth and thin. I held it up to the moonlight. In my palm was a heart-shaped locket on a long silver chain. I held my palm under my nose, running my fingers over the etched surface. My thumbnail traced the groove in the side, and I slid it in, popping it open. There inside was the picture we'd taken of Gabriel. Rodney had trimmed off half of his hands to fit it inside, but I could still see the edges of them, wrapped around mine.

I was struck speechless. Tears welled up in my eyes. Our future was uncertain, but here he was, still taking care of me in just the right ways, not the stupid, damaging ways that I kept trying to take care of everyone else.

"I thought," he said, "that this way, you could always carry him with you."

I couldn't take my eyes off the tiny picture. "Thank you," I said.

"I've decided," he said, "that maybe doing kid portraits wouldn't be such a terrible thing, you know? We could still do art photos on the side."

I looked into Rodney's eyes. His face was serious; he wasn't speaking hypothetically. I saw it, then: the ways our future might unfold in front of us. We could have that future together, and we didn't have to wait. We didn't have to pretend that wasn't where we were headed. We could start building it now.

I'd never wanted anything so much. "Yes," I said. "Let's do it."

Rodney wrapped his arms around my shoulders, and I leaned my head on his shoulder, my forehead resting against his jaw. And then he did something he'd never done before. Another first for us.

He just held me. Before, I would have made out with him, or pulled away, or made a joke out of it. Anything to push back my nerves, to convince myself that it wasn't serious. But today I just relaxed against him, floating in his arms, and let him hold me.

I couldn't remember anything feeling as good.

Acknowledgments

As always, this book was not written in a vacuum. Many people read various drafts. Thank you to all of you, for your feedback and your support.

Many thanks to Lisa, Eddie, and Krystyna at JABberwocky, for their candid and honest critiques. Eddie—you put up with so much from me. Thank you.

Thanks to Carol, Tessa, Erin, Sandra, Kara, and Isaac, who loved the book even before I rewrote it from scratch, and gave me most excellent advice to help with that rewrite. Thanks also to Kathy, Theresa, Emily, and Megan, for their reads, feedback, and encouragement.

Thanks especially to the Seizure Ninjas—James, Sandra, Jenn, Heidi, Lee Ann, Cavan, Alex, and Heather—for their glowing praise and unrelenting criticism. Your critiques of this book can be summed up in five words—It's brilliant! Now rewrite it!—and I love you all for that. You guys give the best prescriptive feedback around, and all my books would be much worse without you. (You know; you've read them.)

Thanks to Isaac, for his fantastic design advice and his InDesign expertise. But most of all for his friendship and support over the years.

Thanks always to Brandon, who taught me everything, and continues to astound me with his generosity.

Thanks to my husband, who has heard me think aloud about this book for nearly four years, and has endless patience for my constant rounds of "what if…" Thanks also for not laughing at me when I finally figured out what this book was about four drafts in. Sometimes I'm special like that. And thanks to my daughter—I didn't even know toddlers could be so patient, but you are. Thanks for putting up with your working mom. I love you.

Thanks most of all to my amazing editor Kristina Kugler, who helped me turn a pretty good draft into a polished finished work, and the incomparable Melody Fender, whose beautiful design work you see on the cover. Thanks, both of you, for your kindness and patience with me. You are both amazingly good at what you do, but more than that, you're incredible people. I am honored to work with you.

Janci Patterson is the author of two other contemporary young adult novels: Everything's Fine, which won the Utah Arts Council award for Best Young Adult Novel in 2007, and Chasing the Skip, which was released by Christy Ottaviano books in 2012. For more about Janci, visit her online at jancipatterson.com.

Kira thought she knew everything about her best friend, Haylee. But when Haylee commits suicide immediately after her first date with her longtime crush, Bradley Johansen, Kira is left with nothing but questions, and a gaping hole in her life where Haylee used to be.

Kira is sure that the answers to her questions must be written in Haylee's journal, but she's not the only one searching for it. The more Kira learns about Haylee's past, the more certain she is that other people grieving for Haylee are keeping secrets—especially Bradley, and Haylee's attractive older cousin Nick. Kira is desperate to get to Haylee's journal before anyone else finds it—to discover the truth about what happened to Haylee—

And to hide the things that Haylee wrote down about her.